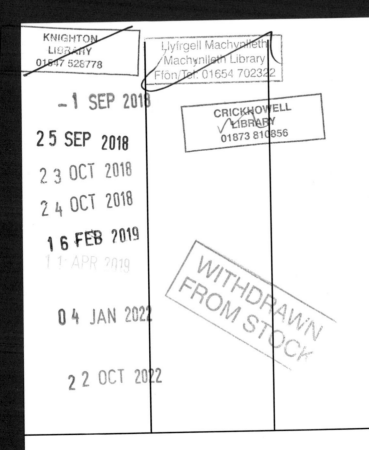

Our Friends
in Berlin

ALSO BY ANTHONY QUINN

The Rescue Man
Half of the Human Race
The Streets
Curtain Call
Freya
Eureka

ANTHONY QUINN

Our Friends
in Berlin

JONATHAN CAPE
LONDON

1 3 5 7 9 10 8 6 4 2

Jonathan Cape, an imprint of Vintage,
20 Vauxhall Bridge Road,
London SW1V 2SA

Jonathan Cape is part of the Penguin Random House group of companies whose
addresses can be found at global.penguinrandomhouse.com.

Penguin
Random House
UK

First published by Jonathan Cape in 2018

penguin.co.uk/vintage

A CIP catalogue record for this book is available from the British Library

ISBN 9781787330979 (hardback)
ISBN 9781787330986 (trade paperback)

Typeset in 13/15.2 pt Fournier MT
by Integra Software Services Pvt. Ltd, Pondicherry

Printed and bound in Great Britain by Clays Ltd, St Ives PLC

Penguin Random House is committed to a sustainable future for our
business, our readers and our planet. This book is made from
Forest Stewardship Council® certified paper.

For Doug Taylor

March 1941

I

The pub, on a cobbled street off Cheapside, would empty in the early evening as City people hurried home to beat the blackout. The upper room had a low-lit, secretive air, which he had come to realise was something the new recruits preferred, the danger notwithstanding. There was nothing like a creaky staircase and Victorian gas brackets to enhance the mood of conspiracy.

Dressed in his ARP warden's overalls, the tin helmet shading his brow, Hoste had passed through the work-weary crowds unnoticed. Back in civilian life he had been unremarkable too, a man of average build, five nine, with close-cropped brown hair, pale eyes, 'no distinguishing features'. It was not uncommon for him to meet someone three or four times before they actually remembered who he was. He had learned the advantage of his anonymous looks; you could be absorbed into a crowd without the least trouble. People would squint at him, wondering when – where – if – they had met before, and shrug. They couldn't swear to it.

Through the pub's window, criss-crossed with white blast tape, he saw the lights of office buildings gradually wink out. The landlord came up the stairs, muttering to himself. As he unfurled the blackout curtains to shield the windows, an air-raid siren started up its vile drone. 'I can time it to the minute,' the man said, with a morose half-laugh. Hoste sat there watching him, and took a swig of his pale ale. It was odd how extraordinary things became so quickly the norm. London had experienced its first raids only last September, and yet it felt like they'd been blacking up windows and hiding lights for years. They lived like moles, burrowing through the dark. Before returning downstairs the landlord dimmed the wall lamps, as if the room were being prepared for a seance.

His guest arrived some minutes later. He was a shortish, pudgy man, perhaps fifty, sweating beneath his heavy tweed suit. Wary eyes darted behind his spectacles. He gave his shirt collar a loosening tug, pinking the flesh on his neck. Hoste inclined his head in greeting and gestured to the chair opposite his own. The man looked around the room, evidently relieved to find themselves the only occupants.

'Mr Kilshaw?' Hoste didn't offer him his hand. 'Jack Hoste. I believe we have business to discuss.'

Before they got down to 'business', Hoste asked him for some personal information. It was standard procedure in recruitment, he explained, to run background checks; it helped him weed out cranks, fantasists, delusional types. Doing this straight away saved so much time. Kilshaw responded with a comradely chuckle. It seemed to break the ice. He was a director at an engineering works in Watford, he explained. Married, with two children. Secretary of his Rotary Club. When Hoste asked whether he had ever belonged to a political party, the man hesitated, then shook his head. 'Will that count against me?'

'On the contrary. It makes you less liable to suspicion.'

Once the preliminaries were done, Hoste leaned back in his seat and spread his hands in invitation. 'So. What do you have for us?' A little twitch of excitement flashed across Kilshaw's face. This was his moment. Living in Bushey, he began, had enabled him to keep watch on developments at the de Havilland aeroplane factory at Hatfield. He had been apprised of the latest prototype, known as the 'Mosquito', supposedly capable of a speed of more than 400mph. It was still at the planning stage, he gathered, but once production began it would not take long to get them operational. Hoste asked whether the prototype was being developed as a bomber, a night fighter or a photo-reconnaissance plane.

Kilshaw shrugged: he didn't know. Hoste said, 'Such intelligence would be of significant use. You have access to the factory?'

'No. But as an engineer I have contacts there.' His voice dropped to an undertone. 'Are you intending … ?'

Hoste shook his head. 'That's not in our remit. My business is to build a network of loyalists. This is a long game.'

They talked on for a while, mostly about the fifth column. Hoste assured him that, in the event of a successful invasion, those loyal to the Fatherland would be already equipped with means of identification – papers, or a discreet badge. By the end of their meeting Kilshaw evidently felt emboldened, for he now said, 'Would there be any form of … remuneration? For the risk, I mean –'

'Of course. Depending on the value of the intelligence a stipend is possible. We are more than obliged; we *want* to reward our agents for their work.'

Hoste decided they should conclude there. It was important not to rush this sort of negotiation; it required stealth, a degree of nous. He knew well the danger of committing oneself too early: recruiter's remorse. He stared over the rim of his glass at the new man and, feigning unconcern, said, 'By the way, one more thing. Have you ever come across the name Marita Pardoe?'

Kilshaw protruded his lip, repeated the name, and grimaced. 'I'm afraid not.'

'No matter,' Hoste said briskly. They both rose and stood facing one other across the table. He saw Kilshaw tentatively lift his hand to shake on the deal. Hoste knew better than that. Straightening, he raised his forearm in a stiff salute.

'*Heil Hitler.*'

Kilshaw, momentarily thrown, stole a glance at the door. The risk! When he saw the coast was clear he mirrored Hoste's salute. '*Heil Hitler.*'

*

'Hardly got a wink last night, they was making such a racket.'

Hoste was seated behind a couple of women on a bus bumping along to Waterloo. They were talking about the night's five-hour raid by the Luftwaffe.

'Yeah, I know. Between that and his nibs snorin' his 'ead off . . .'

There was a long pause before her companion replied, her tone more meditative than indignant, 'This war. I can tell you, gives me the sick.'

The bus had halted, the road ahead a minefield of broken glass and debris. It stuttered forward again, steering around a huge crater. Hoste gazed out of the window. The city seemed to him like some creature woken from a terrible dream, stunned to find itself so bedraggled and bruised. As he stepped off the bus the morning air stung his eyes with its bitterness. Greasy coils of black smoke and brick dust drifted off the bombed buildings about him.

Around the corner, a shift in the usual perspective stopped him in his tracks. Sometimes, when deep fatigue set in, his dreams would start up their hallucinatory dance while he was still awake. He blinked, sharply: this was no dream. One entire side of Medway House had disappeared, exposing a wall of mauve Victorian brick unseen in sixty-odd years. A fire crew were just packing up, their hoses coiled like green intestines about the pavement. Hoste was still in his ARP uniform – he had been on duty all night himself – so he ducked beneath the rope and approached. His footsteps crunched over glass. He looked up at what remained of the block's scarred face; every window had been blown out, like eyes made sightless.

Another ARP warden had noticed him standing there.

'Direct hit. Took that side clean off. They've only just put it out.'

'Casualties?'

'Four dead. Some injuries. Most of 'em had gone to the shelter.'

6

Hoste continued to stare, apparently in a daze. The man looked at him again.

'You know the place?'

After a pause he nodded. 'I live here ... I mean – lived here.' He wasn't looking at the man, but he caught his whistling intake of breath.

'Sorry. That's bad luck.'

'Not really,' said Hoste. 'On another night I might have been in there.'

He began walking towards the wide front door, which was hanging off its hinges. Behind him he heard the man mutter a warning about its being unsafe – falling masonry – but Hoste ignored him. He stepped inside the ruined shell and looked around. A chaos of plaster and wood and brick lay strewn about. Black cinders whirled down mockingly through the air, and a steady drip of water came from where the firemen had drenched it with their hoses. He clambered across the hall to check the staircase, its iron banisters twisted and buckled from the blast. How often had he tramped up and down these stairs? He looked up, and saw a gaping wound that let in the sky. His rooms had been on the sixth floor, and he tried to imagine the scorched and blackened husk of what remained. What had he lost? His clothes, of course, photographs, nothing of any great value. Some books, a few German Baedekers, which he wouldn't be needing in the foreseeable future anyway. The furniture was the landlord's. The rest – his files, papers, correspondence – was locked up in his office at Chancery Lane. It was the luck of the draw. Buildings like this came down overnight, every night, and people had to go and live elsewhere. He wondered if it said something about him that he wouldn't miss it much.

Back outside he took another long look. They were unlikely to let it stand, such was the damage. He could feel the brick dust at the back of his throat, and he spat. As he walked away he remembered, on his bedroom wall, a little watercolour of the Bay of Naples. His mother had painted it when she was on her honeymoon. He hadn't really looked at it for years. But it occurred to him now it was something he'd have liked to save.

It was only when Hoste was heading back across Waterloo Bridge that he realised it was a Saturday. There would be no use in calling at the Section. His chequebook was at the office, but his keys had been in his rooms and the banks were closed. He stopped to think. Was there anyone in London he might apply to? The problem in his line of work was that you didn't tend to make many friends. It hadn't bothered him before – it didn't bother him now – but he did feel in need of a wash and brush-up.

He remembered then that Traherne lived in St James's, not far from here. It was just the sort of place he would live, now he thought of it. He checked in his pocket for coins and stopped at a telephone box on the Strand, but he couldn't reach the operator. The lines were down; the raids had probably hit the exchange. He would have to take a chance. Bone-weary, he caught a bus trundling west on the Strand.

'My dear man,' cried Traherne, rearing back at the sight of him. 'You look like you've been dragged halfway round the park.' Hoste began to explain what had actually happened, but was cut short. 'Come in, come in!'

Traherne, in his dressing gown and pyjamas, presented a boyish figure. His fine, caramel-coloured hair was tousled from bed. He led his guest through a panelled hallway and up a flight of stairs, chuntering away. 'Bombed out, eh? I did hear the place getting fairly knocked about.'

As he pushed open the door to his flat he turned suddenly to Hoste. 'How did you know to come here, by the way?'

'Oh, I recall you once told me you lived on Jermyn Street, so I walked up and down looking for your name on a doorbell. There it was.'

Traherne looked at him slyly. 'Trust you to chivvy a fellow out! Here, sit down, I'll make us some tea.'

While he was gone Hoste took in his surroundings – the marble fireplace and its fender, art deco mirrors, glinting drinks trolley, old master prints on the walls, the soft patterned carpet underfoot. Hoste had not encountered taste in such casual abundance. He supposed there must be family money to go with his education (Christ Church) and his spell with the Guards. Traherne was in his early thirties, a shrewd, raffish, clubbable sort of man who belonged so comfortably to the world of 'influence' that no one seemed able to resent him for it. Hoste still regarded the younger man as his patron; they had become friendly with one another, if not actual friends. All the same, he could never have imagined himself pitching up on the man's doorstep like this to beg for help.

'Here, drink this,' said Traherne, pouring his visitor some tea. 'I'll run you a bath. I dare say you'll need some fresh kit?'

Hoste gave a grimacing smile, and plucked at his sleeve. 'This uniform is all I have left.' And it reeks of dirt and smoke, he thought.

Traherne looked wonderingly at him for a moment, and laughed. 'Well, that – and your sangfroid. Must say, I've never seen a fellow so nonchalant after losing all his worldlies ... We should put you on a poster promoting the "Blitz spirit".'

Ten minutes later Hoste was submerged in a steaming tub. He wasn't sure how Traherne had finessed such luxury – this wasn't the usual couple of lukewarm inches of bathwater – but he had no intention of objecting. The bachelor ease was evident, too, in the bottles of cologne, the Floris soap, the badger-hair brush and cut-throat razor. 'Help yourself,' he'd said, and Hoste did so, giving himself what his barber in Holborn would call 'a right old shave'.

'I've dug out a few things for you,' Traherne said as he emerged from the bathroom. 'Lucky we're about the same size.'

'This is awfully good of you,' said Hoste, following him into the bedroom. On the bed, laid out with military regimentation, was underwear, socks, twill trousers, a shirt and collar and tie, even a pair of conker-coloured brogues.

'They might be a squeeze,' Traherne said doubtfully. 'I have improbably dainty feet.'

The shoes pinched a little, but Hoste was too grateful to pass them up. Once he was dressed Traherne pulled open his wardrobe, revealing a long queue of coats and jackets, of a quality Hoste could tell at a glance was far beyond his means.

'Not the velvet smoking jacket, I think,' Traherne said, pushing it down the rail with a snigger. 'Here, this might suit. Relic of Oxford – done stout work for me!'

It was a jacket of dark green tweed, nicely tailored with leather buttons and a neat ticket pocket on the right. A scent of hair oil and warm afternoons rose from it. Hoste put it on, and Traherne took an admiring step back.

'My word, you do cut a dash.'

They returned to the living room and had another pot of tea. It felt strange to be sitting there in another man's clothes, like an actor in rehearsal. Since they knew little of one another personally the talk soon turned to work. Traherne was eager to know how the latest recruitment had gone.

'Promising, I should say. Engineer, lives near Watford. Reckons he can get out blueprints of the Mosquito – from the de Havilland factory.'

Traherne squinted in surprise. 'D'you believe him?'

Hoste nodded. 'He seemed too nervous to be making it up.'

There was a pause before Traherne spoke again. 'How soon can you complete your report on him?'

Hoste made a brief calculation. The only key to his office had been lost in the inferno of his flat, so a locksmith would have to be found. 'Tuesday lunchtime.'

'Good. I think we should move quickly on this one. Will you send it directly to me?'

They were preparing their goodbyes at the threshold of the flat when Hoste remembered something else.

'He hadn't heard of Marita, of course.'

'As a matter of fact there's news on that front. We have a lead.'

'What is it?'

'All in good time. Castle will send you the memo. First you must go home and get some –' He caught himself, and slapped his hand to his forehead. 'Beg your pardon, my dear fellow, I wasn't thinking. Where *will* you go?'

'Oh, a hotel, for the moment.' He cut a glance at his colleague. 'I'm sorry to ask this, after all you've done, but I'm rather – short –'

'Of course! – I should have thought.' He dashed back down the hallway, returning moments later. 'There's five pounds and some change. Will that be – ?'

'It's plenty. Thank you. I'll get it back to you on Monday –'

Traherne waggled his hand in dismissal of this delicacy. But Hoste was scrupulous, and would insist on repayment of the loan at his earliest opportunity. It was a rule with him never to be beholden to anyone, least of all a colleague. Having said their goodbyes, he wandered out again into the morning and breathed in its sulphurous air. The all-clear had gone an hour ago. From a few streets away came the wail of an ambulance, hurrying on to the scene of another disaster from the night before: a collapsed building, or a damaged shelter, or a body found blown into a basement. There was no end to it; you kept going, because there was nothing else to do. A line he'd overheard a few hours ago recurred to him – *This war would give you the sick.*

He smiled, and shivered, and walked on.

2

Amy put down her pen and rested her chin on joined hands. This was getting them nowhere. From below the window rose the honk and grind of traffic on Brook Street. She suddenly wished herself down there, striding along the pavement. You could forget, during the raids, what a wonderful thing it was to be able to roam about the London streets. Instead, she looked across the desk at her client – first of the day – a lawyer's clerk named Sidney Kippist, short, bald, fortyish, fussy. Dismay must have registered on her face because he leaned towards her and said, 'Is something the matter?'

'To be honest, Mr Kippist, yes – there is. When we ask our clients to list their requirements, we expect a mixture of positives and negatives – "I would like this sort of lady, but not that; I prefer this sort of personality rather than that." You see?' She looked at his registration form again. 'Yours are all negatives – "Not lazy or common. I don't like them 'made up to hell'. Must not chew gum ... Not too old, not too fat. Not American." It doesn't seem to me the best frame of mind in which to set out on the road to matrimony. After all –' *you're no bloody oil painting yourself,* she wanted to say – 'a successful marriage is based on mutual tolerance. Give and take.'

Kippist shifted in his seat. 'I thought it would be better to establish straight away what I *didn't* want. Besides, they aren't all negatives, as I recall –'

'Well, yes,' conceded Amy, 'but I don't think "a lady with capital preferred" is much to go on. A lot of gentlemen we interview "prefer" someone with money. It's not very original. Can you tell me what *personal* qualities you admire? Someone modest and quiet, perhaps? Someone who likes to play the piano, or takes an interest in animal welfare, or likes to go for walks, or ... what?'

He protruded his lip thoughtfully. 'Yes. Someone like that.'

Amy stared at him. *Well, which, for heaven's sake?* 'I'll just have another look through my files, if you'll wait a moment.'

As she riffled through her papers, she heard a thin clicking sound from across the desk. Kippist was gazing off into the middle distance, seeming not to notice the irksome noise his false teeth were making. Oh, the poor woman who got this one ... She wished she might spare her.

'I've three more for you. How about this – twenty-eight years old, Londoner, convent-schooled. At present in the WRNS –'

'No one from the forces, sorry,' Kippist said firmly.

Fair enough, Amy thought. It was hard to plight your troth to someone who next day might be dispatched to the other end of the country. She returned it to the file and opened another.

'This lady, thirty-seven, runs her own flower business in Walworth –'

'No'.

Amy tilted her head enquiringly. Did he object to Walworth? she wondered. Or to the fact she was in trade? Or to her being thirty-seven? Kippist wasn't saying; he merely folded his arms and looked blank. She put it aside, and opened the last one.

'Twenty-nine. Slim, dark-haired. Music teacher. Friendly, outgoing ...' She glanced up at Kippist, who had leaned forward in his chair.

'Do go on,' he said.

'Lived with her parents in north London until recently, now shares a flat with two girls ... Would like to meet a gentleman between thirty-five and forty-five years old.'

Kippist was nodding in approval. 'Does she mention anything about children?'

Amy read down the form. 'Says she would like them, but would understand if her future husband would prefer not.'

By now he was rising to enthusiasm. He began to crane his head around, hoping to peek at the file for himself. 'What's this lady's name?'

'Miss Ruth Bernstein.'

At that Kippist drew in his chin sharply. He stared at Amy as though she had made a dreadful faux pas. 'Oh, Miss Strallen – a Jewess?!'

Amy blushed, though not for herself. 'There is nothing on your application to suggest you objected ...'

He shook his head. 'I should have thought that was *understood*.'

A silence fell between them. Amy closed Miss Bernstein's file and put it back in her drawer. She wondered if she ought to apologise, but decided that graciousness would be wasted on him. She rose and smoothed down her skirt.

'I'm afraid that's all I have for you at present, Mr Kippist. We'll be in touch when another suitable candidate comes up.'

Kippist gave a little sigh of disappointment. 'The search goes on, then.' He was turning to go when something apparently occurred to him. 'Will you amend my form regarding, um ... ?'

Amy said, with a tight smile, 'Noted. And if you think of anything else to include on your proscribed list be sure to tell our secretary, Miss Ducker.'

He hesitated a moment, perhaps hearing an insolence in her tone. But he said nothing, took up his hat and left.

Once she heard the door to the street close Amy went out into reception and, with a quick double knock, put her head round the door of the adjacent office. Johanna looked up from her desk, strewn with registration forms she was busily matching up in pairs. Since there was no client in the room Amy sidled in and, with an exasperated oath, threw herself full-length onto the horsehair couch.

'Sometimes I could just strangle them,' she said to the ceiling.

'Oh dear,' said Jo. 'Who's been in?'

'Kippist. The lawyer's clerk.'

'Ah, yes. So what did he want?'

Amy half snorted a laugh. 'A fantasy! A feminine paragon – like the rest of them. You know, it never fails to amaze me how a certain kind of man considers himself absolutely entitled to a woman half his age – and twice as good-looking.'

Jo smiled. 'Women can be unrealistic, too.'

'But not like men! Honestly, if you'd seen this fellow, just sitting there dismissing one nice girl after another, as if he were some Adonis ...'

'I know. Just think of it as a business transaction. We have his five guineas, that's what matters. When's your next?'

Amy glanced at her watch. 'Midday.'

'Right, that gives us an hour for matching. Pull up that chair.'

'Matching' – or 'mating' if they were feeling silly – was their term for introducing people on the basis of their registration forms. They had been running the marriage bureau for just over two years. Johanna Quartermaine, born of a well-to-do family that expected nothing of her beyond marriage and children, had sickened of waiting for Mr Right and decided to put her mind, and social skills, to some use. Aware of the legions of single people (like her) on the lookout for a suitable partner, she saw the potential in setting up an agency that would do the matchmaking for them. Drawing on a small inheritance from a late aunt, in the spring of 1939 she rented run-down premises in Bruton Place, bought a few sticks of office furniture and devised a short brochure.

There is no reason to feel ashamed because you wish to marry the right person. In fact, you ought to rejoice in your good sense for knowing it is better to seek out opportunity rather than simply wait in hope. You would consider yourself weak-minded and irresponsible if you did not make provision for other aspects of your life. How much more important is this question of making the right match!

The Quartermaine Marriage Bureau will put you in touch only with people who fulfil the requirements you specify. It is our job to remove the inconvenience and embarrassment that so often block the path to romance. We cannot guarantee the ultimate prize of matrimony, but we promise to give you the best possible chance of it.

Price on application to 36 Bruton Place, W., or telephone MAYFAIR 1629

Her enterprise was rewarded even sooner than her optimistic spirit had bargained for. By the end of the first week, she had received fourteen applicants; by the end of the first month she had nearly a hundred. Once it became apparent she would not be able to cope with the numbers on her own she advertised for a business partner. From the moment Miss Strallen sat down opposite and offered her one of the cakes she had bought en route at Fortnum's Johanna had a feeling she was the one. Her instinct was not misguided. Amy had been raised in a large gregarious family and would spend holidays with cousins organising theatricals and concerts. In her youth she had shown promise as a musician; she liked to play the violin and also had a fine singing voice. Her school thought her good enough to apply to the Royal College of Music, but in the event the examiners considered her playing 'exuberant' rather than accomplished. She bore the disappointment lightly, thinking they were probably right.

Her good sense did not desert her as she grew older. She developed a shrewdness about people, and how best to deal with them. She put the shy ones at their ease and the cocky ones in their place. Her natural warmth, combined with a streak of irreverence, made her a favourite with clients, who began recommending the Quartermaine Marriage Bureau to others even if their own marital ambitions had yet to be realised. People continued to pour in, and the QMB moved to larger premises round the corner on Brook Street. A secretary was hired to deal with the appointments book. The *Daily Mail* ran an article reporting on the venture's success.

As the summer rumbled to a close, however, events in Europe might have spelled the end for the bureau. With war declared, Jo and Amy assumed that the lowering mood of dread would put paid to thoughts of marriage. Yet instead of a downturn in numbers, the business actually boomed. Young men about to take up arms urgently sought out wives they could write to – dream of – while they were away. Women, conscious of the previous generation's loss in the Great War, wanted to secure a husband before it was too late. In fact the only danger to the bureau was the physical one from the sky; during the autumn Blitz their office building had had two close shaves. They discussed the possibility of moving to the suburbs while the bombing continued, but in the end neither of them could bear to leave Brook Street.

As midday approached Miss Ducker called in to tell Amy she had three more appointments that afternoon.

'I thought it was only two.'

'Gentleman just telephoned to confirm. Four o'clock. His cheque's come through, but no registration form.'

'Righto.'

Her twelve o'clock was a pretty twenty-year-old who worked in the office of a munitions factory nine till seven, Monday to Friday, and helped in a forces canteen every other Saturday afternoon – she barely had time to go out and find a man. Her two o'clock was a fiftyish stockbroker who had lived with his mother until her death last December; it transpired that her last wish was for him to find a wife. He himself seemed unenthused by the prospect. At three she interviewed an RAF pilot, a type so in demand she was able to present him with a choice of ten female clients straight off. Amy had talked about this with Jo, who reckoned that pilots were sought after because of their sense of proportion. 'You can't risk death in the air every day and still have a mind for petty quarrels.'

Her last client of the day arrived at four o'clock on the nail. She was feeling rather beat, so she made herself a quick cup of tea in the tiny kitchen upstairs. Stubbing out her cigarette she cracked open her office door and asked Miss Ducker to send him in.

He entered and met her eye with a little nod, which she interpreted as a sort of modesty, his way of saying 'I am grateful for your help'. He was of average height, wearing a smart tweed jacket and club tie. Slightly pasty skin, but not bad-looking. He had a very deliberate way of checking his place, eyes to the left, then to the right, as if he were casing the room. She asked him to take a seat, and uncapped her fountain pen.

'We'll just go through the formalities of registration,' she said brightly. 'It's Mr ... ?'

'Hoste. Jack Hoste.'

She began writing. 'Date of birth?'

'January the 20th, 1899.'

'Address?'

'The Russell. In Russell Square.'

She looked up. 'You mean – you live in a hotel?'

'For the time being. I was bombed out a couple of weeks ago.'

After a murmured consolation she continued the questionnaire, though his answers came in a distracted, halting way. He was more absorbed in looking about her office, his eyes glinting as they settled on this or that object. It was as though he were trying to memorise the whole room.

'So, you've not been married before, Mr Hoste?'

'No.' He smiled at the idea.

Amy smiled back, put down her pen and folded her hands on the desk. 'May I ask what sort of lady you hope to marry?'

He blinked at her, evidently taken by surprise at the question. The quizzical light in her eyes disconcerted him. 'I'm open to suggestion.'

She stared at him, equally puzzled. 'How d'you mean?'

'Well, I thought you had all the data – that is, the relevant information.'

'I think you've got this the wrong way round. Our bureau is set up to match clients with suitable partners. The *type* of partner is decided by the client, not by us. We don't know what you want until you tell us.'

Hoste realised he ought to have been briefed. Preparation was key in his line of work; forewarned was forearmed. He had read the words 'marriage bureau' on the Section memo and ignored them, possibly because he didn't know what a marriage bureau was. His long delay in replying prompted Amy to fill the silence.

'You must have *some* idea of the lady you're looking for ...' Her tone was encouraging, which made him want to help.

It was not a question he had considered in some time. Now he heard himself reply as if it might have been a stranger speaking. 'I should hope for someone – a woman who – if it were possible – would like me.'

He really hasn't got a clue, thought Amy, who nonetheless felt touched by the pathetic simplicity of his reply. 'That's perfectly reasonable. But you need to be a little more specific.' She saw his blank expression and pressed on. 'We look at things like compatibility. For instance, when a farmer has applied to us –'

'You get farmers here?'

'We get all sorts. As I was saying, with a farmer we will try and match him to a woman who enjoys country life, fresh air, looking after animals, and – clearly – doesn't mind hard work.'

'The farmer wants a wife,' said Hoste with a wondering air.

Ignoring this, Amy continued. 'Of course compatibility involves so much more than one's occupation – there's also age, religion, social standing, family commitments, a preference for town or the country.'

'That's a lot to consider.'

'Indeed it is. And that's before we even address matters of temperament and personality. Do you want someone who's the life and soul of the party, or the quiet and homely type?' For a moment Hoste thought she was asking him a direct question. Amy saw the confusion in his eyes. 'It was a hypothetical point. May I ask you a personal question, Mr Hoste? You've had lady friends, I'm sure ...'

(Though based on present evidence she wasn't sure, at all.)

'Yes, yes. Though not recently. The last one was about five years ago.'

'I see. Can you perhaps describe her to me?'

He squinted at her. 'You mean – as a person?'

'If you wouldn't mind.'

He hadn't thought of her, of Jane, in a while. Was it five years – or six? A nice girl. He wondered what she was doing now. As he was describing her, though, he found himself looking more closely at the woman, Miss Strallen, across the desk from him, concentrating. She had a funny way, in repose, of resting her tongue on her teeth. He supposed she was late twenties, maybe thirty. Her hair, mid-brown, shoulder-length, was very shiny. How did she get it like that? She had neat, slim hands, he noticed; altogether not bad-looking. He could not help warming to her open, approachable manner; it was so very different from his own.

He was jolted from this reverie by the sound of her voice. 'So from what you've told me, this Miss Temple – Jane – was confident and gregarious. She liked tennis, travel, cookery. Keen on dogs. Quite well off. Very interested in you and your work. I must say, she strikes me as an ideal girl!'

'She was, I suppose,' he agreed.

'Perhaps, then, we could try to match you with someone similar?'

She saw his face cloud. He looked away, and gave a slow shake of his head. 'I don't think so.'

'But why ever not?' she said, perplexed.

There was a pause while he searched for the words. 'Because ... because I don't think I could bear to disappoint someone like that again.'

She frowned, staring at him. 'What makes you think you'll disappoint her?'

He smiled, but sadly, and rose from his chair. 'Just an instinct I have. I'm sorry, Miss Strallen, I'm not really the right sort for your ... business.'

He held out his hand, which she took, somewhat at a loss. Like a lot of men he hadn't really understood what her 'business' was – the idea of a marriage bureau was a new one – but he seemed suddenly eager to be gone.

'Well, if you're sure. I'll have our secretary return your registration fee –'

'Don't worry about that. Keep it. I'm sorry to have wasted your time.'

He touched the brim of his hat, and was gone.

I could have handled that better, he thought, on his way back through Mayfair. His ending of their interview had been too abrupt – graceless. She had looked quite shocked ... But he had sensed her interest in him, or at least in the irreducible oddity of his character.

Shopkeepers were putting up their boards for the night, blinds were being drawn down in readiness. They had had three weeks of heavy raids, not just in London but all over the country – a spring Blitz. You could almost tell from people's faces, from their hurried movements, that they were in for another night of it. Under the vast encircling dark, the streets, shaken from last night, vibrated with apprehension.

Back at the hotel room he began to change into his ARP uniform and pulled the blackout curtains closed. He had rather enjoyed staying at the Russell – the impersonal mood of hotel life suited him – though of course it was too expensive to maintain in the long run. He unlocked the desk drawer and took out the memorandum Castle had sent him. As usual there was no heading, no date or signature, no clue as to where it had come from.

> A record has been located of MARITA Pardoe (née Florian) travelling from London to Germany, September 1935. On this occasion accompanied by a Miss AMY STRALLEN: friend or colleague, status uncertain. Duration of stay four weeks. Both resident in Berlin, later travelling to Nuremberg and Munich. At present, STRALLEN working at office in Brook Street, Mayfair – marriage bureau (?). May still be in contact with MARITA.

He took the flimsy memo into the bathroom and placed it in the sink. He lit a match, held it to the paper's edge and watched the flame curl around it, browning into black, eating up the white. Flakes of charred nothing floated up. He glanced at himself in the mirror, the embers making an eerie chiaroscuro of his face. It was not unlikely that Miss Strallen had thought him rather sinister today. The flame went out, and the room went black.

3

Walking along the seafront Hoste stopped to look at the barbed-wire defences ranged on the shore. He wondered if the Germans would think them as puny as he did. The light in Hastings this morning was the drab white of laundry that had been through the mangle once too often. Seagulls wheeled above him, calling each to each.

He spotted a pub at the far corner of Warrior Square and went in. The saloon smelt of last night's lock-in, mingled with the tang of fish and vinegar. He drank a pale ale very quickly and ordered another. He hated these 'away days', but he knew that his ring of disloyalists had to be kept in good order. Most were quite manageable, but now and then you got a few unstable ones, talking too loudly in public, making a nuisance of themselves. You had to take that sort in hand if you didn't want the balloon to go up.

He finished his second beer and checked the address in his notebook. Outside, he saw a bus pass along the parade, the single bit of traffic he had noticed since his arrival. You could die of the quiet in a place like this. He began walking west up the hill, past a dairy, a bank, a butcher. A woman pushing a pram went by. He reached another terrace of shops, and found the one he was looking for: Norman Antiques Emporium. He pushed open the door, setting off a little bell, and waded into the cavernous resting place of a thousand unconsidered objects. From inside glass domes, stuffed birds – a kingfisher, a puffin, several types of owl – trained their sightless gaze upon him.

He picked his way through a jumble of gloomy Victorian furniture to the proprietor's desk. In a wicker-backed chair sat a dumpy, rosy-faced old dear who looked up from her knitting at his approach. She gave him an expectant smile.

'I am here to enquire about a pair of duelling pistols,' he said with heavy significance.

'Just down those stairs, dear,' she replied, not bothering to acknowledge the coded phrase by which she should recognise him. (Her reply was supposed to run 'I'm sorry, they've already been sold'). She clearly preferred her knitting to the cloak and dagger.

He descended the narrow flight of stairs, inhaling the scent of ancient dust and rising damp. A single bulb illuminated the basement passage. Voices rose and fell from behind a wall. Someone must have heard him, for a door at the end cracked open and a shadowed face peeked round.

'Mr Hoste? This way, sir.'

He followed the summons. The room he entered was a musty old parlour, with a fireplace and cherrywood table redolent of an eighteenth-century coffee house. Brasses and prints, some of actual coffee houses, decorated the lime-washed walls. A patterned rug had been worn through by immemorial footprints. At the single window hung a pair of ratty net curtains. The smell of damp persisted. Around the table sat four people he recognised, and one he didn't. The man who had spoken to him was Ernest Dorling, tall, gaunt, with an ingratiating manner that didn't match his restless troubled eyes. Having assumed the role of host he began reacquainting him with the assembled. The ferrety man with brilliantined hair and sallow complexion was Gleave, and the slot-mouthed woman in the brown cardigan and spectacles was his wife, Eileen. Next to her was Alfred Herzig, a jowly, stiff-looking man with a moustache that might have done duty on a Prussian cavalry officer. On his right was Franks, a morose young bruiser with pitted skin and a twitch that made Hoste feel sorry for him.

'And I don't believe you've met Mr Scoult,' said Dorling, gesturing to a heavyset fellow of about forty with a ruddy complexion and wavy grey hair. He stood up and shook hands with Hoste. Scoult radiated a chummy air, as if he'd rather have been meeting in the saloon bar Hoste had just left.

'Heard a great deal about you, sir,' Scoult said, with a wink. His accent was northern, possibly from Yorkshire. 'I might have some information that will interest you –'

'We'll come to that in due course, Mr Scoult,' Dorling cut in, his tone slightly agitated by the newcomer's pushiness. 'First of all, I'd like to present our esteemed guest – if I may address you so, Mr *Hoste* –' a nervous tinkle of laughter went round the room – 'with a report on recent activity in the district of Hastings and St Leonard's. Mrs Gleave has agreed to keep the minutes of this meeting.'

Mrs Gleave, poised with pen and paper, returned a nod.

There had been, said Dorling, a number of tip-and-run raids by German planes in the last month. Some had hit their targets: a church, a library, several local businesses and shops had sustained bomb damage. The most significant was a direct hit on a school clinic, resulting in casualties. Mrs Gleave observed, with a satisfied grin, that a pregnant mother and two young children had been killed – several more had been injured.

'So that information we gave you at our last meeting clearly did the trick. The pilots knew where to bomb.'

She was still smiling rather proudly. Hoste, staring at her for a moment, gave a slow nod. 'Intelligence regarding the layout of the town has been very useful. Our friends in Berlin are pleased.'

Scoult pulled a demurring expression. 'And yet the raids continue to miss targets more often than they hit them.'

'Many *near* misses in the last two weeks,' said Dorling, trying to sound positive, 'including a narrow squeak for the ARP headquarters. A great pity.' He asserted that the tip-and-run raids were worthwhile, all the same. 'For the record, four hundred houses have been made uninhabitable, and over a thousand people in Hastings are now homeless.'

Murmurs of approval greeted this statistic. Hoste looked around the table, their expectant faces tilted towards him. 'Unavoidably, night raids are prone to error. Bombing in built-up areas cannot be exact, even when supplied with coordinates. But, as I've said before, your willingness to gather intelligence is vital to the Luftwaffe.'

Discussion then turned to the likelihood of invasion. While debating the relative strengths of the Wehrmacht they put forward theories as to why Hitler had so far refrained from the great thrust – *fahren gegen England*. Rumours were still abroad that troops would be parachuted into the country wearing disguise, though no one at the table seemed to take this very seriously. Germany would only invade once they had control of the skies, and after the Spitfire Summer of last year that objective had been shelved. Still, Britain was vulnerable in its coastal defences – South Wales, East Anglia – and the Home Guard, for all their pluck, could not be expected to mount a proper resistance. Gleave, the best informed of the company, wondered if Hitler had turned his sights in a different direction: Russia, for instance.

Hoste was fascinated by what they knew, and what they didn't, though he seldom volunteered an opinion of his own. It was his policy to listen, to absorb, to remember. When Herzig asked him if he had received any private assurances regarding the Führer's plans, he gave a self-deprecating half-smile. 'You flatter me, Mr Herzig, by suggesting I might be privy to such information. And even if I were, I know you are too much of a professional to believe I would readily disclose it.'

Herzig laughed, and the others joined in. He had taken the rebuff in exactly the spirit it was intended: we are men of the world, let us not fall out over matters of protocol. Up to this point the mood had been agreeable, albeit what they were agreed upon was the violent overthrow of the British government and the immediate institution of Nazi rule in its place. It was only when the name of Oswald Mosley came up that the atmosphere began to change. Mosley, focal point of British Fascism, had been detained in Brixton Prison for almost a year. His wife, Diana, was imprisoned at Holloway. There was no sign from Whitehall that they were about to end their internment – a cause of outrage to the company. Franks, hitherto almost silent, now spoke up.

'We wouldn't be in this mess if Mosley had seized his moment. The BU should have stuck it to the Jews before the government and the police got involved. If he'd been a bit more savvy about using force we could have imposed ourselves – could have scared the life out of 'em.'

There was a pause before Scoult said, 'I'm afraid you're talking rot, young man. Mosley did as much as anyone could. Times were against him.'

Franks's thin, pockmarked face coloured angrily. 'What would you know about it? Ever had a battle on the streets with the commies and the Jews? Half of what's wrong with this country is it doesn't want to get into a fight.'

'We appear to be in a fight at the moment,' remarked Gleave drily.

'You know what I'm talking about,' muttered Franks, whose hatred struck Hoste as virulent even by the standards of this company.

'It's important that we focus on the long term,' said Dorling, aiming for a conciliatory tone. 'We are agreed that the one hope of salvation for this country – and the world, come to that – lies in a National Socialist victory. To this end we must continue to do all we can for Germany.'

'Hear, hear,' said Mrs Gleave. 'It won't be long before the whole of Europe realises that Germany was right – Jewish Bolshevism is the enemy. Even if Hitler is attacked on all sides, the struggle goes on. Isn't that right, Mr Hoste?'

Again, Hoste sensed a hush descend whenever he was consulted for a view. It was a taste in miniature, he thought, of what actual power must feel like. There were people out there who not only liked to be ruled; they longed to be. He wondered if there were many of them. Enough to foment a Nazi revolution? Mrs Gleave was still looking at him eagerly.

'The struggle *will* go on, Mrs Gleave. But in common with Mr Franks I fear the BU has ceased to be a dependable ally. Their members are monitored by the police, and associating with them will only invite suspicion onto us.'

There followed a long discussion about how best to serve as a fifth column. Hoste rejected the efficacy of leaving lights on in buildings during a raid: they might just as likely be a decoy tactic of the Home Guard tempting German planes to waste their bomb-loads. He advised against other domestic acts of sabotage such as scrambling local radio signals. That kind of meddling might be traced to its source and jeopardise other cells of resistance.

'Caution should be our watchword,' he said, concluding. 'Do not draw attention to yourselves, whether in loose talk or disruptive behaviour. The best way you can serve the cause of National Socialism is to keep supplying reliable intelligence. Think of me as a direct conduit to the planning rooms in Berlin.'

Once the meeting was ended, Mrs Gleave went off to the kitchen to make tea. While they stood and stretched their legs, Scoult took Hoste aside. 'A useful meeting, I should say,' he began, appraising Hoste from beneath his brow. 'May I ask – being a newcomer to this company – is it true that you're –'

'Gestapo,' said Hoste, anticipating his question. 'At present their single agent at large in this country.'

'What happened to the others?'

'They were caught, Mr Scoult. Most are interned, but a few, unwilling to be taken, paid the ultimate price.'

Scoult nodded gravely. 'How have you managed to ... stay undetected?'

Hoste, with a shrug, said, 'One of course depends on luck. I've had some close calls in my time. The best safeguard, however, is discretion. You learn to judge who can be trusted, and who cannot. An agent lives or dies by his ability to know.' He waited a beat for this to reverberate. 'But tell me, what's this information you have?'

Scoult had been filling a pipe as they talked, and now lit it. A whitish-orange glimmered within the bowl, and he shook the match out. 'Dorling here told me about a certain person you've been trying to locate. Marita Pardoe?'

'You know her?'

'From before the war. She and her husband Bernard were at a number of British Union meetings I attended. We got to know each other a little.'

'I see. Are you still in touch?'

Scoult shook his head. 'Last I heard he was picked up by the police. I gather he's at the internment camp in the Isle of Man.'

'And what of her?'

'Not sure. Someone told me she'd left London for Ireland. But it's also said she got back to Germany.'

'So she managed to escape ...'

'Oh, Marita is too clever to get caught. Rather like yourself!'

'Can you describe her?'

He pulled a doubtful expression. 'Tall, quite imposing. Well dressed. She's not really like anyone I've ever met. One of those people who seems to look right through you. Articulate, a lot of cunning, knows her own mind. Impatient, I'd say –'

'With him?'

'No, no. I mean with the British Union – she thought they were completely ineffectual. Hopeless. She had quite sophisticated ideas about subversion – not just inside Whitehall but in business, and industry. Infiltrating the top levels and working through the whole structure. A plan for the long term, she said. In the meantime, she wanted to stir up unrest on the streets and get the government on the run. That would be the first step to installing a dictator.'

Hoste nodded. 'Ambitious.'

'Aye. Though unlike certain folk –' he flashed a look across the room at Franks – 'Marita had thought it through.'

It sounded like the woman Hoste had been tracking. The more he heard about Marita the more he found his interest piqued – it was the mark of an exceptional agent to have remained elusive for so long. He thanked Scoult and handed him his card.

'If you hear anything more about her – anything at all – do give me a call. I imagine Mrs Pardoe and I would have much to talk about.'

It was time to leave. Dorling made his usual speech of thanks to him for his visit, and assured him that they would be 'working night and day' to accumulate intelligence. They all stood in anticipation of his departure.

'My thanks to you all,' said Hoste, and raised his arm. '*Heil Hitler.*'

As he exited the room he felt, not for the first time, like a priest who had just dispensed his blessing.

The train back from Hastings was slow, delayed by broken signals from the recent raids. Arriving at Charing Cross he walked down to the Embankment and stepped onto a tram. As it halted in the Kingsway tunnel another tram was arriving at the adjacent platform. He stared out at the faces through the glass, pickled in the dim aquarium light of the car. They seemed to him lost souls, passing one another every day, every night, pressed together by necessity yet utterly alone in their needs, fears, longings. The human face was a window, but it was also a wall. What secrets did they keep locked behind it? And behind the wall of the face, the vault of the heart.

Picking up his key at the hotel reception, he was informed by a desk clerk that a gentleman was waiting for him. He passed down the corridor into the panelled bar, still hushed at this hour. A few residents – he recognised them by now – were installed. At a table near the window sat Castle, reading *The Times*.

'Ah. There you are,' he said, folding up his newspaper and fixing Hoste with a pleasantly sardonic smirk. Castle, at fifty-nine, was the old man of the Section; his face was pouchy and lined, in contrast to his dark sleek head of hair. Hoste wondered if he dyed it. His manner was studiedly calm, and his eyes had a slow droop suggestive of a foreign dignitary involved in a discreet negotiation. He raked his gaze around the room.

'Hotel accommodation ... have you come into funds, old boy?'

'It's temporary,' replied Hoste. 'I've been looking round for digs.'

'What of your old place – did they recover anything?'

'Not a stick. Got so badly hit they pulled the rest of it down.'

A waiter approached and took their order. Once he had gone Hoste looked enquiringly at his colleague. 'To what do I owe the pleasure?'

'Two things. Kilshaw's story has been verified. Seems that he does indeed have someone on the inside at de Havilland.'

'Good. Though I should warn you – he hopes to be rewarded.'

'Hammond can look after that. In the meantime, make him feel appreciated.'

Hoste returned an impatient nod. 'What else?'

For answer Castle bent down to his briefcase and withdrew a buff-coloured file, which he handed over. Inside, Hoste found a single photograph. It showed a group of four young women, in holiday mood, posing for the camera; they stood in front of a tourist coach, evidently about to board. He studied the picture for a moment. It had been taken some years ago, but he was almost certain that the tall smiling girl in tennis shoes was someone he recognised.

'That, I believe,' said Hoste, squinting, 'is Miss Strallen.'

'Correct. And that one –' his fingertip hovered over the black-haired girl next to her – 'is Marita Pardoe. Florian, as was.'

He looked up sharply. 'Are you sure?'

Castle, enjoying his surprise, nodded slowly. 'As sure as we can be. Taken on Beaumont Street, Oxford. You can just see the Randolph Hotel in the background.'

Hoste stared at the face – thin, dark-eyed, watchful, aloof. After two years of searching this was the first picture of her he had ever seen.

'Dates from '34, we think,' Castle continued, 'when she and Strallen were at secretarial college. According to our researches a group of them were going on a day trip. These two must have got on well, because the following year they went on another – to the Fatherland.'

It wasn't much, but given how little else they'd got on Marita, it was significant. This was a woman who had made a point of covering her tracks – no letters, no documentation and, until now, no photographs. Recruiting her would be his greatest coup yet. Castle seemed to read his thoughts.

'You've got that bloodhound look. Anything doing at Hastings?'

Hoste shook his head absently. 'Scoult knew that the husband had been interned. No clues about her. Looks like I'll have to try Miss Strallen again.'

'I don't understand. Why didn't you ask Strallen in the first place if she knew Marita?'

'Two reasons. First, we know Marita is a crafty operator. If she gets wind that someone's looking for her she might turn tail and disappear for good. Second, we can't be sure yet where Miss Strallen's sympathies lie. They may have a bearing on whether she'd be prepared to direct us to Marita.'

'How will you manage it?'

Hoste's expression was pensive. 'With the utmost caution. Miss Strallen is still our only link – we mustn't scare her off.'

After a pause Castle said, 'What's this "marriage bureau" she runs, by the way?'

'Hmm? Oh, it's a peculiar sort of agency that introduces people who, well, want to get married. I showed up pretending to be a client, which backfired somewhat.'

Castle's arch smirk gave way to a laugh. 'Now that I'd like to have seen. She'd have her work cut out finding *you* a wife.'

Hoste laughed along, conscious of being an object of light mockery to his colleague. But it had done the job: unpromising – inept – though his introduction was, he had made contact with her. As he watched Castle chuckling he was already planning in his head a way to secure the confidence of Amy Strallen.

4

The music lifted and rang around the vaulted ceiling of the National Gallery's octagonal room. Amy glanced down the row of listeners, their faces uptilted, perfectly still. Some held their penny programmes on their laps. Not a seat unsold. The steam of damp clothes, with their damp dog smell, had slowly receded. She had had to queue in the rain for today's lunchtime concert, but she didn't mind and nor, it seemed, did anyone else – a solo performance by Myra Hess was worth getting soaked for. The final swirling cadenza approached; the notes were like tiny steps up a hill, surefooted as they neared the summit, then that trembling pause just before the purling descent down the other side – the wisdom and feeling of Chopin clinched in that lovely final chord.

An ecstasy of applause.

As people began to move around her Amy remained seated, trying to hold on to the fleeting sensation of joy. Just the merest trace lingered, then it was gone. She rose, folding her mackintosh over her arm, and joined the shuffle for the exit. She had just got through a knot of people chatting about the concert ('awf'ly good') when a man stepped in front of her. His distant smile suggested that they had met once, but for a moment she couldn't place him at all. When he spoke she faintly recognised his voice.

'Hullo again,' he said. 'Remember me?'

And now she did remember – his face, but not his name. 'Oh, hullo. You came to the bureau ...'

'Indeed I did. And you were very patient with me.' He held out his hand. 'Jack Hoste.'

'Yes, hullo ...' She gestured with her eyes at the people streaming past on either side of them. 'You've been at the concert?'

He nodded. 'I drop by when I can. May I – ?' He indicated that he might accompany her out of the room, and they fell into step. The gallery walls, denuded of their paintings, prompted him to say, 'I always feel melancholy when I see the blank frames here, don't you? Like a lot of small emptinesses inside one large emptiness.'

'But it's not empty – look at all these people.'

'True. I meant empty of things – the things the gallery was built for.'

Amy squinted at him. 'Yes, but they've filled it with music instead. Or do you think that has less value than paintings?'

He heard a note of challenge in her voice, and smiled. 'I just miss looking at the pictures. But you're quite right. Myra Hess and Chopin are excellent compensation.'

She nodded, apparently satisfied by his concession. They were now approaching the main entrance; outside on Trafalgar Square the rain had continued to fall. I'm going to be soaked, thought Amy, pulling on her mac. Hoste too was hesitating on the threshold. He wore a hat but no coat. They pushed through the doors and descended the steps.

'So how's business?' he asked. 'Fixed up any more farmers?'

She smiled and shook her head. 'No farmers lately. This morning I set up a garage owner with a lady who manages a shoe shop. Then I matched a solicitor with an antiquarian bookseller.'

Hoste listened, and said quite seriously, 'I suppose you have to be quite careful in your business. I mean, you couldn't risk matching a dentist to a manicurist, for instance.'

Amy frowned at him. 'Why ever not?'

'Well, because they'd fight tooth and nail.'

He waited a moment for it to sink in, and was pleased to hear her laugh – a surprisingly throaty laugh, at odds with her prim dark clothes. 'That's very silly,' she said, almost accusingly. 'But very funny.'

He inclined his head in acknowledgement. As they quickened their step towards the edge of Charing Cross Road, a bus rumbled over a puddle, nearly spraying them both in its slipstream.

'For God's sake,' Hoste exclaimed, and turned to Amy. 'What d'you say we get a cup of tea and wait for this rain to ease off?'

She glanced at him, hesitating. It seemed rather presumptuous. But the rain was awful, and she didn't have another appointment till four o'clock ...

'There's a Lyons just round that corner,' he added.

'All right, then.'

Arriving, they found the place full to the door, the windows steamed up with people crowding in from the rain. Their eyes met one another in a forlorn way, and they laughed. She supposed this would be the moment to part, but Hoste sensed an opportunity.

'What am I thinking! There's a flat I've rented up the street – we could have our cup of tea there for nothing.'

'I thought you lived in a hotel?'

'I did. I moved out a few days ago. Come on – it'll save us getting drowned.'

A port in a storm. He didn't look a dangerous type, though the childlike watchfulness of his manner was disconcerting. He was what her friend Bobby would have called a rum cove, and yet rather compelling too, in a way she couldn't yet fathom. She gestured for him to lead on. As they hurried up St Martin's Lane they talked about the raids, and she thought: the war has allowed us to behave like this – to accept a sudden invitation to tea from a near stranger. They turned into a paved court lined on either side by bookshops. On reaching an unmarked door halfway along, Hoste let them in and led her through a narrow hallway to the stairs.

'I should warn you,' he said, as he put his key to the lock, 'it's not very homely.'

She walked in, prepared to see a chaos of unpacking. But in fact it only looked bleak; dust sheets shrouded the furniture, and the walls sported ghostly blanks from the previous tenant's pictures. Unopened crates stood around. Naked bulbs depended from the ceiling, and the windows were uncurtained. He seemed to have adapted the front room as an office; papers and files were stacked in wobbly ziggurats on the carpet. A smell of dust and neglect coated the air. He was right about one thing, she thought – there wasn't a trace of homeliness in it. But then he *had* lost everything at his last place.

Grimacing in apology, he whipped the dust sheet off an armchair like a matador with his cape and asked her to sit down. 'I've had to work here, too, as you can see. The electricity at my office has been out from the raids.' He removed another stack of papers from the chair next to her.

'I think – I seem to remember – you're an accountant,' she said.

'Something like that. I work at the Inland Revenue – involves a lot of chasing unpaid taxes.'

Before he repaired to the kitchen, Hoste did a little more stacking and squaring off, though as far as Amy could tell it was merely a light rearrangement of the mess. While he was gone she took a cigarette from her case and lit it. There was no bookshelf to view, nothing for a visitor to browse, and no pictures or photographs to brighten the room. It wasn't just unhomely – it was woebegone in its sheer anonymity. She would never have allowed a stranger to inspect such a scene.

Her gaze, starved of interest, happened to fall on the heap of files he had just been tidying. A name on the very top file leapt out at her, and she picked it up in disbelief. BERNARD PARDOE. Unable to resist she peeked inside at the client details. No question: it was him. What were the chances of that? Still with the file in her hands she didn't hear him come back into the room.

She looked up, startled. 'Oh, I'm sorry – nosy of me. It's just that –' she held up the file – 'it's the strangest coincidence.'

'What's that?' said Hoste, not looking at her as he balanced the tea tray on another cairn of papers.

'Well, this man. Bernard Pardoe. I know him – or rather, knew him. He married a friend of mine.'

He looked at her keenly. 'Really?'

'Yes. Marita Pardoe. Marita Florian, as she was.'

'You still see her?' he asked, keeping his tone casual.

'Not for years. I was at a secretarial college with her. We were quite close for a while ...' He nodded, encouraging her to go on. 'We went on a couple of holidays together before the war – one of them to Germany, as a matter of fact. Marita was very eager to go to Nuremberg, for the rally.'

'You saw Hitler?'

She nodded. 'From a long distance. Quite a spectacle. This must have been in '34. Or '35. Most of the time we were walking in the Alps.'

'Ah! I used to go on Alpine holidays. *Kennen Sie Tirol?*'

'Er, no. You speak German?'

He nodded. 'We used to have summers in the Tyrol – I dare say it'll be a while before we see another one.'

They both fell silent at that.

'So what happened – with Marita?' he went on.

'Oh, well, she got married. And got rather involved in politics. The British Union of Fascists. She and Bernard were both party members.'

'Did you ... fall out?'

Amy paused for a moment, squinting at him. 'You seem very interested in this, for some reason.'

Hoste, excited by the tug on his line, had got ahead of himself. Her expression had become clouded with suspicion. It was absolutely imperative he didn't rush her now. He sat back, and began pouring them each a cup of tea. 'You might be able to help me, that's all. Pardoe has been in the wrong tax category for years – he's owed a considerable rebate. But he's dropped out of sight. My best chance of tracking him down would appear to be through his wife.'

She tweaked her mouth in regret. 'As I said, I haven't seen her in years. I know she and Bernard lived in Germany for a while. The last I heard of them was just before the war – they were back in London working for the BU.'

She sensed him mulling over this information. It was a pity that Pardoe was not traceable – tax rebates were probably quite rare, and he and Marita had often been short of money. She sipped her tea and cast a look around the room. Without quite meaning to say it out loud she mused, 'It must be hard to start all over again.'

'I beg your pardon?'

'I mean, losing all your possessions. I wouldn't know what to do with myself.'

He looked at her as though he hadn't considered the problem before. 'Oh, it wasn't such a disaster. I didn't really own a great deal – I've never been a collector of anything. Some stamps, when I was a boy, that's all. I find it simpler not to be attached to things.'

'But what about basic things – clothes?'

'I bought some more. There's government relief to be had, eventually, and my mother was kind enough to send me a few things that belonged to my father.'

'You mean –'

'He died a couple of years ago. It was rather fortunate that she hadn't thrown it all out.'

Her eyes strayed involuntarily over what he wore today, and she did notice something slightly old-fashioned in the cut of his jacket, and the shoes. A dead man's shoes ... She was impressed by his sangfroid, and somewhat repelled by it, too. It was surely not quite human to sound so carefree. But it fitted with the rest of him, his strange social manner, and the unpredictable shifts from blankness to warmth and back again. He was looking at her in a curious way.

'Tell me, how did you get started in this marriage business?'

She choked off a laugh. 'You say that as if it's something exotic, like snake-charming. I was a secretary in an advertising agency. One day I saw a notice for a situation that sounded ... more interesting. I didn't know what a marriage bureau was – nobody did, really – but I went along and met Johanna, whose idea it was. We took to each other pretty quickly. After a year she offered me a partnership.'

'So you've made a success of it.'

'We've not done too badly.' She tilted her head slightly. 'Are you thinking of trying again with us?'

'Oh, no. No. That's not why I was asking – I was just interested. Are you, um –' he glanced at her hand – 'married?'

She shook her head. 'I know, it seems odd. How can you be an expert in matchmaking when you don't have a husband yourself?'

'Well ...'

She assumed it was what he'd been thinking, and smiled. 'You can be good at something even if it's not part of your experience. You don't have to be able to lay an egg to know whether it's fresh.'

'That's true,' he said.

Amy glanced at her watch. 'I'd better be off – I have a client at four. Thank you for the tea.'

She stood up, and straightened her skirt. He was on his feet, too, and directing at her that look of intense appraisal she found unnerving. 'I'm very glad we ran into one another. Perhaps I'll see you at another concert.'

They were back in the hallway when she saw his ARP tin helmet hanging on the back of the door. 'That must keep you busy,' she said, with a rueful look.

He nodded. 'I'm on duty again tonight. A full moon, I hear. A bomber's moon.'

'Good luck,' she said, and paused on the threshold. 'I don't know if it would be any use, but I might have Mrs Florian's address somewhere – Marita's mother. She lived up in Maidenhead, I think.'

'That could be very helpful,' replied Hoste, holding the door.

'Cheerio, then.' They shook hands, and she left.

Amy got back to Brook Street with five minutes to spare. Her next appointment was a furrier from Whitechapel, in his early fifties. She quickly went through the requirements they had distilled from his letter.

> Not bossy, impatient, or a socialist.
> No bridge players.
> Someone who is 'down to earth' and has no 'airs or graces'.
> Would prefer a working-class girl of refinement.
> Good teeth essential.

Just then Jo put her head round the door. 'You seem to be in a good mood.'

'Do I?'

'I could hear you whistling as you came up the stairs. How was the concert?'

'Lovely. Holst and Chopin. Then I ran into someone I half knew, a client. He turned out to be a music lover, and an Alpinist. We had quite a lot to talk about.'

'Oh,' said Jo, raising her eyebrows. 'Good-looking?'

She laughed. 'Not my type. He was perfectly nice – but he was more interested in correcting tax claims. Takes his work very seriously.' At that moment there was a ring at the door. 'Talking of which –'

From reception Miss Ducker called through that her four o'clock had arrived. Jo suggested that they might finish the day doing some 'mating' (the word still made them giggle). Amy had a quick primp in the mirror, composed herself and asked the secretary to send him in.

Evening was coming on. Miss Ducker had gone home a while ago. Amy and Jo, on their hands and knees, had covered Jo's entire office floor with registration forms, matching this one with that. It was companionable work, and they laughed as often as they rolled their eyes at the vanity on parade before them. Amy had in her hand a report from Mr Woodcock, their most annoying client, about a recent match-up.

'Listen to this,' she said, altering her voice – she was a good mimic – '"She is most agreeable, but I do not imagine I shall ever feel matrimonially inclined towards her. She is too tall, not very comely, rather too old in that she looks her age, walks badly, and her legs, though passable, are far from perfect. Mentally, she is delightful, but I cannot overlook the signal importance of the physical. Would you be so kind as to try again?"'

'Oh, the pompous, conceited oaf!' cried Jo.

Amy gazed off for a moment. 'And yet – there's almost certainly a woman out there who'd be delighted to receive Mr Woodcock's attentions.'

'I know,' Jo conceded. 'God help her.'

She glanced at her wristwatch.

'Goodness, the time! It's nearly seven. Come on, we don't want to get caught in the blackout.'

Jo stood up quickly and hurried out to fetch their coats. When she returned to the office Amy was still kneeling on the floor, frowning over a form.

'Amy, for crying out loud! We must go.'

She was right, Amy knew; the city had taken a terrible pounding in recent weeks. They had cowered at the steady death drone of planes coming from the south-east. There was no sound like it. And yet that fear in the pit of the stomach, the fear it might be your turn – she didn't feel it tonight. What was wrong with her? Outside, Mayfair was huddled in darkness. Windows and fanlights had a poked-out look. Only the pavements still glimmered from the day's rain; moonlight had picked out the puddles.

'A bomber's moon,' Amy said, as they quickened their steps towards Bond Street Tube.

Jo gave a little shiver. 'What a macabre phrase. You know, walking past these old buildings I've been trying so hard to memorise them, in case they're not here the next day. But then I forget, and I'll come across a new lot of damage and not have a clue what's been lost.'

'I wonder how much longer it can go on. Strange, there are still people who believe we should make peace with Hitler – they say he really wants England as an ally.'

'A bit late for that, I should have thought. Who are these people anyway?'

'Oh, nobody I know. That man I met today – Mr Hoste – he told me there's quite a few who think suing for peace is the only way to end it.'

'Sounds like wishful thinking.'

Amy shrugged. 'He says that Germany wants a settlement, and that the real enemy is Russia.'

'But how does he know this? I thought you said he was an inspector for the Revenue.'

'He is. But he seems to know an awful lot about – well, everything.'

Jo gave Amy a look that suggested she had more to say on the matter, but their arrival at the Tube entrance curtailed further talk.

'Goodnight, Amy dear,' she said, touching her cheek before she descended the steps. 'Be careful.'

Amy continued on her way through the blacked-out streets. The sirens had started up their protesting wail. By the time she reached her flat on Queen Anne Street she thought she could hear the distant buzz of the bombers' engines. But it was only her senses playing tricks on her. Later that evening, when the sound became unmistakable, she peeked through the blackout blind in her living room. Searchlights had lit up the sky, their long fingers sweeping the horizon. She thought again about Hoste, who would be out there now, on duty. His self-possession, rather unsettling close up, would be very useful in a raid, she supposed. You wouldn't feel so panicky with him at your side. Any minute now the ack-ack guns would cough into life. To the west she saw the pale moon hanging there, and she wondered how something that beautiful could be so fatal.

5

Unlocking a hidden drawer, Hoste took out a scroll of paper and spread it across the desk. It was a detailed blueprint of the RAF's new Mosquito night fighter. The focus was smudged here and there – whoever had operated the mini-camera was no expert – but otherwise the copy was quite legible.

They were in his office on Chancery Lane, where from below came the sound of rubble being cleared. Hammond had been leaning over the desk to scrutinise it. Her silent absorption fascinated Hoste: the way her gaze pored over the document was positively carnal. A minute or more went by before she relaxed her shoulders and glanced up.

'No doubting it. This is the real thing,' she announced.

'I never *did* doubt it,' replied Hoste with a faint smile.

'Clever of you to find Mr Kilshaw. We must keep hold of him.'

Kilshaw, family man and Rotarian from Bushey, Herts, had somehow got his hands on a bona fide piece of sensitive material. It had everything but TOP SECRET stencilled across its face.

Hammond sat down again, her expression still clenched in thought. After a moment she said, 'Does anyone at de Havilland know there's a leak?'

Hoste shook his head, and sensed her satisfaction. Tessa Hammond, senior member of the Section, was in her mid-thirties. She projected a critical beadiness that would sharpen of a sudden into acerbity. The first time he had met her, six years before, he recalled some bland remark he had made being pounced on by her. 'That's a very conventional way of looking at it,' she had said haughtily; it had made him cautious around her ever since. Yet he liked her, even admired her. Her dark shoulder-length curls framed an oval face that was carefully – perhaps too carefully – made up; the application of powder and lipstick felt somewhat effortful, as if she were trying to conceal rather than enhance something. Her figure was good, and she knew how to dress. But behind her capable front Hoste thought he discerned a brittleness. He had heard stories of her romantic failures.

She was looking at him in a quizzical way. 'That jacket you're wearing ... Have I seen it on someone else?'

'Traherne lent it to me the morning I was bombed out. I tried to return it the other week but he insisted on my keeping it.'

'Hmm. I can see why. Rather suits you.'

From the street rose a noise like the seething hiss of a wave – glass being swept up from the pavement. Holborn had been a major casualty of the raids. Hoste went out to make a pot of tea. On returning he found Hammond studying the photograph Castle had given him, the one of Marita with Amy Strallen.

'So which of these is your woman?' she asked.

'If by that you mean Miss Strallen, she's second from the right.'

Hammond screwed her eyes a little, and said with a sniff, 'Pretty.'

'I suppose she is,' he said mildly.

'Can she be recruited?'

He tipped his head back. 'Not sure. She knows Germany – visited Berlin and Nuremberg with Marita in '34 or '35. I haven't probed the politics yet.'

'I see. And ... how old?'

'If you're that curious you can meet her yourself. She's due to call here any minute – said she has something for me.'

Hammond returned a knowing look. 'Better not. I don't want to queer your pitch, now you have your claws in.'

Hoste sighed. 'You make me sound rather predatory. I assure you, the lady has suffered no clawing – or pawing – from me.'

They talked on for a while, mostly about last night's raids, until they heard a ring at the door below. Hoste made claws of his hands in a gesture of wolfish menace, and Hammond, with a smirk, took her leave.

Amy, stepping off a bus on Fleet Street, had found Chancery Lane heavily knocked about by the night's bombing. The raids had lasted nearly until dawn, and she had listened to them from the basement at Queen Anne Street. At times the thud of the bombs seemed very near, and the walls of the building had trembled from the shockwaves. When she left the flat this morning the air swarmed gritty from the dust and debris.

On her way up the stairs of his building she passed a woman whose candid once-over nearly stopped her in her tracks. Hoste's office was located at the end of a corridor. He stood up to greet her. It had been a couple of weeks since they'd run into one another at the Myra Hess concert.

'I've just passed a lady on the stairs – do you know her?'

'Ah. Dark hair, about so tall? – yes. A colleague of mine.' He invited her to sit down. She looked around her; it seemed awfully tidy for a government office. She noticed an adjoining room through an open door.

'Looks like this place had a lucky escape last night,' she said, gesturing with her eyes at the chaos outside.

'That's what I think most nights,' he replied. 'How goes the marriage market?'

She detected again that sceptical note in his voice when he asked about her job. It made her wonder why he had ever applied to the bureau in the first place.

'As a matter of fact we've been getting more business than we can handle. Marriage has never seemed so à la mode.'

'Despite the mood of gloom?'

'Or maybe because of it. Johanna – my colleague – thinks that the war has made people reconsider their priorities. They look at marriage as a kind of insurance against disaster.'

'There may be something in that,' he said thoughtfully. He renewed his gaze upon her. 'So you mentioned that you had news ...'

She pulled a dubious expression. 'Well, I wrote to Mrs Florian, as I told you. I received her reply yesterday. She said Bernard has been interned in the Isle of Man. Marita, last she heard, was living in Ireland – but she's not been in touch for over a year.'

'Do you think she's telling the truth?'

Amy looked at him in surprise. 'About Marita? Why ever would she not be?'

'She may be covering for her. Marita's half German, so she may fear internment herself.'

After a long pause she said, 'It must be a lot of money they're owed for you to be pursuing them like this.'

'I can't be specific about the sum, but – yes, it's a fair amount.' Hoste steepled his fingers together. 'I've been wondering about Marita, actually. When you knew her, was she very ... fanatical?'

She considered the question. 'She was certainly interested in Germany, and Hitler. It had always been her plan to go to Nuremberg.'

'What did you think of her views?'

'Her views about what?'

'Well. The Jews, for instance.'

Amy stared at him. It seemed as though he wanted to provoke her into an argument. 'I'm not sure what this has to do – you must understand, I haven't seen Marita in years. I don't know what she's been up to since. I'm sorry I can't be of more help to you.'

Hoste softened his tone. 'And I'm sorry to pry. I become rather fixated at times. Forgive me.'

Mollified by this, she smiled. 'Don't worry. You take your work seriously. That's a good thing.'

'I'm glad you think so. Some of my colleagues aren't so understanding.'

'Like the lady I passed on the stairs?'

'Just so. I'm thought of as the department's bloodhound.'

She glanced at her watch, and rose. 'I should go. But here, there's something I want to give you.' She reached into her handbag and took out a slim package, cased in brown paper.

He looked startled as she held it out to him. 'For me?'

'It's nothing much, just – well, open it.'

He undid the string and slowly unwrapped the paper. He stared at what lay there – a small framed pencil sketch, about four inches by six, of a mountain range. He was silent for so long she thought he was embarrassed by it.

'It's of the Tyrol. You remember, we talked about it –'

'Of course I remember,' he said, though he still seemed in a kind of trance. She had found the thing in an antiques shop in Marylebone. It was modest but pretty, and she had paid ten shillings for it.

'I thought – I hoped – it might be something you'd like,' she went on, not quite sure any longer.

He nodded slowly. 'It's ... delightful. And exceptionally kind of you.' His gaze lifted from the picture, and he smiled.

'When you talked about summers in Austria and how you wouldn't see another for years, it felt so sad. It isn't much of a substitute, but at least when you look it may remind you ...' She didn't add that it would at least do something to brighten his dismal billet.

A few minutes later, as he was showing her out, Amy said, 'So what now? Is the Pardoe file closed?'

'Oh, I dare say we'll keep an eye out. The Revenue never sleeps.' His tone became coaxing. 'If in the meantime you happen to –'

'Yes?' She had a sudden inkling he was going to ask her to dinner.

'– come into contact with Mrs Pardoe, do let me know.'

She reproached herself. This one was a professional to the last. They shook hands, and she left.

On her way back through Soho Amy stopped at an Italian grocer's on Berwick Street. She bought a pitiful sliver of sausage meat, a few tomatoes and a small wedge of cheese – the ration was beginning to pinch. All the shops looked starved. War had cleaned them out.

As she was leaving the place she saw a notice in the window announcing 'The proprietors of this shop are British subjects, and have sons serving with the British Army'. It reminded her that she had not called recently on the Pruckners, a middle-aged German couple who lived in the flat below hers. The previous summer, when paranoia about 'enemy aliens' was at its height, the couple had suffered grievously. Despite being resident in England for the last fifteen years Paul Pruckner and his wife Gertrud were targeted under Churchill's directive to round up Germans, Austrians and Italians more or less indiscriminately. They were sent to an internment camp in the north-west. Their son, a journalist of leftish sympathies, was considered a security risk and packed off on a ship of internees to Canada. The trials of separation had exacerbated the mother's heart condition, though the family's plight cut no ice with the authorities. When Mr Pruckner was finally released he had asked Amy, his neighbour, for help in seeking information about their deported son.

Of course she had done what she could, wrote letters to the relevant offices, and eventually word came back that the son was safe, albeit on the other side of the Atlantic. Yet Amy still felt indignant on the Pruckners' behalf, and embarrassed that they should be so grateful for her small act of charity. Out in public, their German accents had made the couple objects of contempt. They had been taunted, shunned, spat at. She had thought of them again during this morning's interview with

Mr Hoste. It was hard to tell if he approved of the present treatment of émigrés or not. He had seemed fascinated by Marita and her allegiance to Hitler – though that was before the war, when it was still acceptable to talk about Germany as a civilised country. She couldn't imagine that Marita, even with her 'fanatical' temperament, would be one of those who still regarded the Reich as a friend.

But then, how could she know? She tried to remember their holiday together in Germany back in '35. The signs of hostility against the Jews were too prominent to ignore: the graffiti, boarded-up shops, notices in public places forbidding their entrance, the sense of a whole society turning its back on former neighbours. At the time it had struck her as a matter of curiosity. In Nuremberg, at the rally, they had watched the marching and the displays of military might. They had even joined in the Nazi saluting, because it didn't signify anything. She hadn't connected it then with a war machine that would try to bomb them into oblivion. Naive of her, she realised now. Back in England Marita had stepped up her involvement in Fascist politics once Bernard came along, and the ties of friendship began to loosen. Yet even then she didn't consider Marita a true anti-Semite; she had joked about the Jews, deplored their ways, but so did many other people she knew.

She had crossed Regent Street and was idly glancing into a shop window when a distant reflection loomed in the glass. She turned round to look. Strange, but she thought she had seen that man's coat earlier in the day. The man himself had turned on his heel, without showing his face, and was lost again in the crowd. Had he been following her? She would have dismissed it as coincidence, only she had felt her footsteps being dogged on other occasions recently. She was a good noticer of things, especially of clothes – a combination of blue worsted coat, striped tie and trilby might imprint itself for a few seconds, and however unexceptional she would be able to recognise it again hours later.

But why would anyone be following her?

It was a question Johanna naturally asked when Amy voiced her suspicion later that evening. They were having a meagre supper at Amy's flat.

'I don't know,' she replied. 'But it isn't the first time I've felt it of late.'

'Is it the same man?'

'I'm not sure – I really can't tell.'

'It sounds very queer, darling.' Jo paused a moment, uncertainty in her eyes. She then said in a changed voice, 'Didn't you say you were meeting that chap again – the one from the Revenue?'

Amy nodded. 'I thought I might be able to help him with some information, but it didn't work out. You remember me telling you he was bombed out a few weeks ago? Well, I bought a little sketch for him – as a housewarming present. He doesn't have much else.'

'Nice of you. Did he like it?'

'I think so. Yes. Though he didn't overwhelm me with thanks.'

A knowing smile had tweaked Jo's mouth. 'But worth persevering with ...'

'Maybe. I have a feeling our acquaintance doesn't matter to him one way or the other. Something rather monkish there – one can almost imagine him living in a cell.'

Jo sighed, shook her head. 'Look at us. We run a marriage bureau, matchmake people Monday to Friday, yet neither of us with a man of our own. Not a good advertisement!'

Amy laughed. 'I suppose it's like being an outfitter. You know what looks nice on other people but can't always find the right thing for yourself.'

After supper they sat in front of the open window and had a cigarette. Amy had kept her ears pricked for the sound of planes, but all had been quiet. It seemed that London was to be spared this evening. The German air force had been concentrating its recent attacks on cities further north. It was a respite, but not one she could feel sanguine about; it would be their turn again soon enough.

Amy had received that morning a letter from Bobby, best friend and indefatigable partygoer, now stationed up in Scotland with the WAAF. Bobby's latest story of romantic entanglement, this time with a Scottish laird named Angus, had so tickled her that she recited it to Jo.

'I love this bit where she talks about dancing a reel – "Angus and I went at the thing so wildly that my suspender belt snapped in the middle of it! Front suspenders only, thank God – so I carried on regardless, like a plane on one engine."'

They both burst out laughing. Good old Bobs, thought Amy. It had gone eleven when Jo glanced at her wristwatch. 'Right, time to toddle off, and leave you to dream of your mysterious Mr Hoste.'

Amy rolled her eyes tolerantly. She sensed in Jo's teasing a vicarious interest; if she couldn't find romance for herself she would plot one for Amy instead. They belonged, both of them, to that multitude of odd women – not odd as in 'strange' but odd like a glove, or a shoe: missing its pair. They said goodnight on the doorstep, and Amy looked up at the velvety night, marvelling at the peace. No guns, no searchlights, no drone of engines.

She had just turned off the gas when she heard the doorbell ring from below. She presumed it was Jo, returned to collect something she'd forgotten. Hurrying down into the darkened hall she unlocked the door – and reared back in surprise at the sight on her step. It was a stranger, a man – no, a woman in a blue worsted coat. She wore a man's trilby over her brow, which she cocked to reveal her face.

'Hullo, Amy,' she said, and Amy knew the voice at once, though she could hardly believe her eyes.

Standing there, with a half-smile she used to know well, was Marita Pardoe.

6

Her hands had trembled as she poured them each a drink –
Scotch, she'd asked for. Amy had felt herself being scrutinised
as she carried the glasses to the couch. She sat at one end, her
guest at the other. Marita had cast her appraising eye around
the room, and in doing so seemed, to Amy's discomfort, to
comprehend exactly what she'd been up to in the time since
they'd last met. She had removed her hat to reveal glossy black
hair done up in a chignon. Her face had retained its somewhat
pointy allure; a pale forehead sat above dark, dark eyes, while
the red-lipsticked mouth was made emphatic by the sharp jut
of her chin.

'It must be – you were at our wedding, of course – five
years?'

'Almost exactly. Spring of 1936.'

Marita nodded, smiling. 'I remember you gave us that exquisite water jug.'

Amy remembered too. It *was* exquisite – and extravagant,
given their subsequent disappearance from each other's life.
They stared at one another for a moment. Amy's gaze dropped
first – nobody could outstare Marita. It transpired that Mrs
Florian, despite claiming ignorance of her daughter's whereabouts, had in fact passed on Amy's letter enquiring about her
erstwhile friend.

'It's true I was holed up in Ireland for a few months. A safe
exile – though what a country. A superstitious, priest-ridden
wilderness. And the incessant *talking*. I managed to slip back

here at the end of last year. Under an alias, naturally. I'm obliged to be cautious.'

'Yes, I see that. But you surely didn't think I would –'

'Hand me over to the authorities?'

Something now occurred to Amy, who narrowed her eyes. 'Have you been ... *following* me?'

Marita's smile turned pitying. 'Forgive me, *meine Liebste*. I had to make sure you weren't in the pay of – I am determined not to end up like Bernard in some godforsaken camp.'

'How is he?'

'Furious. Miserable. He was taken by surprise. I, on the other hand, saw which way the wind was blowing.'

'Whereabouts are you?' asked Amy.

'Ha. Between the living and the dead. I'm afraid my address is classified – even among old friends.' Marita looked at her, and chuckled. 'You think me paranoid, I can tell. But there's the devil to pay for anyone who was involved with Mosley ...'

As they talked Amy began to remember why she had once been so bewitched by Marita. It wasn't simply that she was bright and quick-witted – Marita had something else, a charisma, a confidence that gripped and overwhelmed. It was combined with a force of personality that was almost glandular. She looked through people so easily it inclined her to arrogance; even friends she could take a vicious delight in crushing. Amy thought Marita saw through her, too, but for some reason it was her company Marita sought out above anyone else's. Indeed, it was she who had first befriended Amy, not the other way round.

She was just replenishing their glasses when Marita said, in a tone that carried more edge, 'So I'm still wondering. What *did* make you get back in touch?'

Amy, seeing no need to dissemble, said, 'As a matter of fact I was hoping to do you a favour. It seems Bernard is owed a substantial amount of money – a rebate – by the Inland

Revenue. An inspector wanted to know your address, and the only person I could think of applying to was your mother.'

Marita looked disbelieving. 'A rebate? That seems highly unlikely.'

'Why?'

'Because Bernard's tax affairs were in disarray. He was always in debt – the bailiffs would turn up at the door.'

Amy pulled a doubtful expression. 'The inspector I talked to assured me there was an error in the accounting.'

'But how on earth did this inspector know to get in touch with you?'

'Well, that's the funny thing. Quite by coincidence I happened to see Bernard's file lying there in his office – and I mentioned that I knew him.'

Marita's stare had hardened, and Amy knew something was wrong. 'Tell me exactly how you came to meet this man.'

So Amy went through it, from her first meeting with Hoste at the bureau and their accidental encounter at the National Gallery a few days later, to the cup of tea at his flat – *not* his office – where Bernard's file happened to be lying around. Marita listened in silence. It was the cold, measuring silence of someone who knew her own power. Amy remembered it of old. It wasn't just that she had respected Marita: she had been rather frightened of her, too.

She felt a distinct relief when at last Marita spoke. 'I find it difficult to believe that this Hoste is from the Revenue. Anyone working there could have found out that Bernard had been interned. From what I can gather he seems to be more interested in what I have been doing.'

Amy, thinking back, agreed this was the case, though it hadn't struck her at the time. 'He was a queer sort of fellow,' she said. 'But he seemed plausible.'

'They always do,' Marita fired back.

'Who are "they"?'

'Police. Snoops from the Home Office. The sort who would like to put me in prison.' Presently she said, 'Where may I find this Mr Hoste?'

Amy went off to fetch her diary, a sense of alarm gathering in her. She found his Chancery Lane address and wrote it down on a scrap of paper. Marita read it aloud, musingly, then tucked it in the pocket of her mannish trousers. Amy watched, and wondered – things might not go so well for Mr Hoste if Marita took against him. The idea of him being an impostor was baffling. Why would anybody claim to be a *tax inspector* who was not one? But then she remembered his curiosity about the Pardoes, a curiosity that didn't quite fit with his alleged line of business.

Marita asked her for a cigarette, and lit up. Through a veil of smoke she considered her old friend. When she spoke again her tone had reverted to the affectionate irony of earlier.

'Amy Strallen. I never imagined seeing you again. I was certain that you would be married ...'

Amy laughed and told her more about her work at the bureau with Johanna. Marita listened with a smiling grimace to stories of their objectionable clients. Her mind seemed to be turning over their previous conversation, though, for she eventually said, 'You told me Hoste came to you first as a client. Did you ... find him a match?'

Amy shook her head. 'He was rather awkward about the whole thing. But the afternoon we ran into one another he seemed altogether more ... agreeable.'

Marita took this in with a squint, as though Amy had implied more than she'd intended. From outside came the distant toll of the Marylebone Workhouse bell. Two o'clock. Marita softly put down her glass and rose from the couch. She walked over to the window and peeked through the blind onto the street.

When she turned back Amy was looking at her in puzzlement. 'Surely there's no one out there?'

'No. But I'm in the habit of checking. It has saved me before.'

'Really?'

'I'm on the police's list of enemy aliens – one of their "most wanted", I gather. Fortunately they have no recent photograph of me.'

'You sound like a regular Mata Hari,' said Amy admiringly.

Marita had shrugged on her coat and opened the door. 'Unlike her, I won't get caught.' Her gaze fell squarely on Amy. 'I still trust in the discretion of my friends. Hoste may be harmless, but while there is doubt I must be on my guard. Should he contact you, don't let on that I've been here.'

'Will we ... meet again?'

Her back was to her as they descended the stairs, but she could hear the smile in Marita's voice. 'Depend on it, my dear.'

Hoste was already seated in the Corner House on Coventry Street when he spotted his man coming through the door. Kilshaw seemed to carry himself with a good deal more confidence than he had at their first meeting in the pub. His step was almost jaunty as he made his way through to Hoste's table.

'Mr Kilshaw.' He shook the man's podgy hand and gestured to the chair opposite his own. They were meeting to discuss the filched blueprints from the de Havilland factory. Hoste explained that it had taken a while for their authenticity to be verified.

'But now they have been, and our friends –' he twitched his brow – 'are very pleased with you.'

Kilshaw sat back, spreading his hands in a cocky gesture of beneficence. 'Anything to help the war effort.'

'In acknowledgement of your services,' Hoste went on, 'I have been instructed to give you this.' He slid an envelope across the table to him.

Kilshaw peeked into the envelope, which contained five pounds. He counted them. Disappointment clouded his face.

'I'm grateful, Mr Hoste, don't misunderstand me. But last time we talked of a weekly stipend, did we not?'

Hoste returned a patient smile. 'Of course. I remember. But we need a guarantee that intelligence is provided on a regular basis before we make any long-term arrangement. There are other agents to finance, Mr Kilshaw – our resources are not unlimited. If you keep supplying us, we will ensure that you, as it were, go on the payroll.'

'I see,' said Kilshaw. 'So, you still consider me on probation –'

'Come now, that's not it at all,' said Hoste placatingly. He looked around the cafe, bustling and indifferent: no one was paying them the least notice. 'I have something else for you, as a matter of fact.' He produced another smaller envelope and handed it to him. 'Look, but don't take it out.'

Kilshaw did so. Inside was a discreet enamelled lapel pin, crimson and silver, embossed with a black swastika. He stared at it for a few moments before looking to Hoste for an explanation.

'It will help to identify you in the event of our friends' ... arrival,' said Hoste, dropping his voice low. 'I wear mine just here.' He indicated the hidden reverse of his lapel.

He could see that Kilshaw was appeased, like one who had received the equivalent of a Masonic handshake. Emboldened, he began to probe Hoste for more information about their 'friends', and what might be their long-range intentions. He had heard that the possibility of invasion looked less likely ... Had Hoste picked up any rumours from his masters?

'I'm as much in the dark about it as you. In the chain of command my position is not one that would merit such disclosures. Should I fall into hostile hands, it's better for me that I *don't* know. You understand?'

'Yes, yes, of course. Pardon me. But with these raids going on, it would be a mercy to know one way or the other. My wife's nerves, I'm afraid, have been pushed to the limit ...' He looked embarrassed for a moment by his own candour.

'The raids have been hard,' said Hoste. 'The building where I lived was reduced to rubble. We live in the dark, but we endure. What else is there to do?'

A few days later Hoste received a letter at Chancery Lane.

> Dear Mr Hoste,
>
> I have been advised through a third party that your office is dealing with the tax affairs of Mr Bernard Pardoe. As Mr Pardoe's accountant I am charged to pursue any outstanding payments on his behalf. My client is out of the country at present and unable to discuss the matter in person. I am available as his proxy, however. Would you be kind enough to visit me at the above address at a time of your convenience?
>
> Sincerely yours,
>
> Martin Fischer

Hoste wrote back to Fischer, indicating his willingness to help. With the trail to Marita going cold he supposed it was worth a try. On the day before they were due to meet, Fischer's secretary had telephoned to ask if their appointment might be rearranged. The firm had moved to temporary premises after bomb damage to their office building.

The premises were a grim, soot-smeared Victorian paperworks just off Curtain Road in Shoreditch. Hoste initially thought the building was derelict, but then noticed lights on in the upper storeys. He ascended an echoing stone staircase, following the handwritten notice that pointed to Fischer & Co. On the second-floor landing he found the door and knocked. He heard a voice calling him to enter. The office was austerely makeshift; a desk, a filing cabinet, two chairs, no carpet or curtains. A telephone stood sentry on the desk. A pile of correspondence waited to the side, a letter knife glinting on top of it. Presently a woman entered from an adjoining room. She was an imperious figure, mid-thirties, above average height, dark hair in emphatic contrast to her pale skin. Her movements were as studied and precise as a dancer's.

She introduced herself as Miss Berens, and invited him to sit down. 'I'm afraid Mr Fischer has been delayed. But I'm fully apprised of the case, so perhaps we can begin?'

Hoste had a queer feeling he had seen the woman before, but for the moment couldn't place her. 'Are you the lady I spoke to on the telephone?'

'That's correct,' she replied. 'May I see the papers relating to our client?'

Hoste had not expected to be drawn into the detail so quickly. But he had taken the precaution of mocking up a few sheets of figures on Inland Revenue notepaper just in case, and now handed them over. While she looked through them he studied her, the straight back, the animal quickness of her gaze, the stern self-possession.

'Interesting,' she said, looking up from the papers. 'I mean, "interesting" that you should imagine these documents might fool me.'

Hoste stared at her. 'I beg your pardon?'

'They are forgeries, Mr Hoste. They have not come from the offices of the Inland Revenue and nor – I am certain of it – have you.'

'Where do you suppose I've come from?' he asked pleasantly, though he felt a tiny quiver of apprehension.

'That is to be determined. First, however, I would like to know why you are interested in my client.'

The hesitation between her last two words was vanishingly brief, but Hoste had caught it, and now the thing had dawned on him. He felt an abrupt thrill of anticipation that was quite close to fear. 'To tell the truth, it isn't Bernard Pardoe I'm interested in. It's his wife. You, in fact. I presume I am talking to Marita Pardoe.'

She stared at him in disdain. 'Who are you? Hoste – is that your real name?'

61

He laughed. 'I'm rather offended you don't know it.'

'Why should I?'

'Because we have friends in common. And a cause.'

'Explain it, then.'

'Very well. It involves the covert organisation of a fifth column in this country. We are united in a conviction that National Socialism is all that can save us from the Jewish–Bolshevik conspiracy. This means resisting and undermining the British war effort, at least until Churchill and his government decide to make peace with the Fatherland.'

'Most impressive. And what is your part in this?'

He shrugged at her sarcasm. 'I am personally responsible for the recruitment of agents on the Reich's behalf. Their brief is to gather intelligence against the enemy. My brief is to report it to Berlin.'

'*Noch so ein Traeumer,*' she scowled. '*Wie gewinnt man diesen Krieg?*'

'*Um zu gewinnen mussen Sie den Feind kennen.* You speak German like a native. But you are part English, I think.'

'On my mother's side. I was born in this country.'

'Ah. One might suppose your loyalties were divided.'

'One would be wrong.' She paused, squinting at him. Her expression remained cold, unpersuaded. 'So you recruit agents on behalf of the Gestapo, yes? We must know some of the same people. Heinrich Brunner, for instance.'

Hoste shook his head.

'No? Well, then, you have come across Karl Greiser. Or Otto Mohr.'

'I'm afraid not,' replied Hoste. 'You see, I wasn't recruited in Berlin. It was here in London, before the war.'

Marita looked away, considering. She picked up the telephone on the desk, dialled, and muttered a few words before replacing the receiver. She might have been ordering a round of drinks to be sent up, but Hoste suspected something less friendly in the offing. She had said not another word before he heard heavy footsteps approaching down the corridor. A knock came, and two policemen entered. This was not a contingency he had planned for. He had not thought to arm himself.

She stood up and addressed the burlier of the two men. 'Constable Grigg. It's as I warned you. This man is an agent of the Third Reich, reporting directly to Berlin. He has come here today to try to recruit me. I must ask you to take him into custody immediately.'

PC Grigg, frowning, turned to Hoste. 'Got anything to say?'

Hoste, standing, gave the slightest shake of his head. He sensed months of patient groundwork about to be wasted. Grigg went through the formalities about taking him in for questioning. As he did so, Hoste noticed the man's boots, scuffed and worn in a way hardly befitting an officer of the law. And he was pretty certain that a shoulder holster was bulking beneath the man's coat. It made him wonder. The other constable – the killer's accomplice – was preparing to lay a hand on him when Hoste spun him round and locked an arm about his neck. From the desk he snatched up the letter knife and pressed it against the copper's neck. Grigg reared back in surprise.

'Another step back, if you please, Constable. First, remove that gun beneath your coat and place it on the desk. That's the way. Now, those handcuffs of yours – on with them. You too.' He pushed the other copper into a chair, and held the gun over him while he handcuffed himself.

He turned to Marita. 'I'm sorry that you've chosen to doubt me. Though not half as sorry as these two will be.'

'What are you going to do with them?' she said.

'Thanks to you they now know who I am. So I must make sure they don't go telling.'

Grigg, hearing the implication, looked at Hoste in alarm. 'Now see here –'

'Quiet. Step over to that door, both of you.'

Marita, rising from behind the desk, said, 'You're taking quite a risk, abducting two policemen in broad daylight.'

Hoste stared at her. 'You think they're going to see daylight? Goodbye for now, Mrs Pardoe. I feel sure we'll meet again.' At that he pointed the gun and opened the door. 'This way.'

Grigg turned an imploring face to Marita. But she only watched, apparently fascinated. Hoste moved them at gunpoint out into the corridor. 'You. Towards the stairs.' The two men began shuffling up the corridor, as meek as cattle. When they reached the top of the stairwell, Hoste cocked the gun and waited for them to turn. Their faces looked pale.

Hoste glanced down the well. 'You're probably thinking I'm not going to fire. Too many people around, it would attract attention. You're right. Better, as you've probably said to many a miscreant, to go quietly. Over those banisters. A broken neck won't be as clean as a bullet, but ...' He looked at Grigg, then at the other. 'Who's going first?'

There was an awful silence as the two men stood, glassy-eyed, immobile. 'You can't –' Grigg began, but his voice failed him.

'Can't? But I can. And I must.' He raised the gun. He could hear Grigg's breathing go shallow as he backed him against the banister rail. Suddenly Marita's voice, half amused, called them to a halt. She had stepped as silently as a cat up the corridor. 'Mr Hoste. Let them go. These two are not policemen – they are hired players in my little charade.' Grigg and his partner, white-faced, stood looking at one another, relieved. ('Thought I was a goner,' Hoste overheard one of them say while Marita uncuffed them and sent them on their way.)

When she invited him back to the office she opened her desk drawer and took out a bottle of Scotch and two glasses. She poured and handed one to Hoste.

'A peace offering,' she said. 'I apologise for that subterfuge just now, but I had to be certain. The police have spies everywhere.'

Hoste raised his glass. 'I'm pleased to meet you at last. You have quite a reputation among the people I associate with.'

She eyed him over her glass. 'I had often wondered if Berlin would ever succeed in planting an agent here. They have tried before.'

'I know. And all of them exposed. That's why they recruited me – a native.'

'Your circle ... how many do you run?'

'Between twenty and thirty, at any one time. And you?'

'I have a small band of like-minded people to call on. Those two you just met, for example. One has to be careful, though. The remnants of Mosley's mob are generally unreliable. No sense of discipline – or *style*.'

Hoste smiled. 'On that score I fear you may be no more impressed by the type I recruit. But they are loyal.'

Her voice became more confiding. 'And what of Amy Strallen?'

'I hardly know her. As soon as I learned that you two had been friends I kept her under watch. Then it was a matter of baiting the trap.'

'So she believes you're from the Revenue?'

'She has no reason to believe otherwise.'

Marita paused for a beat, then said, 'Did you ever consider recruiting her?'

He shook his head. 'I didn't get the sense she was sympathetic to our – What, am I wrong?'

She pulled an ambiguous expression. 'There was a time, in Germany, I thought Amy was ... susceptible. Attending a rally at Nuremberg indicates at the very least a degree of interest. Sometimes I thought I detected rather more than an interest. An enthusiasm.'

Hoste pictured her in his mind's eye. 'You know her far better than I. My first impression wasn't – but she seemed bright. Capable. If you think she's worth cultivating ...'

'I do. But let us agree – she must not know we have met. Better to work on her independently, then compare our findings.'

Hoste half smiled at her deviousness; like a good chess player, she always planned a couple of moves ahead. He couldn't be sure she was right about Amy Strallen; if she was, he had misjudged her. He finished his Scotch, and rose to leave. Marita watched him narrowly, like a cobra eyeing a mouse. They were allies, for now. But there was no friendliness.

'By the way, that Browning you took from him. May I have it?'

He handed the gun to her. She removed the magazine and examined it.

'So you really would have dispatched two unarmed men in cold blood?'

'Did you doubt it?'

She seemed to consider the question. 'No. That you didn't give me away when you could have done was the moment I knew. I'm glad I didn't have to take any drastic measures –'

'Such as?'

For answer she opened her drawer and took out an old-fashioned revolver. She squinted down the barrel. 'I would have put one right behind your ear.'

Hoste nodded. He knew – he had an instinct – that it wouldn't have been the first time she had killed a man.

7

Amy ran her eye down the list of the day's appointments, who all happened to be women. She regarded their female clients in a kindlier light: they tended to be more accommodating, more willing to take a chance with what was on offer. In interview men could be so brusque – unforgiving. Perhaps they knew that the numbers weighed heavily in their favour. There were far more single women out there searching than there were single men to supply them. Sometimes a sentence in their application forms leapt off the page and caught at her heart.

My sweetheart was killed during the war. If I can find someone like or as near as possible to what he was I should be very grateful.

Someone who will be a pal in every sense of the word.

Someone willing to marry an unmarried mother.

They were not all so sympathetic, of course. Women could be as imperious as the men.

Not a schoolmaster, clerk or parson. Nice hands rather important.

I am private secretary to a duke. Any man must be of my own standing.

No bridge, pub crawling, golf, passion for 'The Club'.

A knock came at her office door, and Miss Ducker announced her ten o'clock client. A woman in her mid-thirties entered, mid-brown hair, neat and well put together but awkward about her height (she half stooped to hide it). The smile she offered Amy was shy, possibly resigned, as if her presence there was the result of a practical joke. Her name was Georgina Harlow. She asked if she could smoke, and Amy pushed an ashtray across the desk towards her. Her voice carried a slight sibilance that reminded Amy of a girl she had known from school with a lisp.

After she had been through her details, there was a long pause before Miss Harlow spoke. 'I'm not really sure I should be here.'

'Oh. Why do you say that?'

'Well, my work as a civil servant keeps me so busy I hardly have a moment for ... anything else.'

Amy tucked in her chin. 'I'm sure even the Civil Service allows its employees some leisure. All work and no play ...'

Miss Harlow nodded, as though she saw the justice in this. But there remained in her demeanour something unresolved, withheld.

'I can't spare many evenings,' she said shortly. 'And with this wretched war one can't be certain whether tomorrow will be here or not.'

Amy put down her pen and looked at her. 'Miss Harlow, forgive me. It seems as though you're putting obstacles in the way before we've even begun. Our job is to introduce people to one another with a view to a long-term relationship. Sometimes they work, sometimes they don't. But we have to ensure your basic willingness to be available. D'you see?'

Miss Harlow looked down and with a movement of her shoulders signalled her unhappy assent. Sensing the need to tread carefully, Amy spent a few minutes discussing the kind of husband she might be looking for. On her application form the woman had been modest to the point of reticence, specifying merely that he should be older, enjoy 'hikes' in the countryside, and not mind that she spend time with her invalid mother.

'That isn't an awful lot to go on. One has to consider a man in terms of his character. What would you say is the most important quality?'

A silence intervened as Miss Harlow stared off into the distance, lost in thought. 'I should like – that is, I should *hope* he was gentle.'

Amy nodded her encouragement. 'That's a start. What else? Perhaps think of men who have courted you before –' It occurred to her almost instantly as the wrong thing to have said. Miss Harlow's expression recoiled in a wince of mortification.

'I'm afraid I have little experience to call on in that respect,' she said quietly. Then she raised her eyes to Amy. 'None at all, in fact.'

Amy tried to cover her surprise, though it must have been clear on her face. That this woman – good-looking, with nice manners and a respectable job – should have gone unclaimed her whole adult life ... 'I'm sorry, I oughtn't to – I find it hard to understand, that's all. You seem to me so ... eligible.'

For a moment Miss Harlow seemed on the verge of tears. But she managed to compose herself. 'I once thought so myself. But over the years I found – I realised – I simply don't fit in. I don't know why.' She paused, and smiled sadly. 'Oh, I've always had friends, and colleagues, of course. I know that I can "get on" with people. But whatever it is that attracts a man, I don't have.'

Amy said, as gently as she could, 'So ... why now?'

'I don't know. Time was when I hoped to have a child. That's probably out of the question now. But I can't quite give up the idea that – well, that I won't go through the rest of my life alone.'

Here was courage, Amy thought, voiced so meekly it might have escaped notice. She had checked Miss Harlow's age:

thirty-seven. That would be no disadvantage for a man; he could even afford to wait a few years. But the approach of forty was a black cloud hanging over a woman still hopeful of marriage. Wasn't this precisely where her job could make a difference? The bureau wasn't merely a clearing station for society's unmarried flotsam and jetsam. It could do people a genuine service in rescuing them from an abyss of lovelessness.

She beamed brightly at her client. 'Miss Harlow, I can understand how you had to nerve yourself to come here. It's not easy to admit to this sort of inexperience. But I'm glad that you have, and in return I'm going to try my very best for you.' She put forth her hand across the desk. 'Shall we make it a deal?'

Miss Harlow, surprised, but clearly grateful, took Amy's hand in her own.

Amy reread the letter she had received a few days ago, hardly more able to credit its contents now than she had then.

> Dear Miss Strallen,
>
> I have been meaning to write to you these last weeks, but business obligations prevented me. I would like to thank you for that most generous gift of yours, and hope you will allow me to take you to dinner one evening. I have in mind a place that does not trouble overmuch about food coupons.
>
> If such an invitation is agreeable to you, would you kindly let me know if next Tuesday would be convenient?
>
> Sincerely yours,
> Jack Hoste

It was typed, somewhat unfortunately, on Inland Revenue-headed paper, and felt like something he might have fired off to a professional acquaintance; its stiff Edwardian tone made her giggle. But then, as she knew, Hoste was a queer sort of fellow, and there was every chance he had composed such an impersonal letter in good faith. She could not deny harbouring a certain curiosity about him.

Tuesday came round, and at seven Amy left the office and walked out onto Brook Street. They had arranged to meet at a restaurant in Soho. The violet light of an early-May evening swarmed over the rooftops, and despite the ruin and rubble of half-gutted buildings that she passed on the way, a feeling of lightness possessed her. She had already made a start on finding a gentleman for Miss Harlow and in the course of an hour's consultation with Jo that afternoon they had picked out three promising candidates. Jo had advised Amy not to raise her hopes, especially in the light of Miss Harlow's particular history, but Amy's enthusiasm was irrepressible.

Hoste was already there. His welcome bemused her, for in those first few seconds it seemed to suggest that they never had met. She was disconcerted, especially since their getting together was his idea, not hers. The wariness in his eyes soon dissolved, however, and he was back to being almost sociable again. They both drank gin.

She gave a little laugh and said, 'I was worried for a moment that you'd not recognised me.'

He made a face. 'Really? Well, if I hesitated it was because you look – I don't know – changed. Your hair, I think?'

'Yes,' she said, smiling. 'I had it coloured, but I thought –' She stopped herself; she had assumed he wouldn't notice. Men often didn't. Perhaps he was more observant than he appeared. 'Not on duty tonight?'

'No. Even an ARP warden gets a pass now and then. That's why I suggested we meet this evening. Ah ...' The waiter had arrived, and they ordered. Cod in a cream sauce, boiled potatoes and beans – as good as a feast. Amy steered her gaze around the dining room, mutterish with talk; people were absorbed, faces canted towards one another, smiling, or earnest, oblivious to all else. She caught Hoste's eye again.

'It's odd, sometimes you look at people and wonder if they've forgotten all about the war – blanked it from their mind.'

'Maybe they have. Most people just get on with it, don't they?'

'Like you. You're very philosophical.'

Hoste considered this. 'Well, I've lived through one before. Fought through it, in fact.'

'*Oh.*' This hadn't occurred to her.

'Joined up when I was eighteen. Stationed at Ypres with the Hampshires, and six weeks later got a Blighty. When I returned to the front more than half the lads I knew were dead. So perhaps it did make me philosophical.'

'But you must have been frightened, too?'

'Of course. I mean, when you're being shelled and you see the fellow in the trench next to you get a –' He halted for a moment. 'But the strange thing was, I knew – for an absolute certainty – that I would survive.'

'How? How could you possibly know?'

He shrugged. 'I've no idea. I just did.'

They were silent for some moments, before she gave a regretful half-laugh. 'Did you ever imagine fighting another war?'

'Well ... what happened afterwards, at Versailles – that was asking for trouble. The Allies oughtn't to have humiliated Germany like that. It made another war almost inevitable.'

Amy narrowed her eyes. 'I was still a girl when the last war ended. You would see men in the street, maimed, or blind, selling matches on trays. I remember thinking how terrible that was, after what they'd been through.'

'Did it make you angry?'

She looked at him, hearing something in his tone. 'I don't know about angry. Ashamed, certainly. We sent off all those young men to fight for us – "for king and country" – and did nothing for them when they came back. Did *you* feel angry?'

Hoste sat back in his chair. 'No. Just relieved, to have got out of it alive. And I was fortunate in having a job to go to.'

'What did you do?'

'I was clerk at a bank in Lewes.'

'Is that where you come from?'

'Not far. A village called Wivelsfield. A proper country mouse.'

She smiled. 'Until you got to London –'

'– and became a town rat.' He said this with an odd emphasis. Their food had arrived, and they both had lager to go with it.

'And yourself? – a Londoner?' Hoste went on.

'Actually, no, I was born in Epsom. My parents only moved to London when I was in my teens. Then I lived in Oxford for a few years while I did secretarial training.'

'Where you met Marita Pardoe.'

'Yes. Did you find out anything else, by the way – where she might be?'

He shook his head. 'I'm afraid not. Probably lying low somewhere. It surprises me, though, that she never got in touch with you.'

Amy paused in her eating. 'Why are you surprised?'

'I suppose because – from what you told me – you were fast friends. Close enough, for instance, to holiday in Nazi Germany.'

'I went there for the walking, not for the Nazis. Much as you did, I think.'

'True. But no one ever took me to a rally at Nuremberg.' She felt him watching her as he spoke. 'Did it not strike you at the time as a queer thing to do?'

She put down her fork and looked at him. 'You've asked me about this before. It may seem odd to you, but at the time I didn't really think about it. Marita was a strong-willed person. She had a way of persuading you to do things, and though it was no personal longing of mine to attend a rally I agreed to go. In hindsight, I suppose it was a mistake.'

'I see.'

'You sound almost disappointed, Mr Hoste. Would you prefer me to be a secret admirer of the Reich?'

He acknowledged her lightly mocking note. 'You'd not lack for company if you were.'

'You're joking. D'you mean to say there are —'

'Of course. You don't believe that Hitler lost all support in this country because we declared war on him? Some still think of him as the future of Europe.'

Amy shook her head. 'I'm not one of them.'

They held one another's gaze for a moment. Then Hoste said evenly, 'Well, then. Let's drink to that.' He took a swallow of his beer. 'I met a chap at dinner the other night who was complaining about the lack of romance in his life, and what should he do about it. I recommended he try your marriage bureau.'

'Nice of you. But your chap says he wants romance. We set people up with a view to marriage.'

'Can you have one without the other?'

'You'd be surprised,' said Amy drily. 'For some clients – men, usually – it's simply pragmatic. They apply to us because they need a woman around the house, or perhaps because they're hoping for an heir. Romance isn't always a prerequisite.'

'You disapprove of that – the practical approach?'

'I don't approve or disapprove. My job is to match people I think suitable. Though I can't deny that my sympathies vary from one client to another. Yesterday, for instance, I interviewed a lady who has suffered such loneliness I've made it a personal mission to find her a man.'

Hoste pulled a doubting expression. 'That reminds me of a line from a play I once saw — "If you're afraid of loneliness, don't get married."'

'Sounds rather gloomy.'

'Yes. You would disagree, I presume?'

'I don't know. I've never been married. But I don't suppose I'd be doing this job if that was my conviction.' Amy tipped her head in a reflective way. 'I still wonder why *you* came to the bureau that day. You don't seem to hold marriage in very high regard.'

'Not true. I merely suggested that it might not be an antidote to loneliness. I don't disdain the institution. My mother and father had a pretty jolly time of it, I think, until he got ill.'

'But you're not inspired by their example. When we met that first time at the office you didn't look like someone desperate to get up the aisle.'

He'll think I'm fishing, Amy thought as she said it. But Hoste only laughed. She hadn't heard him laugh very often – it was most unlike him.

'Shall we have another beer?' he asked, and she readily agreed. The talk turned to music, and Amy mentioned a forthcoming performance of Elgar's Cello Concerto at the Queen's Hall. It occurred to her that they might go there together, if he wasn't busy.

'I shall make sure that I'm not,' he replied with uncharacteristic suavity. He was full of surprises this evening. It wasn't until the waiters began clearing tables that the lateness of the hour was borne in on them. Time had worked its mysterious trick of elasticity, stretching out a whole evening from what had seemed no more than an hour. He had asked for the bill, and she noticed when it came how many lagers they had drunk. When she rose to go to the ladies she felt a pleasant wooziness feathering her blood; not stinko, she thought, but squiffy.

On returning she realised that something had changed. Diners were standing at their tables, and a gathered stillness held the room; Hoste waited there motionless, his ears pricked like a gun dog.

'What's the matter?' she said, though instinctively she already knew.

'A raid,' he said. 'We'd better get out of here.'

As they emerged onto the street she tipsily thanked him for dinner, but her words were drowned by the wail of the siren. Hoste, holding her lightly by the elbow, began walking south down Wardour Street. They both carried torches, though their beams were not much help against the inky immersion of the blackout. People were hurrying across and past them, seemingly taken unawares by the menace overhead. A warden's whistle shrilled, and shouts followed. 'Take cover!' The noise – that terrible grinding of engines – had seemed distant, and now it was near. Amy looked up to see the night sky lousy with planes, lit up eerily by the sweeping searchlights.

At her side Hoste had picked up the pace, still guiding her by the elbow. He was muttering directions under his breath as they moved – 'Just here', 'Next turn' – which gave her comfort. At least one of them knew which way they had to go. The effects of the drink were quickly thinning. From the east could be heard the sound of bombs falling, the whistle, then the impact – the crump. Anti-aircraft guns barked in response. She had never been caught outdoors like this before, and it struck her anew how the sound of a raid – the planes' long drone and the bombs' shrieking descent – was the sound of dread itself, of fate coming for you. It was impossible not to take it personally. They were still in the grid of Soho's narrow streets when a voice nearby cried out in fear, and they looked up to see the silhouettes of bombs against the glowering sky, three, four, five of them, tumbling down, falling almost dreamily. At a junction Hoste brought them to an abrupt halt; the street ahead was dark – and then intensely bright – as a high explosive landed. The ground bucked beneath them, and the shockwave gusted past their faces.

This is too near, she thought, as Hoste took tight hold of her arm and hurried her onwards. Had he meant to get them to a shelter and miscalculated the distance? Perhaps they ought to have stayed inside the restaurant. A ribbon of incendiaries was coming down, and one landed with a clatter on the pavement in front of them. It fizzed in a halo of white sparks. 'Can't leave it to burn,' Hoste shouted in her ear and, disengaging her a moment, stamped it out with the heel of his boot. They had ducked into another side street when a great screech rent the air, so close to them that before she knew it he had pushed her roughly into the doorway of a shop, his body smothering hers. The booming detonation, a thunderclap in her ears, came almost simultaneously with a wave of flying debris. For what seemed like minutes it rained grit and stone and a thousand tiny shards of glass.

Though his body was still tensed against hers in the doorway they could barely see one another, such were the blinding clouds of dust. They were coughing like hags. Hoste had reached into his pocket and taken out a handkerchief to muffle his mouth. Her eyes smarted. 'Hold on to my arm,' she heard him say, and they began to wade through the burning air, footsteps crunching on glass. As the choking dust cloud began to clear they could just make out the pub opposite, which had taken a direct hit. There will be people dead in there, she thought; crushed and buried, or simply obliterated in the bomb flash. A few yards further north and it might have been them. She swallowed, and shuddered. The clang of ambulance bells sounded on the air.

Hoste's urgent pace told her they were not yet safe themselves. They had crossed Cambridge Circus and were still in full view of the bombers, circling, dropping their loads. She had an impression of being seen from a vast height, moving like clockwork toys that had been frantically overwound. Their terrible insignificance. Hoste had stopped to spit the dust from his mouth, and she took a moment to do the same. 'Are you all right?' he asked her, and she nodded. 'If we make a run for it we'll be back at my place in five minutes.' And so she clung to his arm and they began to jog-trot, their torchlights weaving crazily down the empty black gauntlet of Charing Cross Road. Not another soul did they encounter before they gained the cover of his rooms in Cecil Court.

He closed the blackout curtains on entering the living room while she hunted blindly for a lamp. When a light finally came on they looked at one another in stunned silence: they were coated head to toe in dust, as if they had just crawled from a mineshaft.

'Jesus,' he breathed, and asked her again, 'Are you all right?'

'I think so. I mean, apart from –' She looked down at her hands, streaked with soot and dirt. She supposed her face looked much the same.

'The bathroom's through here,' he said, leading her across the room. 'There might still be some hot water.'

In the mirror her eyes were red-rimmed from the smoke. She managed to clean herself up, though she couldn't get the taste of burnt dust out of her mouth. 'Could I possibly have something to drink?' she called through the door.

When she returned to the living room he had poured out a good two fingers of whisky for them, with a jug of water to mix it. She took a great gulp and felt its bite in her throat. Watching her, he gave his glass a quick lift and did the same. 'Oh God!' she cried, hand to her mouth. He had just turned his head, exposing a wound that had leaked dark blood onto his shirt collar. 'Stay still,' she said, edging around him; pincering her fingers she pulled out a shard of glass about an inch long, lodged just below his right ear.

That might have gone through my eye, she thought, if he hadn't been there shielding me.

She asked him if he had iodine, and back in the bathroom she carefully wiped the cut clean and plastered it. The Scotch was making her giddy; she had drunk it too quickly, and had to sit down. Her ears were still ringing from the bomb blast.

Hoste was peeking through the blackout curtain, listening for the guns. 'Sounds like it might be a long one,' he said, and left the room for a few moments. When he returned he was dressed in his ARP serge.

'You're not going out again?' she said, disbelievingly. 'I thought it was your night off?'

'Yes – damned inconsiderate of them to come over this evening! I'm afraid they'll be having a hot time of it up at my station. I ought to go. But you must stay here. There's a divan you can sleep on.'

'Well, I'm not sure –'

'I'm not arguing with you about this. You're to stay. At least until the all-clear. I'll try to get back before it goes. Right?'

She caught his eye. 'Right.'

He smiled. 'Make yourself at home. Have some more Scotch. Or there's tea in the kitchen.' He put on his tin helmet, and gave it a double tap with his knuckle. 'I hope I haven't used up all my luck tonight.'

He had spoken lightly, but his mention of luck caused her alarm. His uniform, too large for his slight frame, made him look suddenly frail, and doomed – like a Tommy about to go over the top. She had stood up and moved towards him.

'Thank you for saving me – I mean it.' She leaned in and briefly pressed her lips to his cheek. 'I hope that brings you luck.'

He stared at her very intently for a moment. 'I should hope it would. And if not, well – it will make a happy memory.' He gave a parting nod, and was gone.

She could hear the raid racketing on outside, the implacable drone of the planes, the muffled explosions like a giant beating a carpet. An open-air madhouse. For how much longer were they going to circle up there? It occurred to her now that she should have gone with him. He was the type who would take risks, not out of bravado but out of that irrational belief in his immunity – *I knew I would survive*. Her being at his side might have made him more circumspect.

A violent shiver abruptly ran through her, and she pulled her coat tight. The ashes in the grate were cold. But she found coal in the scuttle, and spent a few minutes preparing a fire with twists of paper. She felt in her pocket for matches and found none. Surely Hoste kept some about. A few minutes hunting – in the kitchen, in the living room – uncovered not a one. The cold was piercing to the bone. There had to be a fire-lighter somewhere. She opened a door that led into his bedroom. It held his air of monkishness: a lamp at the bedside, but no books. On the wall, by the window, her picture of the Tyrol was a solitary adornment. It touched her that he had bothered to hang it.

A natural delicacy made her hesitate before the chest of drawers. But it was only a hesitation, and soon she was making a sweep of his modest layers of vests and sweaters. There was the odd cigarette card, but still no matches. With a deeper sense of trespass she found nothing in the second drawer but underthings, pyjamas, socks. The bottom drawer disclosed a miscellany of junk, old magazines, correspondence, a round tin of collars and studs, an unframed certificate from his bank, mothballs, ARP pamphlets, a pair of braces, a small bottle of hair oil. He had chucked all sorts in here. Her eye caught the gleam of something at the back, and she inched the drawer a little further out. They were dark leather presentation cases, in pristine condition. Curiosity provoked her to pick one up and undo its tiny clasp.

At first she could hardly understand what she was looking at. Or rather, she knew what it was, but couldn't understand how it had come to be in Hoste's possession. She felt her heart thump hard as she checked each one of the seven other cases, and found the same thing. There, on a black silk mount, lay an Iron Cross, highest decoration of the German military.

8

Amy left the flat before the all-clear sounded. She had been careful to leave no sign that she had been in his bedroom. But she had dithered for a while on the threshold not knowing what to do; whether to await his return or to get out of there. The shock of it had disabled her. Her first instinct was to stay and confront him about her discovery – only she couldn't imagine saying the words, *I know you're an enemy agent.* It sounded too preposterous. But what other conclusion to draw? Then there was the obvious danger she might be putting herself in: if indeed he was a traitor, and his secret was out, he would be left with no choice but to silence her. The alternative was to pretend she knew nothing and continue from the point they had left off – kissing him goodbye, as she recalled, and wishing him luck.

Dissembling was beyond her for the present, and she sneaked out of Cecil Court like a thief in the night. The raid had moved away from the West End by then, but such was her preoccupation she barely noticed the ochre glow of the city on fire, the clang of fire engines and ambulances tearing up the streets. All she could think about was that inconceivable discovery in his flat. From the start she had marked his oddness, though it had seemed to her eccentric rather than sinister. When he had challenged her about Nazi politics and her visit to Nuremberg she had thought it merely an intellectual playfulness on his part. She didn't suspect for a moment he was an 'enemy within'. How could he be, this ARP warden who risked his life fire-watching and herding people into shelters each night?

Unless this was part of some elaborate double bluff, a way of hiding in plain sight. It was quite possible. Hoste had talked only this evening about British people who still believed Hitler to be 'the future of Europe'. Evidently he was better acquainted with the type than she'd thought. In this light, his obsessive interest in Marita Pardoe made sense. Her unapologetic passion for the Fatherland would naturally attract someone sympathetic to the Nazi cause. Had they in fact been in cahoots with one another without telling her? That she herself might be their dupe – it brought her to a halt on the pavement – caused her a sickening dizziness. No, no, it couldn't be; and she began turning the possibilities over again, trying to recall tones of voice, facial expressions, that she might have misinterpreted.

Nothing had been resolved by the time she got back to Queen Anne Street. She let herself into the flat and, in a trance of fatigue and alarm, made some tea. She sat at the kitchen table. Every time Hoste came to mind she fell into a terrible swoon of doubt – and, she had to admit, regret. For it wasn't just that she felt in his debt for having saved her life mere hours ago. That kiss for good luck she had given him had come from an impulse of protectiveness; and from something else, too, possibly something romantic. What's more, his look had seemed to answer in kind. He had felt it, she was sure – *it will make a happy memory*, he'd said. It had crowned the end of an evening when they'd lost all track of time, so beguiling had they found one another. Then, once the raid had descended, he had guided her to safety. That too had felt like more than an act of gallantry. She wished she had Bobby there to talk to. Her last letter had hinted at her feelings for Hoste, and Bobby's reply, begging for more details, had somehow made him even more intriguing to her.

From a distance not far off she heard another explosion. A bomb with a delayed timer, or else some poor devil had been trying to defuse it. A few more to add to the night's casualties. Those death-dealers up there – could it really be that this man she thought she knew was on *their* side? Still at the kitchen table, she made a pillow for her head on crossed arms. She didn't stir from this exhausted position for some time.

They were clearing up for days afterwards, filling the hospitals, the mortuaries. The sweeping up of broken glass sounded like breakers rolling upon the shore. It had been the heaviest raid on London so far, but like a storm blowing itself out, a calm followed. People craned their necks upwards every day and found empty skies. The sirens were still on alert, but the planes that had traced the snaking ribbon of the Thames were gone. In June the Nazis invaded Russia, and a new phase of the war began.

After leaving Amy in his flat that night Hoste had ventured to the station at Holborn; he found all hands to the pump putting out fires. Incendiaries, flaring up with Hydra-headed malignancy, had bathed the area in a ghastly glow. The fire services could not cope with the volume, and often the decision to save one building came at the conscious sacrifice of another. By early morning rescue men, their faces masked, were toiling to extricate bodies from the mangled mass of debris. At one point Hoste saw a line of corpses laid out and shrouded in hopsack, waiting their turn for the mortuary van. He felt the cut on his neck throb, and thanked his stars. An inch or two nearer and the glass might have severed a vein.

When he had returned to the flat, in the poky dawn light, Amy had gone. It surprised him that she hadn't bothered to light a fire; the room was stone cold. He saw that the bed he had made up for her had not been slept in, either. In the kitchen the bottle of Scotch had been replaced on the shelf and the glasses lay washed on the draining board. For some reason this bit of household tidiness depressed him; he'd rather have found the evidence of their camaraderie intact, and her asleep on the divan. When she had cleaned his cut there had been something – a tenderness – that moved him. He had thought she would stay. He had also meant to show her the Tyrol sketch he had hung – to assure her of how much it had been appreciated. Well, next time he would.

As the days and weeks went by, however, he heard nothing more from Amy Strallen. It puzzled him at first, for they had parted on such friendly terms. The kiss he still recalled. In any case, he had no time to dwell on it. Marita, zealous to a fault, kept proposing new initiatives on his recruitment drive. They would meet regularly to discuss fifth columnists she considered worth cultivating. She was deeply intolerant of cranks – 'fantasists' – who merely sought an audience for their crackpot theories. What was needed were people prepared to do the hard work of accumulating intelligence and grooming contacts. At times she expressed her impatience even with Hoste, accusing him of a lack of ambition. Instead of just recruiting spies, he ought to be training them up in subversion – sabotage, of course, but also bugging government offices, lifting classified material, and stalling 'Churchill's propaganda machine'.

Hoste said that he agreed with her in principle, but they had neither the resources nor the remit from Berlin to carry out such activities. Their job was to gather and relay information, no more. Marita would scowl in disgust, but in general they got on pretty well. If he could steer her off the eternal subject of the Jews and their troublemaking she was quite enlivening company. She could talk for hours about art and film and theatre. (She could talk for hours about everything.) She was well read in the classics, though what she loved was thrillers; sometimes when Hoste met her she would be in the middle of a murder mystery or an espionage story. She read avidly but sceptically. Once, a few weeks after seeing her absorbed in a cheap-looking thriller called *Cadaver Non Grata*, he asked her how it had ended. 'I didn't finish it,' she replied. Why not? 'Because I knew what was going to happen. When I know that, I stop reading.' Hoste, without telling her, borrowed the book for himself from the library. He read it right through. The ending came as a complete surprise to him.

He still had no idea where she lived, and she never dropped any hint, even of the district. He had arranged with the Section to pay her four pounds a week, more than any other agent in their employ. This she would collect when they met, at either a cafe or a dining room in the West End. In company it amused him to note her constant animal alertness. When she entered a room unfamiliar to her she would look around to check that it had another exit. She would always sit facing outwards to monitor the comings and goings. Nothing seemed to escape her attention.

Eating together one afternoon he noticed her distractedly scanning the room over his shoulder. She dropped her voice for a moment. 'Don't turn round – there are two police detectives sitting by that window.' He watched her watching them. She was always alive to the possibility of being cornered. Even though the police had no recent photograph of her, she moved through the city like a fugitive. 'How can you tell?' he asked her quietly. Marita gave a little twist to her mouth. 'Instinct. It's not let me down yet.' A table near to them had become free, and they watched as the two men she had identified rose and slouched towards it. One of the men caught his eye as he sat down, and Hoste felt a shiver of dread. Marita was staring off, her face set impassive and hard. The pair of them were waiting – to pounce? A minute, two minutes, ticked by. Slowly, by an unseen signal, the men got to their feet again, and Hoste wondered if this was the moment Marita would make a dash for it. Instead they asked another customer – a man – to accompany them outside. Through the window they watched as a uniformed constable put the man in cuffs.

'That was a close one,' said Hoste. Marita squinted at him, and said nothing.

One afternoon a few weeks later, having arranged to meet at a pub on the Strand, she turned up in the company of a young man, smartly dressed, blue-eyed with brilliantined hair – as suave as a matinee idol. Once he began talking, however, the illusion was broken. His Ulster accent fell menacingly on the ear. Marita introduced him as Billy Adair.

'Marita's been tellin' me abite yew,' he said, widening his sharp, feline eyes suggestively. 'The handler.'

'Is that what she calls me?' Hoste looked at her, but she returned only a long, languid blink. It transpired that she and Adair had met in Dublin during her temporary exile, and found they had much in common. He had been working covertly for the British government as an agent provocateur and became notorious for betraying several prominent members of the Irish Republican Army. His father, he explained, had also been recruited as a spy for the British during the 1916 uprising.

'So you followed him into the family business,' said Hoste.

'You could say.' He smiled for a moment. 'But we never traded under the family name, if you get my drift.'

Hoste listened while the two of them talked about Ireland and its usefulness as a bolthole from the mainland. Adair, having collaborated with the Ulster Constabulary, had now made an enemy of them; London had proved a congenial place to lie low. He and Marita had met at a secret assembly of BU renegades and Fascists just before the war broke out. Something in the tone of their talk inclined Hoste to wonder whether their association had been entirely professional. He was certainly handsome enough, and Marita was possibly not averse to the attentions of cocky young acolytes.

'I wonder if we might put Billy's other talents to use,' she said, turning to Hoste.

'Other talents?'

She looked to Billy, who said, 'Agents of the Irish Constabulary were trained in the use of firearms. It was always handy to carry a pistol on the streets, in case you ran into some blood-thirsty Taig.'

'I see,' said Hoste.

There was a silence, before Marita spoke again. 'Billy's being rather coy. In fact he was so "handy" with a gun that the Constabulary hired him as a special operative. If a Republican politician or union leader was making life troublesome – and there usually was one – they'd send Billy in to deal with him. The best shot in the business.'

Hoste nodded slowly. 'No doubt. But I fail to see how an assassin might be deployed in this country. We're not at present overrun by Republicans.'

Marita gave a sardonic snort. 'You deliberately miss the point, Hoste. This government of ours refuses to deal fairly with Germany. Churchill would rather fight to the last man than sit down and negotiate. We must force his hand. Imagine the shock to them of suddenly losing Eden, or Attlee, or Morrison. "There is a tide in the affairs of men" – well, this is ours. Should we not take it?'

Her question was directed at Hoste, who returned her gaze and held it for a long moment. Then he said, with cold formality, 'Mr Adair, a pleasure to meet you, but would you be kind enough to leave us for now? I have confidential business to discuss with Mrs Pardoe.'

The Ulsterman looked surprised, but with a puzzled glance at Marita he rose from the table; he took up his hat and, with a muttered farewell, was gone. Marita's expression had darkened, and Hoste knew that a critical moment had been reached.

'That was not polite of you,' she said in a low, sullen voice.

'And inviting that man to this table was not wise of you.'

'What? He's a National Socialist and a –'

'He's a thug, and a professional Judas. You think I've not heard of Billy Adair? He's ratted out men on so many different sides I'm surprised he can see straight. What on earth do you think you're doing, bringing him to me?'

Marita, bristling, almost spat out her words. 'I shall tell you. I look at your network of agents and ask myself: what is being done to help the Fatherland? And the answer is – *nothing*. Nothing! What is the point of intelligence gathering if we cannot use it to break this government? An assassination could change the course of the war. Even you must see that.'

Perhaps she expected to provoke him with this little cuff of disrespect. But Hoste didn't flinch. 'You want to associate with a man like Adair, that's your business. But let me make it absolutely clear: my loyalty is to Berlin, and to the running of this operation. If I should hear that you've done anything to jeopardise that, it's over – you're over. The money stops, and you're on your own. Or you're with Billy Adair, which amounts to the same thing.'

Marita's eyes glittered like a switchblade. Her face had gone pale – the pale of repressed fury. He had braced himself for a tirade, but in the end she merely curled her lip, and said in a sarcastic tone, 'Tough guy.'

But something must have registered, because she dropped all talk of Adair.

One evening in late June, Philip Traherne held a small party at his flat in Jermyn Street. A belated celebration of Castle's sixtieth birthday, it later became known as 'the Trimalchio evening', such was the bounty on offer. In this era of food coupons and rationing it was impossible to know how Traherne had come by the cold cuts of meat or the fresh salmon, let alone the champagne and the cognac and kümmel. Even those with decent access to the black market were surprised by the lavishness. But nobody was complaining, least of all Castle, who gulped down a large balloon of brandy while cornering Hoste for a debrief on his latest recruit.

'And she's satisfied with the money?'

Hoste pulled a face. 'I don't think Marita would ever admit to being "satisfied" with anything. But she knows that four pounds a week is a good screw.'

Castle paused to fill a pipe, and lit it with thoughtful little creasings at the side of his mouth. 'We've been impressed by the stuff she's bringing in. The troop encampments on the south-west coast, for instance.'

'I've been wondering how she got hold of that,' said Hoste. 'I asked her whether it could be verified, hoping she'd let slip the name of her contact. But of course she didn't. Far too shrewd.'

'You sound like an admirer.'

'I suppose I am. I can't help admiring people who are good at their job – the will to get things done. Marita is the keenest I've ever met.'

Sweetish clouds of smoke from Castle's pipe billowed across them. 'Quite the tartar, I imagine.'

Hoste nodded. 'We crossed swords the other week. She wanted to bring in an Irish gunman, name of Adair. She's determined to get up an assassination campaign, starting with Churchill's War Cabinet.'

'How did she propose doing that?'

'I didn't ask. I simply told her – over my dead body.'

Castle returned a thin smile. 'I'd watch out. She might take that literally.'

The conversational murmur around them rose and fell. The windows had been thrown open to the night air, and the net curtains stirred lethargically. Through a knot of drinkers Hoste watched Traherne and Tessa Hammond picking a path towards them.

'Evening, gents,' said Traherne, looking from one to the other. He was wearing one of his innumerable smoking jackets and a pair of cream-and-brown co-respondent shoes. 'Hope you two aren't talking shop. This is a birthday party, remember.'

Castle winked at Hoste. 'Matter of fact we were discussing Jack's admiration for a certain lady.'

Traherne raised his eyebrows. 'Oh, anyone I know?' he said, cutting a glance around the room.

'He's joking,' said Hoste. 'Capital spread, by the way, Philip. Seems you've got in everything but a suckling pig. And not impossibly that.'

'Well, nothing's too good for Castle. Happy birthday, old boy.' A few other guests echoed his toast before Traherne took Castle off to make some introductions. Hoste was left with Tessa, who had fixed him with a pert look.

'May I ask — was the "certain lady" just mentioned Miss Strallen?'

Hoste smiled. 'No. I'm afraid Miss Strallen has dropped out of view. Perhaps I offended her, though I can't think how.'

'She's probably just got some new man,' said Tessa shortly, though if she hoped the remark would jolt him it was misplaced, for Hoste only nodded, seeming thoughtful. They were silent for a moment; then Tessa went on. 'By the way, I've been given a couple of tickets for a concert next Tuesday. Schubert. Or is it Schumann? Anyway, I thought you might be ... ?'

Hoste, who had been half listening, focused on her. 'Ah, thanks, but I can't next week —'

'Oh, that's fine,' said Tessa, interrupting quickly. 'Absolutely fine. It was only a — I'll find someone else.'

A waiter bearing a tray of drinks created a distraction, and they began to talk of other things.

9

A voice was addressing her, and Amy came round to it as if from a dream. Johanna stood at her office door.

'Sorry, miles away. Morning.'

'Good morning,' said Jo, with a puzzled smile. 'I was just saying that I liked your dress.' It was short-sleeved and narrow-waisted, with a floral design, something she'd bought a few summers back and forgotten about. She had hardly noticed herself putting it on.

'Thanks,' she said belatedly.

A minute or so later Jo reappeared, this time without the smile. She closed the door behind her and leaned against it.

'Amy? May I ask – is everything all right?' Her tone was gently confidential.

Amy sat up at her desk. 'Yes. Of course. Why – why d'you ask?'

'It's just that these last few weeks you've been so preoccupied. Are you bored with the work? Because if you are I can ask Miss Ducker to –'

'No, I'm not at all bored. Is that how it seems?'

Jo made an awkward face. 'A little. When we used to do the matching you were always so enthusiastic and funny. But lately you seem, I don't know, remote from everything. I just wondered if there was – You're not ... ?' There was a question in Jo's eyes which certain women friends would implicitly understand.

Amy bugged her eyes. 'God, no. *No*. I'm sorry, Jo, really. I can't bear the idea of not pulling my weight. I may have been out of sorts – tired, I suppose – but I will try to buck up.'

Jo gave her a searching look. 'I don't like to think you're unhappy. I wonder – is it something to do with that man you told me about? Mr Hoste?'

Amy didn't flinch. Jo was a smart one, but this was a confidence she wasn't going to win. 'I've not seen or heard from him for weeks,' she replied, 'and that suits me fine.' It was said with a smile, and seemed to be enough for Jo, who responded in kind.

'All right, then. I've got a free hour at four, so have you. What do you say we have a matching session?'

For the rest of the day Amy worked with a somewhat self-conscious diligence; she didn't go out to lunch, and only once visited the kitchen to make a cup of tea. She had been aware of her distractedness these past weeks and had dimly hoped that it had escaped notice. But you couldn't work close to someone as beady as Jo and pretend that you were getting away with it.

In the days following her discovery at Hoste's flat she had tried to rationalise what she had seen. She knew that men were born collectors, and that military paraphernalia were an enduring fascination to some. She recalled her father once taking her to visit an old schoolteacher whose living room was practically a shrine to the obsession – weaponry, of course, but also a fusty array of medals, decorations, cap badges, regimental insignia, all proudly preserved in glass cases. Amy had regarded them politely, and wondered what use they were to him. Did he take them out on a slow afternoon and stare at them? Or were they ornaments intended to beguile his visitors?

The question was whether Hoste might be such a man. She thought not. His private cache of Iron Crosses didn't have the air of belonging to a cherished collection. They had been hidden away in a drawer like things not meant to be seen. So she had to ask herself why someone would have enemy battle decorations in his possession. And the answer – much as she resisted it – was that he must be a Nazi agent. But how could he be? The idea was just too horrifying. Back and forth she argued it with herself. In the end she decided to write it down, in the hope that seeing it in black and white would determine the truth.

1) His interest in Marita – wanted to know about her allegiances, anti-Jewish sentiments, etc.
2) Has visited Germany often; speaks German.
3) Seems to know a lot about anti-government elements, the pro-Hitler types who want peace at any price with Germany.
4) The medals. He could only have come by them in Germany, which means he must be connected to the higher echelons of the Reich.

The evidence pointed one way only.

She was still brooding on it as she entered the bar of Fleming's, where she had arranged to meet Georgina Harlow after work. In the course of trying to matchmake her favourite lonely heart, Amy had become friendly with her. They had been to see a couple of plays in the West End and had dinner afterwards. Even if she hadn't felt obscurely responsible for her client, she found Georgina an engaging companion, and a tremendous source of gossip: working for a junior minister at the Ministry of Defence she was first with the news about the Cabinet's internal squabbling, Churchill's drinking habits, the amorous indiscretions of this or that mandarin. She seemed to know before anyone else about the latest initiatives on rationing and clothing coupons and rehousing the thousands of Londoners left homeless by the Blitz. 'I shouldn't really be telling you this,' she would say sotto voce, and Amy would listen, agog.

She heard her name being called from the other side of the room. In the few weeks since they had first met Amy detected a material change in Georgina's appearance: her skin, which had been sallow, seemed to glow, and she carried herself with a new assurance. Where once her gaze had been fearful and downcast, she now looked Amy directly in the eye. The change was easily explained: the bureau had found her a suitor, and it was very quickly apparent that he was keen.

'So how goes it with Prince Charming?' said Amy, once she had settled herself in the booth.

Georgina smiled. 'I can't vouch for any royal blood. But he does have plenty of charm.' The man in question, Christopher, had made money in a brokerage firm before he decided to quit and open a small gallery in St James's. Amy had liked him on sight, but until Miss Harlow's name entered the books they had not been able to find him a suitable match.

'So it's all looking hopeful,' Amy said encouragingly.

At this Georgina widened her eyes and laughed in a half-embarrassed way. 'I should say so …' When Amy cocked her head, inviting her to go on, she added, 'He wants to marry me.'

'You mean … ?'

'He's asked me. And I've said yes.'

'What?!' Amy said, louder than she'd intended. A few heads turned towards them. 'Georgie – you're not serious. How many times have you actually met?'

'Half a dozen, I suppose. You think it's too soon?'

Amy stared at her, disbelieving. 'To be honest, yes. I mean, what's the rush?'

For the first time that evening her gaze dropped. 'I'm older than you, Amy. As you know, I'd like to have a child, if I can. I've talked to Christopher about it, and he's as keen as I am.' She looked up again and said, in appeal, 'I thought you'd be pleased. You introduced us, after all.'

Amy felt herself caught in a bind. She didn't want to dampen the mood, given Georgina's luckless past. And wasn't this exactly the point of the bureau anyway, to make introductions between people who longed for companionship? This might be the most inspired bit of matchmaking she'd ever done. And yet ... and yet she couldn't overlook the fact that this was Georgina's first suitor. First *ever* suitor. A voice within urged caution. How could they be sure of one another from so brief a courtship? How could anyone?

'I *am* pleased ...' she began.

'You don't sound like it,' said Georgie with a sad little laugh.

'It just seems rather sudden. I was hoping that you'd try a few, before you made up your mind. It never occurred to me that you'd settle for the very first man.'

'I'm not "settling" for anything. I want to be with him.'

'But is he really so wonderful as that? You're going from no man at all – forgive me, dear – to marrying the first one who asks you. I'm glad, truly I am, that you like one another and get on so well. But I can't help feeling you should give yourself more time. To *think* about it.'

Georgina narrowed her eyes slightly. 'Are you telling me this in your capacity as a professional matchmaker, or because you have no confidence in me as a marriage prospect?'

Amy gave a sigh of exasperation. 'I'd say this to any friend of mine who was about to rush into something. Marriage is a huge commitment, and you should be absolutely certain before you agree to it. I'm just thinking of you.'

'Are you?' she asked quietly. 'Only I wonder – is there something in you that doesn't quite trust marriage?'

The question took her so much by surprise that for a moment she was lost for words. How had this become about her? She had not anticipated Georgina trying to turn the argument around, but now that she had, a calm answer was required.

'I don't think I could do my job if I held marriage in such low esteem. Maybe I've been too cautious in my own life –'

'Maybe you have. Has a man ever proposed to you?'

Amy heard a warning sharpness in her tone. 'No. Never. But that doesn't disqualify me from having an opinion about marriage, or from judging whether it's timely or not. I – I sense that whatever I say now is going to upset you ...'

'Then perhaps we shouldn't continue this conversation,' Georgina replied, folding her hands in her lap.

'Perhaps you're right,' Amy conceded. 'I'm sorry, Georgie. I suppose I must have assumed I could talk to you as a friend rather than as a client. If I've offended you ...'

She left the sentence hanging in the hope that Georgina would accept the apology and laugh the thing off. But the silence between them extended a few moments longer, confirming the suspicion that she had indeed offended her. When they got on to another topic she could hear a stiffness in Georgina's voice, and behind it an implication that what Amy had said about her sudden engagement would not be forgotten. Or even forgiven. There was a lesson to be learned here, she supposed, the old one about not mixing the personal and the professional. In most cases where two clients instantly fell for one another she would have been congratulating herself on a quick success and looking forward to a cheque for ten pounds. As Jo always reminded her, they couldn't afford to be sentimental about business.

Amy strove to keep the conversation going for a while longer, but it was uphill work, and when the dinner hour came round neither of them suggested going on somewhere. They parted outside Green Park Tube, and Amy carried home the cold politeness of Georgina's goodnight in her bones.

One morning a couple of weeks later Amy answered a telephone call at the office. It was Marita. She hadn't heard from her in a while, though ever since her reappearance in London she had remained an object of curiosity. For one thing, she still didn't know how Marita managed to support herself; she had no job, it seemed, and there was obviously no money coming from Bernard, still interned on the Isle of Man. Nor did she have a clue as to where she was living; she had been very careful not to let that slip.

'I have a treat for you,' Marita said with a laugh in her voice, though she insisted it had to be handed over in the privacy of Amy's flat. It was arranged that she would drop by early in the evening and perhaps stay for a drink.

She arrived at the appointed hour, and, on entering the flat, as usual, sidled over to the window. She stood at a slight angle, surveying the street below, making sure she hadn't been followed.

'Is it likely that you have been?' asked Amy.

'Not very,' she replied, her face still turned to the window, 'but I live on the principle that doubt is a useful ally. When you are not doubting, you are not thinking.'

Satisfied by her surveillance, Marita left the window and crossed the room to pick up her shoulder bag, from which she took out a small package wrapped in brown butcher's paper. Under her expectant gaze Amy unfolded its layered sheets to reveal a couple of prime cuts of purplish steak, marbled with fat.

'Sirloin,' Marita announced. 'My dear, the expression on your face is a very picture.'

Amy giggled. 'I haven't seen a cut of meat like this in ages. You must have some very good suppliers.'

'The black market, though not directly. I got this in lieu of payment from a man who was in my debt. There are still a few of them around.'

Marita's piercing dark-eyed look seemed to warn off Amy pursuing the story any further. It was quite typical of her to create a little mystery and then drop it within a moment.

Having invited her guest to stay for dinner they moved to the kitchen, Amy carrying the steaks like a votive offering.

A small cube of butter she had been saving now went into the frying pan, and she peeled a couple of potatoes to make chips. She was wondering what they might drink with it when Marita pulled from her bag a bottle of claret.

'Same man?' asked Amy, which received a brief affirmative nod.

While she prepared dinner they talked about the raids and their abrupt falling-off, about the crippled state of London, and the likely direction of the war. Marita believed that as long as America kept out of it Germany would eventually triumph, though the invasion of Russia was a gamble. She spoke with an authority that secretly amazed Amy; it was as though she had been privy to the strategy rooms of Hitler's ministers and generals – her information hot from the dragon's mouth. Her confident projections brought to mind a more recent acquaintance.

'Did you ever track down the tax inspector – Hoste?' she asked, with all the nonchalance she could feign.

Marita hardly blinked. 'Yes, I paid him a call. He'd got those tax arrears quite wrong – there was no money owed to us. Unfortunately.' She waited a beat before continuing. 'And you? I thought I detected just the merest *tendresse* when we last spoke of him ...'

Amy gave a resigned laugh. 'I think it was only curiosity. There was something about him – well, it doesn't matter now.'

She felt that she must not share with Marita anything she knew about Hoste, least of all her theory of his double life. It was an instinct she couldn't explain, but she trusted it. She attended to the stove and began telling her about another client. There had been no further contact with Georgina since their awkward set-to at Fleming's.

'Of course I oughtn't to have interfered. My job was to find her a suitable marriage partner, not to put my oar in about waiting for the right man.'

Marita cocked her head slightly. 'It sounds to me like you gave her good advice. She must be half crazed to fling herself into marriage. A man is allowed to play the field – why not a woman?'

Amy nodded. 'All the same, I feel as though I've ruined something. I didn't know her that well but we really got along.'

When she looked up Marita was staring at her. 'Sometimes we behave in ways that are not quite fathomable to us. The mind plays tricks with our intentions.'

'What d'you mean?'

'Only this – that our unconscious may have the whip hand without our even knowing it. Maybe you believed you were trying to help – Georgina? – but were obeying an impulse to hurt her. To punish her.'

'But why would I want to do that?'

'I have no idea. This woman is unknown to me. But I do recall another instance, not so many years ago, of your withdrawing from a friend. It may not have been a conscious choice, but the effect was the same.'

The implication could not be ignored, and Amy felt herself blush. It was something – no more than an exchange of words – that had happened just before Marita had got married five years ago, and now seemed so lost in time that Amy wondered if it had happened at all. Marita, prolonging the moment with her silence, directed a glance at the sizzling pan on the stove.

'Don't burn the steaks,' she said quietly.

Amy rose and took the pan off the flame; she went to the cupboard to fetch pepper and mustard, and rummaged around in a drawer for napkins – all useful activities to divert them from the minefield just glimpsed. Marita poured them more wine while keeping a stealthy eye on her hostess, and slowly the danger receded, and the conversation took a different tack.

They had eaten the steak and were finishing with a cigarette when a knock sounded at the door. Amy got up to answer it, wondering who could be calling at such an hour. She was greeted on the threshold by Paul Pruckner, her neighbour from downstairs. A faint smile lit his gaunt, stubbled face.

'Miss Strallen, good evening,' he said with a little bow. 'I apologise for the lateness of the hour, but I have something for you.'

'Hullo, Mr Pruckner. Come in,' said Amy. 'I haven't seen you in ages.'

As he removed his thin scarf in the hallway he explained that he had spent the last few weeks working on a farm in Essex – 'from where these beauties come'. He was holding a carton, inside which lay six white eggs.

'My goodness!' she cried. 'I really have hit the jackpot this evening. My friend brought round a steak for our supper.'

'Oh, I didn't mean to disturb –' he began, sensing his intrusion, but Amy was already ushering him into the kitchen. She insisted that he stayed for a drink. Introductions were effected, and Pruckner, with old-world courtesy, made another low bow as he greeted 'Mrs Pardoe'.

'Marita, look what Mr Pruckner has brought.' She laid the open carton on the table, where the eggs' whiteness seemed to glow.

He explained that they were a token of thanks to Amy, who was 'always' doing little favours for him. Whenever he was away, Amy would fetch his wife's medicine – she was an invalid – and sometimes did her shopping. 'Everyone should have such a neighbour,' he concluded with a fond glance.

Pruckner's heavily accented English prompted Marita to ask which part of Germany he was from.

'Augsburg. Perhaps you know it? I think of it still. We have lived in this country for more than fifteen years, but a part of us of course will always be German. The present government will certainly not let us forget it.'

'Mr and Mrs Pruckner were interned, and their son,' Amy said. 'But Marita knows all about that – her husband is still being held on the Isle of Man.'

'My dear lady, I'm very sorry to hear it. Is he too an "enemy alien"?'

'Not exactly. But he was branded a danger to the people.' Marita glanced at Amy, who hoped she would leave it at that.

'Is there any prospect of his release?' Pruckner asked.

'None – at least while we are still at war.'

'Ach, to think that these great countries of ours once came close to destroying each other. Now they are determined to try again.'

'You fought in the First War, didn't you?' said Amy.

Pruckner nodded. 'I was an infantryman. So were my wife's brothers. One of them was killed at Ypres, the other survived and won the Iron Cross.' He gave way to a bitter laugh. 'For all the good it has done. We have not heard from him since the last round-ups.'

A stunned pause halted them. Amy watched Marita's expression begin to dawn.

'Round-ups? You mean – you're Jewish?'

'No,' he replied. 'But my wife is. She fears the worst, of course ...' If Pruckner had chanced to scrutinise Marita at this moment instead of continuing the narrative of his unfortunate brother-in-law he would have beheld a subtle but unmistakable change in her demeanour – a stiffening of her posture, and, what was more pronounced, the disappearance of any friendliness from her eyes. At one point she cut a glance to Amy, who realised she had been slow to head off this potentially disagreeable encounter. But it had only just dawned on her that Gertrud Pruckner *was* Jewish; she had believed the couple were outcasts on account of being German. She hadn't suspected that they were at an even graver disadvantage.

Reaching the end of his story, Pruckner had looked in appeal to both of his listeners, yet with only one of them still holding his gaze he found himself addressing Amy alone. She tried to compensate by showing a greater attentiveness, though inside she was wishing him gone. Marita, to judge from her glowering silence, was wishing him at the bottom of the ocean. When at last he rose to leave she remained seated, her gaze averted; Pruckner looked not so much affronted as confused.

'Madam, good evening,' he said, half extending his hand. This too was ignored, and Amy interposed herself brightly.

'Thank you so much for the eggs, Mr Pruckner,' she said, and walked him out to the hall. The relief she felt almost smothered her mortification. As she opened the door he turned to her, and said in a low voice, 'I hope I did not offend Mrs, um, in some …' Amy might have blushed at the pity of this broken apology: he seemed not to realise that the offence had been against him. She hurriedly confided that no blame was attached to him; her friend was merely preoccupied by her husband's long absence.

'Yes, yes, I see. I should not have –' he muttered. 'Forgive me.' He inclined his head briefly, and was gone.

When she returned to the living room Marita was standing, provokingly, by the window she had just opened. The expression on her face was one of narrow-eyed distaste. Amy began to clear the glasses, then stopped.

'Is there something the matter?' she said.

'I'm surprised you find it necessary to ask,' replied Marita coolly. 'Do you suppose it is a pleasure for me to see you associating with a – degenerate?'

'If you mean Mr Pruckner, he's a very decent man who happens to be my neighbour –'

'Which is why I decided to hold my tongue. You have to live in the same building, after all. But, Amy, to *make a friend* of such a creature!'

'I don't see any shame in it. He's not even a Jew.'

'He's as good as. His children are. He has the Jew's habit of insinuating himself, of wheedling favours out of people. Clearly he takes advantage of you on his wife's behalf, but you are too kind-hearted to see it. Or too stupid.'

The daggered afterthought made Amy flinch. It reminded her of the old days when her friend's uncertain mood would suddenly flame into a black rage. She remembered how it would frighten her. It still did. The best way to defuse the danger was to say nothing, and she continued clearing up.

But Marita was not finished. Her voice took on a more acerbic tone. 'That you offer no argument is equivalent to admitting it. Amy – look at me – are you honestly so blind to the enemy in your midst? Even during the raids the Jews made the most of the opportunities, always first in the queue at the shelters, always the first to claim full rent for bomb damage. But have you ever seen one of them volunteer as a warden or a fireman? Of course not – they're too busy showing off their wealth or getting the best of a deal. As for that lot downstairs, I'd advise you in future to keep your distance. They will have the coat off your back before you know it.'

Amy considered mounting a defence, but one look at Marita was enough to give her pause. She feared this vitriol being turned on her. Trying to keep her voice from quavering she said, 'They're my neighbours. I can't help that.'

Marita gave way to a snort of disgust. She turned again to the window and said, almost to herself, 'Yes ... in my experience I have come to learn there is quite a lot that you can't help.'

She let this remark hang in the air before pocketing her cigarettes and fetching her coat.

10

The music was still playing in her head as she emerged from the National Gallery. Amy hadn't been to a lunchtime concert there in a while – she wasn't sure why. Descending the steps she caught sight of him waiting, scanning the faces in the crowd as they filed past, and realised at once he was looking for her. She lowered her head, and her step quickened slightly; there was a sufficient bustle of people around to shield her from notice.

The sun was out, and a ragged formation of airship-like clouds nosed across the sky. She was walking on, her heartbeat back to normal, when a shadow dropped alongside her and made her jump.

'Hullo there,' said Hoste. 'Sorry, I didn't mean to give you a fright.'

'Oh, hullo ...'

He laughed. 'I thought for a moment you were trying to give me the slip. I spotted you in there and thought, *I know that face* ...' He sounded friendly, light-hearted. She covered her fluster by taking the programme from her pocket.

'Did you enjoy the concerto?'

'Oh, I always enjoy Rachmaninov.'

'You've been going a good deal?'

'Well, yes, since the poor old Queen's Hall went ...' On the longest night of the May raids an incendiary bomb had scored a direct hit and burnt the place down.

Amy nodded sadly. 'My parents used to take me there when I was a girl. I passed it the other day – to be honest, I could hardly bear to look.'

'D'you remember saying we might go to hear some Elgar there?'

She did remember; it was while they were having dinner in Soho, the same night he had saved her life. She wondered if he thought it strange that she'd just disappeared. 'I've been meaning to get in touch,' she began, not sure where this lie would take her. 'I – I'm sorry I haven't –'

'I thought you might still be in the flat when I got back that night,' he said. 'That is, I hoped you would be,' he said, correcting himself with a little laugh.

She stole a glance at him; he was not put out, in fact he was being charming – as if he were pleased to see her. He looked different, somehow. The planes and contours of his face were more defined, his eyes bright with meaning. Not like a film star, quite, but perhaps like someone lower down the cast list.

'What a night that was!' he continued. 'Heaviest raid of the lot. Now here we are in July and hardly a peep from them since.'

'Every time I hear someone say they're over I have to touch wood. Do you think – will there be more?' She thought for a moment he might actually know.

'I couldn't say. After that pounding we took I can't think why they didn't come back and finish us off.' Hearing a doomy note in this he added, 'But if it is just a lull, there's no reason not to enjoy it. I've noticed the shelters are only half full these days.'

'Yes, I'd almost forgotten what a good night's sleep felt like. Although –' her voice turned musing – 'I still wake up and swear I can hear those engines grinding away.'

'I know what you mean,' he said. 'One got so used to the sound.'

They had come to Piccadilly. She was on her way back to the office, and assumed he would turn up Shaftesbury Avenue in the direction of his own. But he asked if she would mind him accompanying her into Mayfair.

'I haven't that much work at the moment,' he explained.

'Oh ...' She braced herself to go on. 'I wonder what you do all day?'

He looked at her in a puzzled way, and she worried that her question had sounded brusque. He mustn't get the idea I'm snooping, she thought. After a moment he said, 'I suppose it's what most people in an office do – nothing of much interest. Just a lot of paperwork.'

She nodded. 'Only ... I recall you saying you had to travel about – Hastings, was it? You still do that?'

Again, there was a tiny pause. 'Yes. I still do some work down there. And at Tunbridge Wells, Rochester, Broadstairs ... Wherever they care to send me.'

They. She would like to have established who *they* were, but he already seemed bemused by her questions. Any more would look fishy. The paradox struck her with renewed force. How could this decent, amiable-looking man, who had shown every sign of supporting the war effort, how could *he* be a Nazi agent? People were mysterious, of course. You couldn't always tell what was going on behind someone's face. In the paper you saw photographs of quite ordinary-looking men who turned out to have committed a brutal murder. There may have been something in Hoste's past that had distorted his mind and tipped his loyalty upside down. His political allegiances were murky, and his interest in Marita still baffled her. But if he were a rabid anti-Semite – and she couldn't rule it out – he had kept it very quiet.

The trouble was, she had let these suspicions brew for weeks on end. If he was indeed an enemy within then who knew what terrible damage he might be doing to the country? He could be giving away secrets, or helping Germany prepare for an invasion. It was her duty to do something – she knew it. But what?

They had reached her office on Brook Street, and she thanked him for his company. He looked at her with a disarming expression.

'I wonder – perhaps I could get us tickets for another concert. You mentioned Elgar, for instance.'

'Erm ...' An intuition had told her that he might ask this, and she didn't have a ready excuse. 'I – I'd like that. Very much.'

'Righto,' he said, and with a tip of his hat he was gone. On her way up the stairs, she realised that she could easily have brushed him off. Instead she had accepted his offer with barely a hesitation. The prospect of going out with him again appealed to her. She couldn't help liking him.

A letter had arrived for her since she had been out of the office. According to Miss Ducker it had been delivered by hand. She opened it and read:

Dear Amy,

Something was amiss between us the last time we met, and I'm sorry for it. I probably took your response to my news the wrong way. I certainly regret the harsh words that followed, because they made a rift in our friendship. May I hope that we can repair it? On one score at least we should no longer disagree – I have broken off my engagement to Christopher. For one reason or another, things had become difficult, and I decided that we should have some time apart to reflect. He cut up rough, which only made matters worse. I have been wretched about it in the days since, and am still trying to convince myself that it's for the best. In the meantime, I would very much like to see you again, and write these words in the hope you will feel the same.

Yours, very affectionately,
Georgie

She put the letter down in a confusion of feelings. Mainly what she felt was relief at the prospect of reconciling with Georgie; she too had brooded over their estrangement. It was ridiculous to have fallen out over a mere misunderstanding. But she couldn't ignore a needle in her conscience. Remembering the argument that had sparked it off, she wondered how much responsibility she bore in the matter. She had only warned Georgie against being precipitate, against jumping into marriage so quickly – the same thing she would have said to any friend. And yet it struck her as a real possibility that she had helped separate two people who loved one another.

Interviews with clients occupied her from three till five, though her mind was elsewhere, partly on the letter from Georgie but mostly on what she ought to do about Hoste. It had got to the point where not acting would be culpable negligence – a crime, in fact. She was packing up for the evening when an idea came to her; with a glance at her watch – nearly five thirty – she hurried out in the direction of Shepherd Market. She had passed the place dozens of times without giving it a moment's thought: now it presented a way forward. It was situated in a narrow set of Victorian chambers whose door opened to her push. A notice stencilled on the wall pointed to *Detective Agency* on the second floor. She met no one on the way up, her shoes clacking and scraping on the tiled steps.

A light was on in an outer office just down the corridor, and she knocked before entering. Whoever occupied the desk here had left for the day. A door off to the side opened and a short, stocky man of about forty put his head round.

'May I help you?'

Amy, with nothing prepared to say, made an apologetic face. 'I suppose I should have made an appointment ...'

The man swung open the door in invitation. 'No need for that. If you'd like to step this way, Miss – ?'

He introduced himself as Moody, and belied his name in seeming perfectly even-tempered, with a soft and confidential voice to match. The merest cockney twang could be heard in it, which she also thought reassuring – it made him sound fly, like someone you couldn't get the better of. He wore a dark gaberdine suit and tie, like an undertaker's. The office in which they sat was orderly but impersonal. A few watercolours of sylvan scenes hung on the walls, but no family photographs or personal tokens, and nothing to identify the nature of the business. Even the carpeted floor seemed to collude in the air of discretion. Moody took out a notepad and asked her how he might help. She took a deep breath.

'Your line of work involves a lot of surveillance, I imagine – keeping a tail on people?' With an open-palmed gesture he agreed that it did. 'There is someone – a man – whom I suspect of ... wrongdoing. I can't be certain of it, which is why I'd like you to establish beyond doubt what he's been up to.'

Moody put down his pen and looked at her. 'This man – would I be right in assuming you know one another?'

'Yes, we do.'

He inclined his head sympathetically. 'Miss Strallen – if I may – we deal with cases like this all the time. Is he in fact your husband?'

She started at this. 'No, no –'

'But you *are* romantically attached?'

'No, nothing like that. I don't really know him well at all.'

Moody drew in his chin. It seemed he was already finding this a bit rum. 'Then what d'you suppose he's guilty of?'

'Well, I'm not sure. That's why I need you to investigate. I think – I have reason to believe – that he's a subversive.' It was the first time she had said it aloud. 'That is, I think he's an enemy agent.'

A sceptical furrow had creased Moody's forehead. 'Based on what evidence?'

She hesitated before recounting the story of being left in his flat during the raid, and her stumbling upon his cache of medals. Moody listened, his small grey eyes sliding over her, seeming to calculate the likelihood of her being crazy. When she came to the end he waited a moment, squaring his pad – on which he hadn't yet made a note – and staring off thoughtfully.

'You're absolutely certain that these "medals" were German?'

'I know what an Iron Cross looks like. I've seen one before.'

'So you'd like me to tail this party, in order to discover … what exactly?'

Amy gave a half-shrug. 'Some indication of what he's doing. Perhaps from the people he meets – I don't know.'

He puffed out his cheeks, then said, 'Why not just report these suspicions of yours to the police?'

'Because I don't want to involve them unless it becomes unavoidable. This man –' she searched for the words – 'he once did me a great kindness. I can't really – It would be ungrateful of me to try to have him arrested on a mere suspicion. That's why I'd like you to … look into it.'

Moody stared at her for a moment, seeming to make up his mind. 'I should warn you, Miss Strallen, this sort of investigation doesn't come cheap. It entails long hours of waiting, watching – you understand?'

'Yes. Perhaps you could tell me …'

He pulled open a drawer of his desk and picked out a card, which he slid across the table without comment. In very small print it listed his rates in pounds and shillings. He was so discreet he wouldn't even mention money aloud, lest it contaminated the air.

'There may also be incidental expenses. It all adds up.'

She sensed he was trying to put her off, possibly out of kindness: the job would be a costly one.

'That's fine,' she said, pushing the card back to him. 'When can you begin?'

They proceeded to the paperwork, and he made a note of Hoste's home and office addresses. He asked her if she had a photograph of 'the party', but of course she did not. He took down a brief description instead, and she tried her best to make him sound distinctive – which, in appearance, he wasn't.

'When may I expect your first report?' she said, rising to her feet.

'Usually I would take two or three weeks to put something together.' Then he added with pointed but not unfriendly irony: 'But given the case may involve the security of the nation, I'll contact you by the end of next week.'

After the incident of Mr Pruckner's visit Amy decided not to think about Marita any more. In the past she had always been quick to smooth any ruffled feathers between them, first because she feared her disapproval, and second because she felt that Marita's impatience was often justified – she was so much the cleverest of all her friends, and it seemed only right that she, Amy, should be the one to appease and conciliate. On this occasion, however, she was unwilling to play the peacemaker, for the simple reason that she had done nothing wrong. Mr Pruckner was her neighbour, and he deserved her friendliness and courtesy whether he was Jewish or not.

In truth she had been shocked by the vehemence of Marita's hostility. It had been clear from the outset that she had no love of the Jews; in the old days, before she had joined the blackshirts, she had limited herself to a mocking aloofness, to sniping and carping. 'They' were always first in a queue, always ready to seize an advantage and bilk the unsuspecting. But never before had Amy heard her use a word like 'degenerate', or speak of them with such disgust in her voice. It was as if their offence to her had become personal, although, as far as she knew, Marita didn't nurse a particular grievance. Following the surprise of their rapprochement she wondered if it was really possible for them to remain friends after all. When they had first got to know one another in the thirties she had been somewhat in awe of Marita – her intelligence, her striking looks, her terrifying social manner. Then had come the break, and during that long estrangement Amy had developed self-assurance, a spirit of independence, mostly through the success of the bureau. She no longer needed someone to look up to.

Perhaps her silence conveyed its own message, because Marita had telephoned a few days later and suggested going for a walk: it was a beautiful Saturday, warm with only the faintest breeze. They met at the south end of Regent's Park and began strolling up the Broad Walk. All around the Nash terraces lay swathes of bomb damage, some of it being cleared up as they walked. The far-off sounds of tapping and tidying floated across the air.

Marita wore a sleeveless dress with a geometric pattern of purple and green. Her hair, pulled back in a ponytail, lent a more playful aspect to her angular face. Amy hadn't envisaged any show of remorse from her, and in this at least her expectations were squarely met. Marita was not one for contrition, except in circumstances when it didn't matter: she could apologise for being late, or forgetful, but she would not yield in any argument about politics.

'You know me well enough by now, my darling. I am not going to make a fuss about what was said last week. Let us draw a veil over the unfortunate matter of your neighbours.'

'Agreed,' said Amy, who could not resist adding, 'I suppose I should feel grateful that you still care to see me.'

Marita heard the slight sarcasm. 'I accept that not all my friends share my view of how the world works. Some of them I am less inclined to judge than others.'

'That sounds like you're granting forgiveness.'

'No, not forgiveness – only forbearance. In time I trust you will come to see that I was right. For now I should rather keep you as a friend than insist upon winning a point.' She gave Amy a sidelong look. 'You've become more forthright since I first knew you. Tell me, what happened to the friend whose engagement you argued over?'

Amy's expression turned rueful. 'I saw her on Thursday, as a matter of fact. She broke it off. She told me she'd had second thoughts, but I feel terrible now for creating a doubt in the first place. They might have got married and lived happily ever after.'

'Most unlikely,' said Marita crisply. 'That this woman parted with her fiancé so soon afterwards suggests your warning was justified. Nobody forced her to break it off. I dare say she has a mind of her own.'

Amy nodded. 'Oh yes, Georgie's bright – she has a pretty important job in Whitehall.'

'Whitehall? You didn't tell me that. What does she do there?'

'She's secretary to a junior minister. Hard work, but she seems to thrive on it.'

'I'm sure,' came the reply, after a pause. 'Well, it sounds to me like you did her a great favour. A husband might not like his wife getting cosy among the mandarins.'

Amy felt far from sure it *was* a favour she had done. On the night they met Georgie had shed tears about the break-up, but assured Amy that she would probably have made the decision even without the prompt of her advice. Christopher had been too eager to rush things along; and it had been naive of her to accept him quite so unthinkingly. Yet a voice within nagged away at Amy, accusing her: she had allowed personal instincts to overrule her professional integrity. As a marriage broker she ought to have put the client uppermost, not the friend. How far should loyalty compete with the demands of duty? She was well aware that the question pertained, more troublingly, to another recent friendship. In choosing to do the right thing you couldn't always absolve yourself of doing the injurious thing.

They had stopped to sit down on one of the benches lining the Walk. Marita took out a slim silver cigarette case and offered one to Amy.

'That's a lovely thing,' she said, admiring the case.

'Bernard gave it me on our first wedding anniversary. He loves to give me presents, jewellery and such, but also little things which have a personal meaning. When we were first courting there was a famous German writer I admired – Bernard contacted the publisher and got a signed copy of his latest book for me.'

Amy found herself wondering, idly, if the book in question was *Mein Kampf*. She hoped it wasn't.

'You must miss him terribly,' she said, putting a hand to Marita's arm.

Marita looked away, considering. 'Of course. But his letters are a consolation to me – and he writes such witty things about the camp, and the prisoners.'

Amy briefly tried to picture Bernard Pardoe. She couldn't vouch for his brilliance as a correspondent, but on their short acquaintance he had not struck her as a wit. In fact she hadn't much liked him at all: his humour was angry and sarcastic, and she faintly recoiled from his narrow, squashed features and his clipped moustache. His devotion to Marita was obvious – no husband could have been more uxorious – but it was never clear to Amy what exactly she saw in *him*. He was possessed neither of looks nor means, despite his way with a gift. She recalled an image of them together at the register office on their wedding day, the bride happy, majestic in navy, and towering over the groom. Of course there was something else that bound them to each other, the same thing that would quickly determine the likelihood of remaining their friend. Amy thought she might not have been the only one to drift away once the Pardoes had wedded themselves to 'the party'; in 1937 Bernard had stood (and lost) as the Fascist candidate in a London by-election. A couple so openly fanatical about Hitler and Germany would require quite some influence to keep up a position in society.

As if overhearing her thoughts Marita said, 'The internments cannot last. Once the tide turns decisively in Europe this country will have to seek peace, or else be obliterated. All that has kept it going for this long is Churchill's stubbornness.'

'You mean we should surrender?'

'No. I mean we should negotiate. How many times must I tell you? – Hitler doesn't *want* to be our enemy. He has long admired Great Britain.'

'He has an odd way of showing it,' said Amy.

But Marita did not seem in the mood for an argument; instead she turned the conversation back to Georgie Harlow and her recent break-up. As they rose to continue their walk she said, 'You know, the best thing you can do for the woman is find her another chap.' She uttered this last word with an ironic relish.

'I'm not sure I dare after what happened. She probably doesn't trust me as a matchmaker.'

Marita's expression was non-committal. After a pause she said musingly, 'If that is the case, may I suggest someone?'

'You mean – ?'

'I happen to know a very eligible man, mid-thirties, not badly off. He's also *extremely* handsome.'

Amy laughed. 'I rather like the sound of him myself!'

'Would your friend be interested, d'you think?'

'I can ask her. But she may be feeling rather bruised ...'

'All the more reason to cheer her up. He's the perfect gentleman.'

Amy felt puzzled. She was certainly selling him. 'What's the name of this paragon?'

'Mm? Oh, William. William O'Dare. An Irishman. I'll arrange an evening – you can meet him, too.'

I I

Amy was back at Moody's office the following Friday. In the anteroom two of his assistants were silently at work; one of them, looking up, indicated by a nod that she should go through. True to his word, the private detective had a report ready for her. She could see on his desk a sheet of paper on which very close writing and several diagrams had been inscribed; the only word on it she could make out was 'sociable?'.

Moody leaned back in his chair and steepled his fingers. 'Because of the unusual nature of this case,' he began, 'progress has been, erm, doubtful. You see, I mostly do divorce work. A simple brief. One keeps watch on a gentleman or a lady with a view to catching them in compromising behaviour. In a romantic sense,' he added, making it sound not very romantic at all.

'I imagine you have some stories to tell,' Amy said, eyebrows raised.

'Indeed.' He pursed his mouth in a tight smile, as if sealing off the glimpsed avenue of reminiscence. 'With this case, I can't be exactly sure what I'm on the lookout for. "Wrongdoing" was your term, as I remember. The party has been kept under surveillance, but so far there's not much to go on.'

He gestured at the closely written page before him. It was, he explained, a record of Hoste's comings and goings each day of that week. He had been obliged to do a great deal of waiting around outside his office at Chancery Lane; Amy sensed the tenacity as well as the tedium involved in the private eye's daily round.

'So he does go out sometimes?' she said.

'Yes. For a tax inspector Mr Hoste is actually quite sociable – likes to meet people in cafes, Corner Houses, a pub on occasion.'

'What sort of people?'

Moody gave a shrug. 'Ordinary people. It would be more satisfying if they were "sinister" or "shifty-looking", I know, but there seemed nothing very remarkable about them at all. Occasionally he meets two or three at once. I've got close enough to eavesdrop on them but, again, the conversation was nothing very unusual.'

'And they talk about – ?'

'The war, mostly. A few made comments about ... members of the Jewish faith. The sort of thing you hear every day. Nothing to suggest subversive tendencies, or a desire to help Germany.'

Amy wasn't quite sure where her next question came from. 'Did any of these meetings strike you as "romantic" in nature?'

Moody's eye twitched: he wasn't sure either. 'I – um – wouldn't say so. The only time I saw him behave in a *familiar* way was with a lady, who I took to be a friend.'

From his description of her Amy thought it might have been the woman she had seen on the stairs that day, the first time she visited his office. 'Or a colleague of his, do you think?'

'Quite possibly. There was an animation in his manner I detected at no other point. The lady seemed to respond in kind.'

Amy bit her lip meditatively. Moody, scrupulous to a fault, had supplied an account of the time and place of each meeting, the number of people, the stray remarks overheard. She briefly scanned the document, and could find nothing of any significance in it. Wasn't it as she had expected? There had never really been much likelihood of catching Hoste and co. flinging Nazi salutes at one another.

Moody had been watching her read it. 'I hope you don't mind that I've appended a few small expenses ...'

'No, of course not,' she replied, with a distracted air.

'I am sorry, miss. I knew you'd be disappointed. Should we conclude the matter here?'

His tone had become sympathetic, underscored by the merest batsqueak of pity – *I was sorry to take the money off her, poor thing* ...

'Give it another week, would you?' she said. 'I don't mind paying.'

He looked at her; inclined his head. 'As you wish.'

It did not take Marita long to follow up her matchmaking suggestion. Amy could hardly recall such eagerness in her. A reservation was made at a little restaurant on Fitzroy Street for four people; Amy would accompany Georgie, while Marita would bring along her Irish friend. Better to make it seem a casual dinner than simply throw two strangers together.

Amy had to screw up her courage before consulting Georgie. At one point she had considered not even revealing to her the motive behind the dinner; then she decided it was better to come clean about it than be caught out later in yet more meddling. To her surprise Georgie had accepted the invitation unhesitatingly. The experience with Christopher, far from discouraging her, had put some steel in her soul. She seemed more worldly; less fearful. On the night of the dinner, Marita had been all charm, and set the tone by ordering champagne. She had not exaggerated William O'Dare's good looks: tall and rangy, his sculpted cheekbones and deep-set eyes lent him a saturnine allure, and a confiding manner blended happily with his not altogether comprehensible Ulster accent.

The evening went well, though doubt had kept tugging at the edges of Amy's consciousness. For one thing, while she had been intrigued to meet O'Dare, she found herself not quite trusting him. His suavity felt like an act, there was too much effort in it, and she couldn't help noticing the quick glances he flicked at Marita. It led her to wonder if the pair had once been something more than friends to each other. And it seemed so very unlike Marita to go out of her way to play Cupid. Hitherto she had always cultivated a cynical amusement on the subject of romance – even Bernard came in for an occasional barb – but here she was promoting O'Dare's merits with all the pushiness of a trader in a souk. The enthusiasm was somewhat baffling. The Irishman himself responded to it with an embarrassed touch of self-deprecation, as if he knew that Marita was overegging it. 'She's not always this nice about me,' he joked, and another look passed between them.

Whatever game they were playing, it worked on Georgie. She looked thoroughly charmed, laughing at O'Dare's unremarkable comic sallies and entering the convivial mood of the occasion. Amy on the one hand was relieved, for it seemed to signal a willingness to put the recent heartache behind her and get on with her life; on the other, she felt alarm that Georgie's lack of experience had made her rather susceptible. She had been too long on the ration where male courtship was concerned. While O'Dare was pleasant, and handsome for sure, she sensed that he was possessed of little to keep a bright woman stimulated. Of course it wasn't necessarily *intellectual* stimulation a woman might be looking for ... but she didn't even want to think about that.

'There's a Mr Moody here to see you,' said Miss Ducker dubiously. 'He doesn't have an appointment but said you'll know what it's about.'

Amy presented her most reassuring smile and asked her to send him in. She and Moody were not scheduled to meet until the end of the week. Something must have come up, though the detective, poker-faced, didn't say a word until Miss Ducker and her thwarted air of inquisitiveness had vacated the room.

'Sorry to drop in like this, Miss Strallen,' he said, his gaze quickly taking in his surroundings, 'but I thought it best to apprise you of developments immediately.'

'Developments?'

Invited to take a seat, Moody produced another of his close-packed reports from his briefcase. There was almost a gleam in his eye as he gathered himself.

'I kept watch on the party, as per your instructions, and found no change in his habits at all – office hours, has lunch in a cafe nearby, takes an occasional stroll to the West End to meet this or that person. Nothing out of the ordinary – only yesterday he met that lady, the one I told you about last time. This was in the Kardomah on Fleet Street. And something rather interesting occurred.'

Amy, almost sick with curiosity, asked him to continue.

'As I mentioned, they appeared to know one another quite well. I got close to them, or as close as I dared. The lady had such a watchful eye I was afraid of being rumbled. So there they were, talking, in voices so low I couldn't hear. I almost gave the thing up, but I'm glad I didn't, because I would have missed a little transaction between them. The party very discreetly handed an envelope to the lady – the work of an instant, unnoticed by anyone except –' He paused, gave a modest cough. 'Indeed, such was the sleight-of-hand by which this was effected one might deduce that the parties were observing a routine. They had done this before.'

'How can you tell?' asked Amy.

'In this business one comes to recognise the signs,' he said, and paused again.

'So what happened then?'

Moody looked momentarily embarrassed. 'I had a close call ...' Despite extreme circumspection on his part he had a distinct sense that 'the lady' had registered his presence. She must have alerted Hoste, because within a minute or so they rose to leave. Moody followed them out in time to see the two of them parting on the street. His objective now was to discover the identity of the woman, and, if possible, the contents of that envelope. The difficulty of this was clear: she had probably noticed him already, and would be on the lookout for anyone dogging her footsteps. 'It's one of the trickiest follows I ever did,' he said, narrowing his gaze. 'She boarded a tram, and got off after two stops to catch a bus going the opposite way. That's when I knew she was on to me. She tried a few old ruses – at one point she ducked into a hotel, and I gambled on her not slipping out the back. I kept my watch in a doorway opposite the entrance, and like a pro she left the same way she came in.'

It took another hour of this cat-and-mouse pursuit before Moody ran his quarry to ground. She entered a library, and after waiting ten minutes he followed in after. Keeping well out of sight he spotted her working at a desk. He waited, and waited. Just when it seemed she would never leave her post she rose and went off in the direction of the powder room. This was his one chance. He quickly occupied the desk next to hers, and thanked the stars that she had taken only her purse, not her handbag. 'She must have thought she had shaken me off,' he said. Amy listened agog as he described his rifling of the handbag. 'The envelope was there, with four pounds inside it. Her identity papers named her as Monica Berens, though they looked to me like a forgery. There was a handwritten letter in there, too, which confirmed that Berens was an alias. You see, the envelope had that name on it, but the letter inside was addressed to someone called *Marita*.'

Amy's sudden intake of breath caused Moody to stop.

'You know her?'

'Yes.' She knew it could be no other.

'It was the name of her correspondent who caught my eye. The letter had come from an internment camp, you see, and the censor had printed the prisoner's name at the top – Bernard Pardoe. One of Mosley's cronies. So your hunch about Fascist subversion may not be wide of the mark . . .'

Amy was still absorbing the shock as Moody talked on. Marita and Hoste – in cahoots. It was incredible, and yet in hindsight perfectly obvious. She thought back to the first time Hoste had introduced – insinuated – himself into her life, the aborted interview at the bureau, then the accidental meeting at the National Gallery and her noticing Bernard Pardoe's so-called tax records at his flat. None of it 'accidental' at all. My God, the act he had put on ... He had used her in order to get to Marita. It had been no overture of friendship, just a coldly calculated subterfuge. She felt a sudden wild plunge in her stomach.

She heard Moody repeat her name, and looked up. 'Are you all right?'

'Sorry, I'm just – um ... stunned. What is – what do you think he was paying her for?'

Moody made a face. 'Who knows – information? Like I said, it seemed to be a regular transaction between them.'

The plunge in her stomach had turned acid. 'What should I do?'

'I believe there's only one thing you can do – report it to the authorities. If it's as we suspect, they're engaged in a serious crime. Treason, in fact.'

'But ... what if we're wrong? If it's just a terrible misunderstanding?'

Moody's sympathetic look cut right through her. 'You don't really think it's a misunderstanding, do you? There's an old saying in our business, Miss Strallen – once there's a doubt, there's no doubt.'

She took the rest of the afternoon off, pleading a headache. Johanna had been very understanding, though she betrayed her own curiosity about Amy's visitor when she whispered, 'Miss Ducker was imagining all sorts ...' Amy fobbed her off with the excuse of 'a family matter', which had the advantage of sounding both vague and too delicate to be divulged.

Treason. The word seemed so antiquated, conjuring images of the Tower of London, of bearded plotters wearing doublet and hose, clapped in irons. But people guilty of treason were *traitors*, which was much more to the point. Those odd conversations Hoste had started with her – about her attitude to the Jews, to Germany, to the war – they played in her head as evidence for the prosecution. That he had seemed unlikely as a Nazi agent now made sense to her, for what better cover was available to an agent than unlikeliness? Hoste's mild-mannered character and his air of trustworthy diligence were cleverly adapted to neutralise the slightest suspicion.

Must she really hand him over to the police? There would be no going back once she did. The consequences of her reporting him offered a bleak prospect either way. If Hoste was innocent of any charges he would never look upon her as a friend again. If guilty, he would go to jail for a long time. She looked out over Queen Anne Street as night fell, turning it over, fretting. There was doubt – there was always doubt; if he were a committed Nazi, why had he taken up the job of ARP warden? Unless that, too, was a cover. It was clear that he and Marita had betrayed her. But had they betrayed the country?

The next morning, after a deep and dreamless night's sleep, she picked up the telephone and asked to be put through to Marylebone Police Station.

12

As Hoste entered the room he felt a distinct edge of nervousness among them. For reasons of security he had rarely visited the headquarters of the Section, and after weeks of silence he would sometimes wonder if they had forgotten about him. But here they were, all three senior members – Castle, Traherne, Hammond – and by the tall window two secretaries facing one another across a desk, at work. The room was almost severe in its absence of homely touches – no pictures adorned the walls, and the parquet flooring made a lonely echo underfoot. Castle, with an expression of kindly regret, gestured him to the oxblood-coloured chesterfield. He sat down, and waited.

'We've had to haul her in, old boy,' he said.

Hoste stared at him, baffled. 'Who – Marita?'

'No, no. I mean Amy Strallen. I'm afraid she's on to you.'

He sat up suddenly, as if prodded by a sharp stick. 'How?'

Castle flicked a glance to his colleagues. 'She hired someone to track you. And she's made a report to the police, so it's serious.'

Hoste thought back to the previous morning, when he'd met Marita at the Kardomah: she'd noticed the tail almost immediately, and they'd cleared out of there. To think that Amy Strallen was behind it … But he couldn't imagine what had given him away. He'd been careful, so careful that in his six years with the Section no one had ever suspected him.

Tessa Hammond fixed him with an odd look. 'You had no idea?'

He shook his head. 'The last time I saw her we talked about going to a concert.' Elgar, as he recalled. He saw Castle and Traherne exchange another look. 'Am I burned?'

'We don't know yet,' Tessa replied carefully. 'That depends on the nature of your relationship with her.'

Hoste now realised where this was heading. 'If you're implying that we were – you're way off.'

'Hard to know how else you were compromised,' said Castle.

Traherne looked at him squarely. 'We've got a heck of a leak to stop up. It would be better for all concerned if you come clean –'

'Come clean about what? I've met Amy Strallen a handful of times. We went to dinner once. There is nothing else to tell.'

A fraught silence followed. Hoste felt indignant that he was not believed, but he knew that protesting his innocence too hotly would damage his case. In the end it was Tessa who broke the impasse.

'The lady may confirm that. I'd better get started.'

Hoste squinted at her. 'She's already here?'

'Downstairs, waiting to be interviewed.'

Once the meeting had ended he followed Tessa out of the room. She was on the turn of the balustraded stairs when he caught up.

'Hammond. Will you let me sit in?' he said.

'I don't think so,' said Tessa smoothly. 'You can listen, if you like.'

'I need to talk to her.'

She pulled in her chin. 'Why? If you really have fooled her all this time she's going to be pretty angry once she finds out.'

'That's why I need to talk to her.' They were on the ground floor, heading for the interview rooms. He put his hand to her arm. 'Please.'

*

Amy looked at her watch; she had been waiting in this bare, windowless room for more than an hour. They had picked her up on the street that morning. She had just left the flat when a car pulled up alongside the pavement and a man in suit and trilby got out. His driver had kept the engine running. She thought at first he wanted directions: in fact, he asked her if she wouldn't mind accompanying them – it concerned a report she had filed yesterday at Marylebone Police Station. 'And what if I do mind?' The man seemed not to hear the question, and held open the car door for her. They had dropped her here, at a municipal building in St James's, without either of the two men addressing another word to her.

Outside she could hear mumbling talk, and then the door opened. The woman who entered was the same one she had passed on the stairs at Hoste's office. She introduced herself as Tessa Hammond.

'I'm sorry they haven't brought you anything to drink. Would you like tea?'

Amy nodded. 'Can you please tell me where I am?'

'Of course. This is a government office dealing with affairs of national security. Your report at the police station was passed on to us ...'

She followed up with questions about Jack Hoste, how often they had met, what they had talked about – and why she had suspected him as an enemy agent. Amy went through her story again, in much the same way as she had to the police, though this woman – Hammond – didn't seem surprised by it, not even by the discovery of the Nazi insignia. A stenographer quietly recorded their conversation at a desk nearby, and Tessa made an occasional note of her own.

'There is one question I'm obliged to ask you, Miss Strallen. Did you and Mr Hoste have a sexual relationship?'

Amy gasped out her surprise. 'Is that what you think?'

'I'm sorry. I wouldn't ask if it wasn't important.'

'Well – the answer's no. No, we didn't. What's happened to him? Has he been arrested?'

The look on her inquisitor's face suddenly softened with pity. 'No, he's not been arrested – because he works for us. A department of MI5. We know it as the Section. Counter-espionage. I am Jack Hoste's case officer. He has in his pocket about two dozen Nazi sympathisers, who believe him to be the Gestapo's man in London. He had been hunting Marita Pardoe for two years before he met you. She's the most dangerous fifth columnist in the country. Your information regarding her whereabouts was absolutely vital.'

Amy was for a moment too stunned to speak. The world had suddenly tilted into confounding new geometries. 'But – the Iron Crosses. Why did he keep –'

'They're fakes. A sop to the recruits. While they believe he's their conduit to Berlin, they'll keep supplying him with intelligence – troop movements, air defences, new developments in radar. It all goes through Hoste, and he "rewards" them with medals – counterfeits. A handful of agents, like Marita, he pays by the week.'

They weren't the only ones to have been fooled, thought Amy. 'It's rather humiliating, isn't it? To have been taken in like that.'

Tessa shook her head. 'Not at all. It's his job. He couldn't infiltrate the ring without deceiving people – good people as well as bad.'

After a long pause she said, 'What will happen to Marita?'

'Nothing. As far as she's concerned, Hoste is the Gestapo's handler in London. No one must make her think otherwise, and that includes you. You must behave towards her as normal – don't give her a hint you know about what's going on. Is that understood?' she said sharply. 'It's why you'll have to sign a few things before we can let you go.'

'Like what?'

'The Secrets Act, for one. You know enough about Jack Hoste now to be a danger to him.' Something in Amy's drawn, troubled face must have moved Tessa, because her voice dropped to a confidential hush. 'You have to understand, this work he does is crucial to the war effort. He didn't *want* to trick you – I believe he's very fond of you.'

Amy replied with a bitter half-laugh. How could she presume to match people with one another when she was such a bad picker herself? They sat there for a while longer, neither of them speaking. Eventually Tessa rose and said that she would fetch the paperwork – they wouldn't keep her for longer than was necessary. 'Thanks for cooperating,' she said at the door. 'This has helped the war effort, too.'

Amy was too deeply sunk in her own thoughts to reply. From outside, the door still ajar, she overheard Tessa remonstrating with someone whose voice she took a moment to recognise. She got up from the chair and walked over.

'. . . she's in no mood to talk to you,' Tessa was saying.

There, in the corridor, was Hoste. His eyes lifted over Tessa's shoulder and seemed to fill with an appeal on catching sight of her. She stood on the threshold, arms folded across her chest.

'Miss Strallen – I'm sorry,' he began. 'I know you must think I'm a –'

Tessa interposed herself between them. 'Stop this, Hoste. You're in enough trouble as it is.'

'I'd just like to talk to her,' he said. 'Five minutes.' Tessa turned round to Amy in silent enquiry. With a reluctant, barely perceptible nod she gave her assent.

'I'll be back in five minutes,' said Tessa, looking rather sternly from him to her. She left them there, facing one another in the doorway. Having pleaded for her time he now seemed at a loss to say anything.

'You must have thought me such an idiot,' she said after a moment. 'Your pretending to be a tax inspector, running into one another at the National Gallery, planting the file on Pardoe. That was all planned, wasn't it?'

Hoste nodded, not catching her eye. 'But I never thought you were an idiot. I'm only grateful you helped me run Marita to earth. If I could have been honest about it I would have been, but this job – it involves being someone else, someone who's not like me at all. It's an act. It's what I was recruited to do.'

'I don't doubt that it's part of your job. But once you'd got what you needed – Marita – why did you keep me under surveillance? What possible use was I then?'

His eyes closed and his hand went to his brow, which he began to knead in frantic agitation. 'Marita had an idea that you might be ... after your time in Germany she believed you might be, I don't know, a sympathiser.'

Amy felt the colour drain from her face. 'You mean – a Nazi?'

'I never thought so,' he said quickly, 'but I had to check, if only to convince Marita I was a bona fide handler.'

She felt a sudden cold grip on her heart: that this man she had – that he could have imagined her capable of such an allegiance. It took a moment to find her voice. 'And was attending an Elgar concert another way of testing me?'

He looked blank for a second. 'No, no. Of course not. I suggested that because – because I hoped to see you again.'

'I should have known,' she said quietly, almost to herself. 'I should have known that very first time you turned up at the bureau. The idea that *you* could have been a partner for someone.'

His little flinch of surprise at this remark might have touched her once. But not now. He had forfeited any claim on her finer feeling.

Well, he thought, *that* was an honest appraisal. 'I realise you'd rather I was out of your sight, but there's one more thing I need to tell you.' She looked at him and wondered if he might save himself. 'Be careful around Marita. I know that you're friends, but you mustn't forget how dangerous she is. She's fanatical, she's devious, and she won't think twice about exploiting you to get what she wants.'

'Is that it?'

'I'm just asking you to be on your guard,' he said. 'We're pretty sure she's responsible for murder. She is absolutely without scruple or conscience.'

Amy laughed miserably. 'Takes one to know one, I suppose.' She held his gaze a moment longer, then stepped back and closed the door on him.

When they let her go at last she walked back to the office through St James's Park. She was in a blinding daze, not seeing the nannies pushing their prams or the boys putting out their toy boats on the lake. She paid no mind to the gravel path beneath her feet or the sunlight glinting through the latticed tops of trees. Nothing impinged on her but the shock of her debriefing – it felt as though she had been in an accident. When she had wavered about reporting him as a spy, the consequences looked likely to wreck any relationship she had with him. But this outcome was quite unforeseen, pitching her into a no man's land of conflicting impulses. There was relief, of course, in discovering that he wasn't a traitor, and an admiration for his courage and cleverness in neutralising the enemy within; wonderment, too, that he had maintained this audacious imposture for so long. Even Marita, the least gullible person she'd ever known, even she had fallen for it. Against this, however, she felt injured pride at having been duped, the more acute for the illusions about him she had harboured.

She thought, as she often did, of the night he had saved her from the bomb blast, and of their bolt for safety down Charing Cross Road. They had sheltered in his flat for what, half an hour? – which at the time seemed edged with a sort of hysterical relief, for they had outrun the danger. Later, before he left for his warden's post, that strange half-hour had breathed into life a tiny flame of enchantment, of encouragement – that they might mean something to one another. Alone in his flat she had sensed, for a few minutes, the possibility of a future with Jack Hoste in it. If she had not gone looking for matches, had not snooped in that chest of drawers, she would never have suspected that he was anything but brave, and honest, and kind ... But now reality had come in a rush through the door, and the flame was out.

On her way out of the office that evening Amy ran into Georgie Harlow.

'Oh, I'm glad I caught you,' she said. 'Do you have time for a quick drink?'

Amy felt so wretched and drained from the events of the morning that her instinct was to decline, but Georgie looked so eager, and perhaps after all a restorative might lift her mood. She had been brooding the entire afternoon. They found a pub just off Berkeley Square and settled with their drinks at a corner table.

Georgie squinted at Amy for a moment. 'You look a bit tired. Is everything –'

'Oh, I'm fine. A hard day.'

Pleased to have her solicitude deflected – as most people are when they have news to tell – Georgie began. 'You know that man we were introduced to the other night – William? Well, he dropped me a line yesterday. He wants to take me to dinner.'

'Gosh,' said Amy.

'I know! Do you think I should?'

Amy smiled. 'I don't know. Did you like him?'

'Well ... I like the fact that he's keen. And he did seem very pleasant that night we met. I can't see why not.'

There was a tentativeness in her voice, as if she were asking for permission. Amy took a sip of her drink and said, 'He did have a certain charm.'

It did not sound, to her own ears, like a wholehearted endorsement. Georgie registered it, too. 'A bit too forward, do you think?'

'Perhaps. But it's hardly indecent of him to *ask*. Did he write nicely?'

She replied with a laugh, and nodded.

'Then maybe you should give him a chance. It's only an invitation to dinner.'

This was evidently the response Georgie was hoping for; she ordered more drinks and began to speculate on what sort of prospects William O'Dare might have. On the night they had met he had talked about working in the export business in Ireland. Did that mean he was well off? Amy listened with a show of interest she hardly felt, offering encouragement and caution in about equal measure. Inwardly she wondered at her friend's naivety, fearing a repeat of the express-like speed with which she had fallen for Christopher. It was strange to find a woman of high professional standing who had so little nous in matters of courtship. But her affection for Georgie, and her residual guilt over the last failure, muffled the distant siren of her misgivings.

They could not be altogether silenced, however, and as she prepared for bed that night something came unbidden to her thoughts. It was Hoste's warning about Marita. *You mustn't forget how dangerous she is* ... He had told her this with particular vehemence. Having tracked Marita for two years he probably knew what he was talking about; and if MI5 regarded her as a threat to national safety then she ought to take it seriously. Was there reason to suspect her friend William, too? Neither he nor Marita had talked about politics on the night – but she remembered telling them that Georgina worked at the Ministry of Defence.

Was that why she had been so keen to throw the Irishman in her path? Hammond had told her that she must behave as normal towards Marita: easier said than done. How was she to behave in front of someone she knew to be an enemy spy, someone actively plotting Churchill's downfall? One false word, one unguarded comment and Marita would notice – because she always noticed. And the stakes were now so much higher. Should the delicate clockwork of his deception be exposed, Hoste would be for it. Amy felt an abrupt surge of panic as a chasm opened up – the nerve it would require to bear all of this secrecy. They were more or less compelling her to act like an agent herself.

This would be her life from now on. Constant vigilance, constant dread. To be the one who gave the game away – calamitous. *The most dangerous fifth columnist in the country*, Hammond had called her. Responsible for murder, according to Hoste. Sometimes it felt like Marita had only to be in her company to know what she was thinking.

She followed her heartbeat into the kitchen and took out a bottle of Martell from the cupboard. Her hand actually shook as she poured a tot. Yes, this was her life now, and as the heat of the brandy spread through her chest she realised that responsibility already had its claws in her. It had to be faced, without delay. She returned to the bedroom and picked up the telephone. At the end of their interview Hammond had supplied her with a number 'in case of emergencies'. She wasn't sure if this constituted an emergency but she imagined that the Section would prefer a warning, even if it proved to be mistaken.

On the third ring a voice answered. Hoste's voice. She almost hung up. 'This is Amy Strallen. I didn't know it would be – I was given this number by Tessa Hammond.'

'Is there something the matter?' His tone was businesslike, almost brusque; it was as though the awkwardness of the morning had never happened. 'This line is reserved for –'

'Emergencies, I know,' she said, determined to match his brisk impersonality. 'You said something about Marita – about how dangerous she was.' She recounted the story of her friend

Georgina, and Marita's eagerness to play matchmaker. Even as she spoke she worried that her suspicions sounded absurd, or, worse, that she was pleading for attention. Perhaps if she had slept on the matter she would have seen it differently tomorrow.

But Hoste in reply didn't sound like someone who was humouring her. 'This Irishman – William – can you describe him?'

'Oh ... good-looking, tall, swarthy. Early thirties, I should say.'

'But you don't recall his surname?'

'I don't, sorry.'

'Has your friend met this chap on her own?'

'Not yet.'

'There may be nothing in it,' he said. 'But where Marita's involved that's never a safe assumption. Tell your friend to be on her guard. She's probably wise to people asking her about the MoD, but the less she tells him about her life the better.'

'If he is one of Marita's cronies mightn't it be best if she just avoids him altogether?'

'I'm afraid that might encourage suspicion. Marita would know something was up.'

Amy didn't like the sound of this. 'Is Georgie putting herself at risk?'

'I don't know,' he said after a pause. 'We'll have to wait and see.'

There was a silence between them, and she wondered if he would make any reference to what had happened. Before he rang off he said, 'If you happen to remember the fellow's name, let me know.'

She replaced the receiver and walked to the window overlooking the street. She half expected to spot somebody down there, in the shadows, watching the flat. But all she saw was the pale reflection of her own face in the glass. Half an hour later she dialled the number again.

'His name – the Irishman's name – I remember now. It was O'Dare.'

Hoste repeated it softly. 'William O'Dare. You're sure about that?'

She was, though she couldn't tell whether it meant something to him or not. They said goodnight.

He had written the name down. *William O'Dare*. One of several aliases that Billy Adair had used. Well, well. So Marita had already put him to work.

The sound of Amy Strallen's voice was still in his ears. He hadn't expected to hear it again, not now – or ever.

Next morning Hoste ran a background check on Georgina Harlow – her record of employment at the MoD, her clearance level, her routine responsibilities. He also got someone to check her appointments diary and noted that the following week she would be accompanying the junior minister on a special train to Shoeburyness, an artillery barracks and key position in the coastal defence of south-east England. He telephoned Castle from his office.

'Any chance of locating the list of personnel due to travel to Shoeburyness on Tuesday week? I gather it's a trip to inspect tanks, ack-ack guns and the like.'

'I'll make enquiries,' said Castle. 'What's this about?'

'Just a hunch. I've had a tip-off about a potential leak at the MoD.'

Castle promised to look into it. When he called back something in his voice had changed. 'The Shoeburyness train. About thirty people from the MoD are listed as travelling, including Georgina Harlow and her boss. Guess who else.'

'Someone from the Cabinet?'

'Only the PM himself. Also Beaverbrook, Morrison, Archie Sinclair. This one's a big number, old boy. Anything you need to tell me?'

'Not yet. It may be nothing at all, but I have to check. Marita could be involved.'

'Ah. I begin to understand. Well, if you need assistance ...'

'I'll let you know,' said Hoste, and rang off.

He stayed about twenty paces behind Georgina Harlow from the moment she left work. She had dressed with a shy twist of glamour this evening, he noticed; a dove-grey summer jacket and skirt, a leather handbag that looked new, and a bright lipstick: she looked attractive, though natural reserve clung to her like a perfume. She entered the bar of St Ermin's Hotel in Westminster, where Billy Adair was waiting. He monitored their initial awkwardness together, which began to dissolve with the drinks (gin and pep for her, stout for him) and faded once they'd sat down to dinner. He didn't get too close lest Adair happened to remember his face, though he sensed he would not. The Ulsterman did most of the talking at first, and little by little drew out his more diffident companion. By the end of the evening they were getting along like old pals. He shadowed them onto a tram heading north. They alighted at Maida Vale and walked another five minutes to her flat, where after some negotiation on the step she invited him inside. The evening had been a success.

By eight o'clock the next morning he was at Fenchurch Street Station just in time to see a black Daimler pulling away, having deposited its ministerial load. The concourse was thronged with police. The 'special' was in fact a regular commuter train intended for Southend but requisitioned for the occasion by the MoD. A guard was directing bemused passengers away from it. Hoste skulked around the station, keeping an eye out for faces he might know. At Smith's he bought *The Times* and started on the crossword. He got stuck on five down, six letters, a word meaning both to *split from* and *become attached to*. How could one word contain virtual opposites? A sudden explosive clatter made him look up: a pigeon was frantically seeking an exit from under the vaulted glass roof. Another knot of VIPs were being escorted across the concourse. Among them he spotted the Home Secretary.

He covered a yawn with the back of his hand. He had got back to his flat at about two thirty and snatched a few hours' sleep before starting out again this morning. On board the train he flashed a card to the police inspector's enquiring look. They had already swept the carriages, he gathered, but he decided to give them a once-over himself. The front one was the dining car laid out for breakfast, the middle two unoccupied, he presumed for the security detail. The back three carriages were reserved for the PM, his ministers and minions. He was about to have another scout along the platform when the guard's whistle blew and the train began to move. Soon they were out of the gaunt, damaged precincts of the City and into the east, flashing past factories and warehouses and the ruins of the docks, the Thames an iron-grey sash in the distance.

He wandered along the corridor, glancing into the compartments. Blank faces turned to him, then looked away. He hadn't yet spotted Georgina Harlow among the swarm of secretaries and assistants. A military policeman stood armed at the head of the last carriage: the PM and his entourage weren't taking any chances.

'Sir, do you have a ticket for this train?' He turned round to see Tessa Hammond grinning up at him.

'I must have left it in my compartment,' he said, patting down his pockets. 'What are you doing here?'

'Castle tipped me off. Thought you might like some company.'

'Ha. I was just on my way to the dining car. Care to join?'

'I have news,' Tessa said as they fell into step. 'Georgina Harlow isn't on the train. She called in sick this morning.'

Hoste stopped abruptly. 'That's odd. She was fine when I last saw her –' he glanced at his watch – 'about ten hours ago.'

'We've checked on her. She is fine, but it looks like she may have been slipped a Mickey.'

He nodded. 'Which means our man is — tell me, are you carrying?'

For answer she tapped her handbag. 'Hope I won't have to use it.'

They had reached the restaurant carriage. A waiter was fussing over a table setting; on enquiry he told them breakfast would be served in ten minutes. They settled at a table opposite one another. Hoste sat close to the window, wary of showing his face.

'Someone once told me I have a very unmemorable face,' he mused.

'I don't think that's true,' said Tessa with a frown.

'It would be greatly to my advantage at this moment if it was.'

They observed one another across the table, companionably lulled by the rocking motion of the train. The Essex countryside slid by their window. Tessa eventually broke the silence. 'Amy Strallen's call was a stroke of luck.'

'Yes. I could tell she was surprised to hear my voice. Given the circumstances she might just have hung up.'

'She's behaved like a professional,' said Tessa. 'I'm not sure many others would have done.'

Hoste heard something pursed in her voice. 'I didn't lay a finger on her, you know.'

'I'm sure you didn't. But one can understand why she felt ... ill-used.'

He looked away, lost in thought. 'By the way,' he said, 'do you know a word that means both to split and to cling to?'

'What?'

'Today's crossword. Six letters, third letter "e".'

She looked at him, wagging her head in disbelief. 'Amazing the way you can utterly dissociate yourself from a subject when it suits you.'

Hoste looked at her in surprise. 'Is that what you think I was doing?'

'My God, you don't even notice!' She paused, then said, '"Cleave" is the word you're looking for. C-L-E-A-V-E.'

The dining car had begun to fill, and two stewards were taking the orders for breakfast. They overheard one of them talking to an assistant dispatched from the VIP end of the train: the PM had asked for breakfast to be brought to his compartment. 'Right away,' came the reply. Some minutes later a breakfast trolley shrouded in a white cloth was being pushed up the aisle by a third steward. Hoste happened to look up and note the man's face. He felt a twitch on the thread. Was there something familiar there? The carousel of mugshots that made circuits in his head was pulled up and inspected. Nothing came to him – nothing except that first twitch of unease. He exchanged a look with Tessa, who was rising from the table almost before he said, 'Let's go.'

He kept his voice low as they followed the steward at half a carriage's length.

'Slow march,' he warned Tessa. He couldn't tell her why they were tailing the man, because he didn't yet know himself. Instinct was driving him along. If he could just get another look at him ... The steward was within sight of the military policeman when he stopped in the corridor and adjusted something on the trolley. His face came into profile, and Hoste knew it at last. PC Grigg, the bogus copper Marita had set on him at their first meeting. He had to move quickly. Looking at Tessa he raised his finger to his lips. As Grigg came to a halt Hoste was soundlessly behind him, and brought down the butt of his pistol on his head. The steward fell in a heap.

The policeman, stunned for a moment, cocked his rifle and yelled at Hoste to drop his weapon and get on his knees. He pushed him to the floor. Not until Tessa was showing him her ID did the mood calm, and Hoste was allowed to pick himself up. Then it suddenly became frantic again when the cloth was lifted from the trolley to reveal a suspect device.

An hour later, after an unscheduled stop on the line and the safe disposal of a home-made bomb, the train continued on its way to Shoeburyness. On arrival the ministers and their entourage debouched on the platform, and through the window Hoste glimpsed a squat, bullish figure clapping a homburg on his head and gazing about at his surroundings.

'Not even a word of thanks,' said Tessa, also watching. 'He obviously doesn't realise how close he came.'

Hoste, finishing the breakfast postponed from earlier, smiled at her peeved tone. 'Oh, I should think he does. But he takes it in his stride.'

'Are you going to join them for the tank inspection?'

He made a face. 'I think I've had enough excitement for one morning. But perhaps we could go for a stroll in the meantime?'

Tessa agreed to wait for him while he went to fetch his hat from the compartment. Making his way back through the empty carriages he couldn't help thinking again about Amy Strallen. Without her tip-off (Hammond was right) today's drama might have gone quite another way. She had a quick noticing eye, sound judgement, a sense of duty, the courage to take risks – in another lifetime she would have made a damned good agent. Too bad he had ruined any chance of being her friend. He thought about the night he had saved her life, the bomb that had come so near. And he thought also of the kiss, later, the natural way she had just leaned in and done it. That was something he should try to remember. Amy Strallen. Even the sound of her name pierced him.

He had just slid open the door of the compartment when he sensed a shadow fall behind him. His first instinct was that a train guard had been following at his heels, checking the carriages, but that proved false the moment a cord slipped over his head and tightened around his neck. Whoever held the cord now shoved him into the compartment, with such violence that his face met the window with a smack. Dazed, choking, he began to tear with his fingers at the throttling noose, but could gain no purchase. Using his upper body he shoved the constricting weight back against the carriage seat, toppling them both at once. But the hands holding the noose stayed tight as a steel trap. His assailant began forcing him to the floor. A voice growled in his ear: 'You're gonna die, ya two-faced *fuck*.' Adair. Of course. Hiding all this time, waiting for his moment. Hoste felt the life being choked out of him, his constricted throat screaming for air. He knew he must fight, must use his elbow or his heel, but the drastic loss of oxygen was making him faint. He wasn't sure if the hissing noise he heard was in his own throat or in Adair's straining breath.

A metallic click sounded from above, and suddenly, miraculously, the savage pressure on his windpipe lifted: air, blessed air! Somewhere he could hear Tessa's voice – clipped, decisive – ordering Adair to raise his hands. Hoste was bent double, still coughing as he got to his feet. Tessa had her gun trained on the Irishman, whose shoulders were heaving. His gaze had murder in it.

'Was the bomb your idea, or Marita's?'

Adair ignored her. He was staring at Hoste. 'You're safe today. But someone's gonna take you *doyne*.'

Hoste shrugged. If – when – Marita got to know of this she would waste no time in organising his elimination. She would probably do the job herself. His eyes met Tessa's: she knew it, too.

'From now on, you'll be lookin' over your shoulder, wonderin' when we're gonna come for yer.'

Hoste found his voice at last. 'I'll take my chances. You've been a marked man for long enough.'

Adair half snorted, shook his head. 'Marked is nothin'. She'll make sure of it. You're a dead man — a fuckin' *dead man.*'

Tessa, widening her stance, told him to take his gun out. Adair stared her out for a moment, then slowly reached into his jacket. He brought out the gun with a goading sort of insolence, and dangled it by his trigger finger.

'You're gonna take it off me?'

Tessa waited a beat, then said, in a coolly formal tone, 'The suspect drew his gun, intending to shoot.'

Adair squinted from beneath his brow, bemused. Puzzlement turned abruptly to comprehension. As he brought his gun arm down Tessa fired. The shot perforated his eye. A small black rosette sprouted over the smoking hole, and after a tiny, eerie delay he toppled back against the angle of seat and window. Blood was leaking down his dead face.

'Forced to defend myself I fired first,' she continued quietly, 'killing him.'

Hoste, his ears still ringing from the shot, returned her gaze. She had won him a reprieve.

May 1935

13

A few tattered blue-black clouds were frowning over the horizon as the train wheezed into the station. The sky had a morose, bloated look, and the rain that had threatened all day started to spit. They heard the guard call out 'Clitheroe'. Amy hauled down their suitcases from the overhead netting while Marita inspected her face in a compact. Outside, on the platform, they looked around for a porter, and found no one. A fusillade of bangs – the carriage doors closing – dinned in their ears. By the time they had emerged from the station the rain had got going in earnest.

The hotel was a few minutes' walk. 'Come on,' said Amy, 'let's make a dash for it.'

Marita made a little exclamation of disgust, as though the very idea of dashing was beneath her. She followed Amy's flailing run at a more dignified, stately trot. The burly landlord of the Swan and Royal gave them a pleasant welcome, though Amy noticed that Marita held herself somewhat aloof from his garrulous bonhomie. She could not always be relied upon to fraternise with strangers, so Amy found herself obliged to perform solo on the social niceties.

'So you've come up all the way from London?' the landlord went on, leading them up the narrow staircase.

'Indeed we have.'

'Changed at Blackburn,' he said. 'Taken you five hours or so, I dessay?'

'Yes, about that.'

'Must be famished!'

'We are quite peckish,' smiled Amy.

'Right then, get settled in while they get your tea ready,' he said, showing them into a room with two neat single beds. But he seemed for the moment unwilling to leave. He enquired as to the purpose of their visit, and on learning that they were here for a walking holiday he voiced his approval, and recommended a few places they should visit. 'Aye, you've come the right time o' year for it!' he cried.

Behind him Marita raised her eyes heavenwards. Amy, keeping the mood civil, thanked the landlord and said that they'd be down presently. When he had gone Marita puffed out her cheeks and leaned back on the bed.

'My God, I thought he'd never *go*.'

'He's just being friendly.'

'Really,' said Marita, deadpan.

Amy could not ignore the sceptical tone. 'It's the north. You'll get used to it. It reminds me of my grandma – she was from round here. They do love to chat.'

In fact she had not been back to Lancashire in years, not since she was a girl. She had had a vague idea of visiting her grandmother's village, for old times' sake, but worried now that it might test her holiday companion's patience. She began to unpack, while Marita continued to lounge on the bed, smoking and reading. She was absorbed in a detective novel she'd bought at a stall in Euston. Amy felt secretly glad that her friend liked to read; it provided a respite from her conversation. Marita had so many opinions that it could be faintly exhausting to keep up.

In truth, they didn't know one another very well. They had met less than a year ago, at a secretarial college in Oxford. Amy had noticed the tall, well-dressed, pointy-faced brunette straight away, but like the others had kept her distance; she had about her an air that was not approachable. By degrees, however, Miss Florian – Marita – would sidle up to talk or share a cigarette.

When the college went on a day trip she made sure that Amy was sitting next to her on the coach. A wary companionship bloomed between them. Amy for her part couldn't help feeling flattered that this stand-offish and somewhat mysterious woman – her senior by three years – had decided to befriend her. As she got to know her better she realised that Marita held their fellow students in as much contempt as she had suspected. 'They're all feeble-minded schoolgirls just waiting to get fixed up with a man,' she said. One of them, a bright, popular girl named Gabrielle Miller, she particularly despised and never tired of descanting on her faults. Once, when Amy innocently remarked on how friendly Gabrielle had been that day, Marita had turned on her with such a withering look that she knew never to mention it again. She couldn't really fathom the root of her dislike, other than the possibility that Gabrielle was the only student who could match her in self-assurance.

By the time Marita put aside her book to get ready for dinner Amy felt weak with hunger. The dining room of the Swan and Royal was not a cheerful one. The mustard-coloured wallpaper and the dusty brown curtains would have looked mournful on a summer's day, but on a night of rainstorms they looked oppressively grim. The ghosts of diners past – single commercial salesmen, exhausted travellers, weekending couples and their fractious children – haunted the room. The service was slow, but the food, when it came, was perfectly decent. She had potted shrimps, then lamb cutlets with peas and potatoes. Marita watched her as she ate, and smiled.

'You eat like someone who hasn't seen food for days.'

Amy dabbed her mouth with her napkin. 'Sorry. "Famished,"' she added in broad imitation of mine host. Marita gave a half-laugh: the one thing guaranteed to amuse her was mimickry, and Amy made a good impersonator.

Marita's appetite was less hearty, and when the waiter hesitated over clearing her half-finished plate she said peremptorily,

'You can take it.' She leaned back, lit a cigarette and fixed her gaze on Amy. 'So ... are you relieved to get away from the birdbrains?' It was her nickname for their secretarial colleagues.

'Rather. Though I don't have such a disdain for them. The girls are perfectly nice –'

'– and perfectly dreary.'

Amy sniggered. 'If it's so awful why do you stay?'

'I require a few basic skills, enough to give me a proper grounding.'

'For what?'

'World domination,' she said crisply, and they both laughed. 'I'd like to stand for Parliament, maybe. Shake things up.'

Amy pouted consideringly. 'You mean in the general election? Which party?'

'I don't know. One that isn't Tory or Labour.'

'Who did you vote for the last time?'

'I forget. How about you?'

'I couldn't. I wasn't yet twenty-one.'

Marita shook her head slowly. 'Even if I were elected I wonder if there's anything to be done with this country. Look at those horrors we passed through on the train – the mines, the disused canals, that hideous black river with the scum on top. So many unemployed, the economy failing, the place is at a standstill. I sometimes think I'd be better off out of it.'

'Where would you go?'

She gave a shrug. 'Germany, perhaps. I admire the way Hitler has got the country back on its feet. He's performed an economic miracle *and* restored national pride. That's the kind of leadership we need here.'

'I don't think we'd take to all that marching,' said Amy doubtfully.

'Oh, that's not relevant,' came the impatient reply. 'All I mean is that we need someone to take the country by the scruff of the neck and shake some life into it. Otherwise we'll simply go sleepwalking into disaster.'

Amy hadn't heard this line of talk from her before. She almost wished they hadn't started. 'Who did you have in mind?'

'Of the present lot only Mosley seems to have the will to change things. If I thought it might help him I would join the party.'

At that moment the waiter came back with the spotted dick and custard Amy had ordered. Marita wrinkled her nose in distaste and lit another cigarette. Mosley and his politics were dropped from the conversation. The landlord put in an appearance, which prompted Marita to retire to the bedroom and gave Amy another twenty-minute test of northern hospitality.

Later, when they were getting ready for bed, they talked about their plans for the next day. If it was fine they would go for a hike; Amy had already picked out a route on her map. She was brushing her hair in the little oval mirror on the dressing table when she noticed Marita sitting up in bed, watching her. Her gaze held a peculiar dark intensity; it was like being observed by a lynx. Her detective mystery was splayed face down on the counterpane.

'How's the book?' she asked, seeking escape from her scrutiny.

Marita glanced at it indifferently. 'Lacking in excitement,' she said flatly, then added, 'Rather like my life at present. Take no notice of what I said about Parliament at dinner. It's just idle talk that comes out when I'm frustrated.'

Amy, taken aback, said, 'Why are you frustrated?'

'Oh, because … I see jobs going that I know would suit me, but they only want men. I applied for one recently, as campaign agent for an MP, and was turned down flat – simply because I'm a woman. Some don't even bother to reply! It's a backward country, this. Another reason I should get out.'

She stopped, and half snorted a laugh, as though to rebuke herself. Then without another word she turned back to her unsatisfying book. Amy finished brushing her hair and climbed into her bed on the other side of the room. The sheets were cold on her skin, and she shivered. She switched off her bedside light and lay there, thinking. Their time together was proving more revelatory than she'd imagined. She had had no idea of Marita's failed job applications, or of her disaffection with the status quo. Her candour had been disarming. Amy stole a look across the room at her friend, haloed in the bedside lamp, silently absorbed in her book.

An unstable mixture of pity and admiration stirred in her, and before she could stop herself she said, 'If you did stand for Parliament, I'd vote for you.'

She saw the back of Marita's head move slightly. But she didn't reply, and Amy, drifting off, wasn't sure if she had heard her after all.

In the morning the rain continued, thinning to a drizzle, but persistent. When Amy returned from the bathroom down the corridor Marita was still in bed, so she dressed and went down to breakfast alone. Over kippers and toast she read the *Daily Express*, poring over the reports on the trial of Mrs Rattenbury. This lady, aged thirty-eight, the wife of a Bournemouth architect in his late sixties, had been having an affair with her teenage chauffeur, a lad named Stoner. The husband had been killed by savage blows to the head with a mallet; both his wife and the chauffeur had at different times claimed responsibility. Both were on trial for the murder. The story of course had created a sensation, and Amy was as gripped as anyone by its startling elements of squalor and ruthlessness. One queer detail in the evidence had impressed itself on her. Counsel had asked Mrs Rattenbury what her first thought had been when her lover had got into bed that night and told her what he had done. She had replied, 'My first thought was to protect him.' A reckless thing to say – and yet a noble one, too.

Amy was still thinking about it as she went back up to their room, where Marita had just finished dressing, quite unbothered about missing breakfast. She made an ironic enquiry as to whether the landlord had been on entertaining form, and Amy laughed.

'He didn't have so much time to gas this morning – every table was taken.'

'Good. Pity about this rain. I propose that we take a walk around the town and see if we can't amuse ourselves.'

The town, prosperous and handsome, was built on sloping streets with any number of interesting little alleyways vectoring off. Amy was surprised to remember quite a lot of it. Marita looked around, in a faintly regal way, at the orderly shopfronts, the solid merchants' houses and the bustle of local life. It felt like a place that hadn't much changed since the Great War, and perhaps earlier. On reaching a quiet backwater Amy gasped, overcome by a sudden recall of the vista. 'I know this street! There's a mill here where my grandmother used to work.' She felt herself drawn down the pavement as if by a magnet, and with every step her memory of it grew stronger. She would know it as soon as she saw it. Marita followed, half smiling at her friend's excitement.

And there it was, set off the street, a large stone building with wide double doors, Low Moor Mill. It had about it a becalmed air, and Amy took another moment to realise that the clouded windows told the story. Her shoulders slumped in dismay.

'Oh ... they've closed it,' she said in a small voice. 'This was one of the oldest cotton mills in Lancashire.'

Marita looked up at the building's plain, weathered face. 'When was your grandmother here?'

'Before the war, years before. She was retired when we were last here – I remember someone telling me this was where Grandma used to work.'

'You can tell her that you visited.'

Amy looked at her. 'I'm afraid not. She died a few years ago.'

She continued to stare at it. There would have been hundreds of jobs lost. To think of all those people like her grandmother, the years they had spent here weaving and spinning and printing – all that labour scattered to the winds. She walked up to one of the blinded windows and peered in, but there was nothing to see. On her shoulder she felt Marita's consoling hand.

'The way of the world. Yet another industry that's gone kaput.'

They walked back up the street, the paving stones dark from the rain and oily underfoot. At the top of the main street the castle loomed, and they followed a winding path to the keep. A spiral staircase took them to the top, which offered an aerial prospect of the town and its pitched slate roofs. The sky, off-white, was smudged here and there by a pewter-coloured cloud. Moments later they heard behind them a din of voices coming up the stairs. They were young voices, reedy and trilling, laughing, and soon the calm was shattered by a wild stampede of schoolchildren. They roamed about, capering, as unselfconscious as monkeys. For about three minutes Amy and Marita stood there, silent and immobile, as the children scuffled about them, and then the teacher's voice sounded across the air, and – just as abruptly – they were gone. The racket faded to an echo.

Amy said, after a moment, 'Have you been following the Rattenbury case?'

'Of course,' Marita replied. 'What made you think of that?'

'Oh, those kids, and something I read in the paper today. They say Alma Rattenbury shared a bed with Stoner in the same room where her child slept.'

Marita gave a wintry laugh. 'The jury won't like that. It's bad enough that she's twenty years older than the lover. She appears determined to sign her own death warrant.'

Amy nodded. 'And yet this woman – I don't know – there's something about her I find horribly moving. You know she was once a songwriter, before all this? The press have treated her very badly, they more or less call her a –'

'Nymphomaniac? Well, she's been a fool, but I agree, they've ganged up on her. I don't care much for her chances.'

Amy sighed, and felt a low mood gather. 'How can there be so much hatred? She's just a woman who made a mistake.'

'But she's party to a murder, even if she didn't swing the mallet herself. As for the hatred, you're too nice to understand. Hatred comes easily to most people.'

'Does it? To you?'

'My dear girl, you of all people should know ...'

'You mean Gabrielle Miller? I don't understand that. I mean, she can be a bit overbearing at times –'

'A bit?! She's pushy and scheming and out for whatever she can get. Like all her kind.'

An uncertain pause ensued. 'What d'you mean, her kind?'

Marita looked at her almost pityingly. 'My God, you're so naive! She's a Jew, can't you tell?'

Amy fell silent. She had believed Marita's antipathy towards the woman was sparked by a clash of temperaments: both were forceful personalities, and always likely to provoke one another. But it seemed this was not a resentment based merely on personality; it ran deeper, darker. She really must be naive, because it hadn't occurred to her that Gabrielle Miller *was* a Jew; the name was hardly an indication, and Amy had not been in their company often enough to know. Her school had been Church of England, and growing up in Epsom she knew of Jews more by rumour than by sight. They were the butt of jokes about money and sharp practice, and little else.

'Would you hate her if she wasn't a Jew?' Amy said eventually.

'Yes. Only without the certainty that she couldn't help being so repulsive.'

Amy turned away. She cast her gaze once more across the sea of slate roofs, slick with rain. Some line of confessional intimacy had been crossed which, for the moment, was best dealt with by her not saying another word. She hardly knew Marita at all, she realised, and she was too afraid of her to risk further debate on the matter.

The next morning they had packed and paid at the Swan and Royal and were on the bus out of town. The landlord had seemed sorry to see them go, and expressed a hope they would come to stay in Clitheroe again. 'We may,' called Marita, muttering under her breath as they left, 'but not with you.' The sky had cleared at last, and the short journey took them down winding country lanes of dripping trees and greenery brilliant from the rain. Fields hemmed with hedgerows climbed away on either side of them. Amy read the paper while Marita stared indifferently at the passing scene. On reaching Whitewell, which comprised no more than an old coaching inn and a small church, the driver helped them down with their suitcases before puttering off again.

Their room here was homelier than at the Swan, with horse brasses and hunting prints on the wall. It looked out onto a wide sloping meadow, grazed upon by sheep and skirted by a beck. Over the following three days the weather was capricious, alternating rapidly between gloom and glare. A morning that began in sunshine would of a sudden darken, and rain clouds rolled in; the sky could not settle upon a mood from one hour to the next. Marita seemed not to mind being cooped up at the hotel; she lay on the sofa or slouched in an armchair, reading. (She had packed another detective novel.) Amy, restless indoors, eventually defied the lowering sky and set off on a walk, only to be caught half an hour later in a crashing downpour; she took cover under a gigantic oak, raindrops trickling down her neck, before trudging damply back to the inn. She was shivering by the time she got to the room.

Marita, lounging in the armchair, shrieked out a laugh on seeing her. 'You look like you've been dragged from the river! Sit here and I'll put this fire on.'

She went off to the bathroom to fetch a towel while Amy peeled off her stout boots and socks. Despite the frustrations of the weather the mood between them had been buoyant. They had not mentioned Gabrielle Miller again; Amy was wary of provoking her companion, and kept the conversation as light as she dared: she didn't want to be thought a 'birdbrain' like the rest. Outside the afternoon light was shrinking, and the rain still thrashed the windowpanes. She sighed and dozed for a while, lulled by the gas fire. She woke with a start and decided to go in search of a newspaper. Down in the bar a few locals were on the first drink of the evening. On her way out she met the hotel porter, who found her a copy of the *Evening Telegraph*. Her heart jumped on seeing the headline, RATTENBURY VERDICT: WIFE ACQUITTED. She found a table in the lounge and fell on the story.

'So the chauffeur will hang?' Marita mused, when Amy had returned to the room, bursting with the news.

Amy grimaced. 'He's been convicted, but the jury has recommended mercy on account of his age.'

'Well, well. That was not the outcome I expected.'

'Nor anyone else, I imagine. The woman was drunk and hysterical when she told the police she'd killed him. She really was trying to protect the boy.'

'You sound positively elated, my dear. D'you suppose justice has been served?'

'Maybe. I couldn't bear to think of Mrs Rattenbury suffering more than she has already. It's felt like a witch-hunt.'

'Ah, yes. I gather witches are something they know all about round here.'

They returned to the subject of Mrs Rattenbury over dinner that evening. Amy felt more relieved about the acquittal than she could quite fathom. 'In her early years in Canada she was a talented musician – she wrote songs.'

'You told me that,' said Marita.

'And she was brave. During the war she joined the Red Cross and served as a nurse in France. She was wounded twice and won the Croix de Guerre.'

'You seem very preoccupied by this woman, Amy.'

'I know. I can't help it. She ought never to have got involved with that brute Rattenbury – I wish she'd had someone to advise her.'

'Mm. To have married three times before the age of thirty suggests an odd partiality.'

'But her first husband died in the trenches –'

'You told me that, too.'

Amy made a face. 'Sorry. It's dreadful, isn't it, to be so bound up in the fate of one woman when you consider twenty thousand and more have just been killed in that Quetta earthquake? It's callous, but – but it's how I feel.'

'It's not callous,' replied Marita. 'Merely honest. Those twenty thousand are a statistic. Natural disasters, however terrible, haven't the power to move us like an individual tragedy. Quetta will be forgotten soon enough. But I don't think the Rattenbury case will.'

Amy nodded, impressed. If some other friend of hers had dismissed the loss of twenty thousand people as 'a statistic' she might have felt disgust, or shame on their behalf, but Marita's tone of cool authority was somehow compelling. No wonder she wanted to go into politics – she would crush the lot of them.

'I was talking to a man at the bar –'

'I noticed. What did he want?'

'Oh, nothing. He just told me that it's set fair for tomorrow.'

'At last! I know how you love this part of the world, but you must agree that its weather *stinks*.'

The next morning Amy slipped out of bed and took fearful steps towards the window. Peeking through the curtains of their room she rejoiced at the sight of a low, sombre sun shouldering over the hills: not exactly basking weather, but it would give them a chance to walk. She returned to her bed, and after dozing for a while she took up the postcard she'd bought in a little grocer's back in Clitheroe. The photograph on its reverse showed the town high street in a strange sepia light.

'Writing to your sweetheart?' Marita's voice from across the room made her jump.

She gave a half-laugh. 'It's actually to my parents.' She dashed off a few sentences while Marita went off to the bathroom. She hesitated over mentioning her discovery of the shutdown mill, and decided it was too sad to tell. A postcard should be jolly.

After breakfast they took up the landlord's offer of a couple of bicycles, which conveyed them through sleepy villages and winding lanes to Bolton-by-Bowland. It was another of the places Amy remembered from childhood, and it cheered her to see the pub and the village school unaltered. They parked the bicycles round the back of the local church, reasoning that they were less likely to be stolen from holy ground. Then they continued up the hill and turned onto a long avenue of mature trees. Marita was suavely attired in a light tweed jacket and knickerbockers (Amy loved the way she dressed) and had a long stride that set a more challenging pace than her companion had anticipated. Amy's own clothes – a woollen cardigan and skirt under a mackintosh – were making her sweat. They crossed a low stone bridge and joined a road lined with yew trees. As the road dropped away it revealed the outline of Pendle Hill on the horizon.

'Ah, where the witches lived,' said Marita when Amy pointed it out.

As the distance between them expanded and contracted, their talk became desultory. In the woodlands they tracked through Amy liked to pause and admire the flowers – bluebells, wood anemones, dog violets – the names learned from her mother. Marita was impressed.

'What about these, the pink ones?'

'Those are red campions,' said Amy. 'Also known as the cuckoo flower, because they announce spring.'

Marita, hands on hips, smiled wonderingly. 'A cuckoo flower! That's very quaint. I had no idea you were a botanical whizz.'

'Oh . . .' Amy waggled her hand dismissively, and they walked on. The truth was, flowers were perhaps the single area of knowledge in which she had an advantage over her friend. Compared with what Marita knew about books and clothes and politics and history – about everything, in short – Amy was quite clearly the dunce. It was embarrassing, for Marita herself could hardly be unaware of the gulf between them; and yet she made no great thing of it. Maybe she enjoyed being so much brighter than her friends . . .

And so much fitter, too, she thought, watching the figure ahead of her advance at a very smart bat. She had taken charge of the map, stopping to consult it now and then like a soldier on manoeuvres. Even granted these pauses Amy struggled to keep up. One wide sloping field gave way to another, the tussocky grass still damp from the rain. In the next field stood a herd of cows, mooching, their gazes blank and steady. After a while the sound of the river floated across the air. She couldn't see it yet, but the water seemed to be chattering with itself. The sun had tweaked its dial a little higher. They had passed through another kissing gate when she hurried to catch up with Marita.

'Shall we have a rest?' she asked, somewhat breathlessly. She sank down on a dip in the grass.

Marita gave a shrug, and sat down just behind her, propped on her elbows. She wasn't tired in the least; walking holidays in the Bavarian Alps, she explained, were much more demanding on the legs and lungs. 'It's my favourite place in all Germany. I hope to go back this year.'

'Your father has family over there, I suppose?'

She nodded. 'Some distant cousins I hardly know. Things might have been very different. My father had gone to work in London for a year. He was about to return to Berlin – literally, he had two or three weeks left to go – when a young secretary started at the firm. They took to one another immediately, which was fortunate. That secretary was my mother.'

'How romantic! Did he consider taking her back to Germany?'

'He may have done, but my mother wouldn't have gone. She had close family, up in Maidenhead. And a very strong will.'

That I can believe, thought Amy, who closed her eyes as the sun broke from behind a cloud and warmed her face. Lying there, she felt a rush of pure contentment. The weather had been atrocious, but this one day had rescued the whole trip. Shielding her eyes she looked across to Marita, whose expression had become pensive.

'What business was your father in?' Amy asked presently.

Marita seemed to wake from her reverie. 'Munitions. He ran a factory. It did very well, of course, when the war came. He might have become very rich.'

'Why didn't he?'

A pause followed. He was a victim of sharp practice, she explained. Two years after the war a new programme of extracting nitrogen pioneered by German explosives experts came to light. Under the terms of the Armistice the Allies took it over, and a contract was tendered – it should have gone to a number of competing businesses, but instead a large fertiliser company named Crewe-Devlin got the entire thing. Nobody knew how, until it was revealed that Sir Alfred Lawton, a government minister, had arranged the contract privately. He also happened to be a director at Crewe-Devlin. 'So they got the monopoly on this new nitrogen technique, kept the price of fertiliser high and eventually drove my father out of business. He had to start again, at the bottom.'

'That must have been hard,' said Amy quietly.

Marita nodded. 'It was. There will always be war profiteers, though few have been as successful as Lawton. And do you know how he got away with it?'

Amy shook her head, and waited.

'Because, my dear, Sir Alfred is a Jew, and enjoyed the protection of his powerful Jewish friends. It's the old story. So remember it, next time you think I'm being too harsh on the Chosen Race.'

Two more hours of walking took them back in a circle to the village. They wandered about the lichen-shawled headstones in the church graveyard, before reclaiming their bicycles round the corner. Amy's legs ached as they pedalled back to the inn; again she lagged far behind Marita, who breezed along the lanes without appearing to break a sweat.

As they were readying themselves for dinner Amy returned to the subject of holidays.

'So you'll definitely be going to Germany?'

'Yes. Late August, if I've saved enough by then.' There was a pause. 'You should come with me.'

Amy smiled; in truth, she felt flattered by the suggestion.

'Maybe I should.'

It being their last night, they had drinks in the bar after dinner. The man who had tipped off Amy about the weather the previous evening stopped by their table. Had they enjoyed their walk? Amy assured him they had, and after a further exchange of pleasantries he wished them a good night and withdrew.

After a moment Marita said archly, 'I believe that fellow is very sorry to see you go.'

'What? I don't think so.'

'My dear! He clearly wanted nothing more than to sit here and flirt with you all evening. Why deny it?'

'Because it's not true,' said Amy, incredulous.

'Then why are you blushing?'

'If I am, then it's because I'm embarrassed that you should misread a perfectly ordinary moment of friendliness.'

Marita pulled a face and fell silent, as if she were backing away from an argument. Amy stared at her, wondering how this wild misapprehension had suddenly come between them. Absurd to think the man had been flirting with her! For one thing, he was a good twenty years her senior. For another, he had addressed his few remarks to both of them, not just Amy. She took a deep swallow of her gin and lemon.

'Let's not fall out,' she began gently. 'You know, it's nothing to me whether he was flirting or not. I wasn't the slightest bit interested.'

Marita nodded, warily appeased. 'I have a suspicious nature – I'm sorry. Though I'm surprised you seem not to notice men "giving you the eye". You are, if I may say, rather innocent.'

Amy gave a shrug. 'Perhaps I'm just slow on the uptake. To be honest, a man would have to make a dead set at me before I got the message.'

'But why? Why be the shrinking violet?'

'I don't mean to. But I'm not confident, really. Not like you.'

'You must have felt twitches on the fishing line ...'

'A few. There was one chap I was keen on, but he – well, I think he lost interest.'

Marita stared at her appraisingly. 'Then he was a fool.'

Later, back in their room, Amy felt licensed to turn the enquiry around. 'That man you introduced me to a few weeks ago. Is it serious?'

'Oh, Bernard. We get on pretty well. He's witty, and clever, and ambitious. Knows his own mind, too – he says he adores me.'

Amy laughed at her nonchalant tone. 'Do you reciprocate the feeling?'

Marita pulled an ambiguous expression. 'Too early to say. Bernard wants to hurry it along, but he'll have to wait. I'm not yet ready to cash in my chips. There's no telling who may be round the next corner.'

'There may not be anyone,' said Amy uncertainly.

Marita smiled distantly. 'That's a gamble I must take.'

Amy went off to the bathroom to prepare for bed. As she undressed she felt a wave of fatigue crash over her, the cumulative effect of the day's walking, the fresh air and, possibly, the strain of long hours in Marita's company. All things considered their first holiday together had been a success. But the awkward little tiff in the bar just now reminded her of the need for caution; with a nature as prickly as Marita's there was no telling the ways in which one might give offence. If she could fly off the handle over a stranger's small talk how would she cope with actual misbehaviour?

On returning to the room she found her absorbed in her book. With a yawn Amy brushed her hair, put some cold cream on her face and got into bed. She called goodnight across the room, but Marita seemed not to hear her. Amy shifted herself to face the bedroom wall, hearing only the soft flip of another page being turned. When it stopped she waited for the sound of Marita getting ready for bed. Instead, her footsteps padded over, and she perched herself on the edge of the bed, like a mother about to read her child a story. Amy looked round, startled.

'Is something the matter?' she asked.

Marita shook her head. It was too dark to make out the expression on her face. Without warning she placed her hand very tenderly on Amy's head. 'Such lovely hair you have.' She began to stroke it. Amy, disconcerted, lay very still. Then: 'You should let someone take care of you.'

There was an appeal in her tone as she continued to caress her hair. At a loss for something to say, Amy simply waited. She felt – she knew – that a response was required of her; and that what she was minded to say would not please Marita. The silence lengthened. When there came a pause in the stroking, Amy said, as softly as she could, 'Goodnight, then.'

Marita stayed there, for some moments, watching her. Slowly, without a word, she rose and returned to her own bed. Amy lay in the dark, not daring to move. She had been about to drop off – but no longer.

In the morning they dressed, and breakfasted, and returned to their room to pack. What had passed between them last night was not mentioned; it was as though it had never happened. Marita seemed quite normal, indeed a little cheerier than usual – they had had their fun, and now she wanted to get back to London. It was Amy who sensed a breach in the mood, the hangover of something unacknowledged, like a death one couldn't talk about. She felt her speech to be slightly mechanical, her movements self-conscious. Much as she wished to forget all about it, she couldn't.

Fearing a silence between them she filled the bus journey back to Clitheroe station with a determined flow of chatter. It sounded, to her own ears, inane. Relief came once they had changed for Euston and settled themselves opposite one another in a compartment. Marita had her detective story to finish, and Amy buried herself in the *Manchester Guardian* with unwonted concentration. The landscape, and the hours, rattled by.

On the steam-swathed platform at Euston they hauled their suitcases along. The dreary station bustle soon enveloped them. In years to come Amy would remember the peculiar burnt-tar smell of the place – works were going on – and the dim glare of the lights beneath the arches that confounded day with night. They had reached the entrance to the concourse when they saw it, a newspaper placard, with its inconceivable headline: MRS RATTENBURY STABBED AND DROWNED.

Amy cried out in shock. She could almost feel the blood drain from her face as she stood there, rooted to the spot. Marita, frowning, bought a copy of the *Standard* and shepherded her stricken friend to a bench against the wall. The woman had killed herself. Amy tried to take in the details as Marita read out the report – Alma Rattenbury had stabbed herself five or six times, then fallen into the River Stour at Christchurch. It had been witnessed by a passing labourer, who had hurried down to drag her from the water. When he reached her she was already dead.

But why? thought Amy. *She'd been absolved of the crime, she was free ... Why did she have to kill herself?*

She found that she was shivering, and numb, though it was a June evening. And she felt suddenly the terrible loneliness of the world, bereft of comfort or kindness, except for Marita, hand in hers, muttering *Don't cry, don't cry*. It was the ideal moment for a prayer, really; but in her distress she couldn't even think of the empty phrases that might once have consoled her.

14

The jovial little foursome entered the bank just before closing. They loitered in the central hall, with the air of men used to being waited upon. One or two of the tellers shot them a noticing look. Eaves, whose view from the desk was obscured, first registered the changed atmosphere when the assistant manager almost skidded to a halt behind him. He quickly opened the side door to step out and welcome the men before leading them away to the manager's office. The ripple of interest the newcomers had left in their wake widened across the floor.

Belton, who sat next to Eaves, whistled softly. 'You know who that is, don't you – the stout party in the brown fedora?'

'No idea,' said Eaves.

'That's our sainted chairman. Monteith.'

Eaves, who had only joined the Euston Road branch eight months before, could excuse himself for not recognising the man. His minor position was no more likely to earn him a personal audience with Sir Alexander Monteith than an infantryman with his general. Belton was now talking across the table to one of the clerks, who reckoned that the other 'older feller' in the party was an MP, though he couldn't honestly put a name to him. The bantering speculation continued while they closed up. Was Mr Bowman, their manager, about to be promoted? Or sacked, even! Maybe he was going to take retirement. God knows he'd been there long enough …

Ten minutes later the assistant manager returned to the floor and made a beeline for Eaves. 'The manager would like to see you in his office,' he muttered, and with a glance added, 'Straighten your tie.'

Belton, who had overheard, was now staring at him. 'Oh my aunt! What's this about, Eddie?'

Eaves, fiddling with the knot, shrugged. He looked down at his shoes, which hadn't been polished in a while. Too late now. As he rose from his desk he felt quizzical glances fasten on him from all sides of the room. Pity mingled with relief; somebody was for the high jump, but not them. It reminded Eaves of school, of being called up before the beak.

At the end of the stone-floored corridor he stopped and knocked. The manager's name was inscribed across the door in gold leaf. A muffled voice called, 'Enter.' The men he had seen arrive were seated in a huddle around the fireplace, where Mr Bowman himself stood in proprietorial ease. Cigar smoke, and the scent of alcohol, permeated the room.

'Do join us, Mr – er –' he began, beckoning him over. As he reached the fireplace Bowman clapped him on the shoulder. 'This, gentlemen, is one of our deputies – Edward Eaves.' He had recalled the name just in time.

He introduced his guests: Sir Alexander Monteith; next to him Roland Hoyle, MP; opposite them on the sofa Monteith's private secretary, Lewis. In the corner, watching from the window seat, was a man of about Eaves's age, dressed in an expensive-looking navy pinstripe. This was Philip Traherne, who greeted him with a lazy waggle of his cigarette hand, as if they had known one another for years. Bowman meanwhile had started to recount the story. The branch had for some weeks been subject to fraud. Certain wealthy clients were systematically targeted, and huge sums of money had disappeared from their accounts. No one at the bank could understand how it was happening, until one employee took the initiative and began his own investigation. He made a study of the clients' signatures and realised there was an expert forger at work; what's more, he was plying his dishonest trade around several other banks in the vicinity. By degrees, the employee-turned-detective compiled a dossier of names and accounts that were being plundered and worked out a common link: they all used the services of the same Savile Row tailor. The trail led him eventually to the tailor's accounts manager, whose professional intimacy allowed him access – literally – to his customers' pockets while they were being fitted for a suit. Wallets, documents, signatures: he had in his hands all the material required for his nefarious project.

'And he might have pursued his scheme indefinitely had it not been for that employee – who I'm proud to say is this fellow here.' He beamed at Eaves, who had not yet been invited to sit down. Perhaps they only wanted a look at him.

Hoyle, a plumpish, plain-faced man with watery eyes, rose from his armchair. 'Well, I've a personal reason to thank you,' he said, offering his hand to Eaves. 'Mine, as you know, was one of the accounts looted by the swine!'

Laughter rang around the room. Monteith also stood to shake his hand, and called him a good fellow. At the same time he chaffed Bowman for not hiring a professional snoop to catch the thief, to which Bowman replied, 'I thought it incumbent upon me to save the bank money, sir.' More laughter, and more chaffing, as the men digressed to talk about an upcoming game of golf on which money was riding. Eaves wondered for how long he would have to keep the smile pasted to his face. It was him they had asked to meet, but it was themselves they wanted to talk about. The only one who hadn't yet spoken, Traherne, now took him aside.

'You still haven't told us how you snared the fellow,' he said with a smile that hid a shrewdness.

Eaves explained: he had presented himself at the tailor's as a customer, D. Strawson – a name he had dreamed up for the purpose. He wrote the accountant a cheque as part instalment on the togs he was supposedly purchasing, and he waited. Sure enough, the forger showed up at the bank the following week with a cheque, signed by and made out to D. Strawson: a perfect forgery, but drawing on an account that did not exist. Eaves had got his quarry cold, and after contriving a short delay he telephoned the police from the bank's private vestibule.

'Bravo,' said Traherne, squinting at him. 'Seems you're in the wrong business! But it must have taken a while to put the plan together?'

'A bit of legwork,' he admitted. 'But once I was on the trail I rather enjoyed it – the imposture, I mean.'

Traherne nodded, scrutinising him. 'I'm sure you did. One other thing – your manager here said that you pursued the plan entirely on the q.t. He didn't know about it, nor did any of the staff. Why's that?'

Eaves paused, and gave a quick backward glance to check they weren't overheard. 'I couldn't rule out the possibility that the forger had an inside man. If I'd shared my suspicion I might have been playing into an accomplice's hands. So I kept the thing strictly to myself. It's safer.'

Something twitched in Traherne's expression. Again he nodded, seeming to approve, and might have spoken had not Hoyle intruded his tubby frame between them.

'Capital work, sir,' he said. 'You've saved me and your bank a small fortune.'

Eaves returned a polite smile. 'Just doing my job, sir.'

'Sounds more like you were doing someone else's job,' murmured Traherne, with a sidelong look at Bowman. A look passed between Traherne and Hoyle, who then consulted his pocket watch. 'Better get back to the House. May I drop you somewhere, Philip?'

The meeting was over; the bank's unlikely hero had been saluted; now they were back to work. Feeling little sense of triumph, Eaves returned to his desk. He'd been told to expect a letter of commendation from the board, and that, apparently, would be his lot. But he was not aggrieved. He had undertaken his bit of crime-busting because the prospect had intrigued him, not because he sought any personal advantage. The thrill of running the culprit to earth was reward enough.

He had taken his seat when Belton leaned in, his expression ablaze with curiosity. 'So – what was that about?'

'Damned if I know. Most of the time they were talking about golf.'

'Golf? Why did they need you?'

Eaves spread his palms. 'Dunno. I thought they were perhaps going to ask me to make up a four. But they didn't.'

Belton's frown deepened. 'What the – I never knew you played golf.'

'I don't,' he replied, and laughed, and returned to his work as if there had been no interruption at all.

One Saturday a few weeks later Eaves was just finishing a breakfast egg when his mother brought in the post from the hall. She handed him a letter that carried the unmistakable stamp of officialdom: the name and address had been typed, and the postmark announced it had been sent from London S.W. This, he supposed, would be the board's promised expression of gratitude.

24 May 1935

Dear Mr Eaves,

I had the pleasure of being introduced to you some weeks ago at Euston Road. Your sleuthing impressed us all mightily, of course, and had circumstances allowed I would have liked to talk more. May we do so anyway at a time of your convenience? I have a proposition that may be of interest.

If you'd be kind enough to write, or else telephone me on the number written here, we can arrange a meeting.

Sincerely yours,

Philip Traherne

Eaves called to mind his correspondent. Traherne had been the youngest of the visitors that day, the dapper one; he'd also had the nicest manners. A varsity chap, he imagined, at ease in the world of influence. But he couldn't recall what he actually did at the bank.

'Anything interesting?' asked his mother, drying her hands on a tea towel.

He shook his head. 'Just a letter from a bigwig at the bank.'

'Oh. I hope they're offering you a promotion.'

'Unlikely. And even if they did, I'm not sure I'd want it.'

His mother paused, frowned, seemed about to speak. Instead she continued with her kitchen chores, as if she saw no use in remonstrating with someone so determinedly eccentric.

Eaves had never been inside a members' club before. The Nines, in Mayfair, had been founded by Dickens, Thackeray and others of note, and prided itself on a reputation for raff-ishness. It was generally thought more relaxed than the other gentlemen's establishments that clustered around Pall Mall and St James's. Women were known to have dined there.

On arriving he was directed up the balustraded staircase, peered at by former grandees of the club from inside their gilt frames. In one of the upper rooms he spotted him, lounging on a chesterfield, absorbed in *The Times*.

'Hullo there,' Traherne called, on seeing his guest, and slowly put the paper aside. 'Just been reading the latest on the Rattenbury trial. Something irresistible about a murder case.'

'My mother would agree with you. She's talked of little else for days.'

'Rum show, isn't it? I suppose it's the age difference between the lady and her, um, paramour that has outraged people. If it was the other way round, and *she* was eighteen – well, no one would bat an eyelid.'

Eaves gave a conceding nod. 'It is unusual. But I don't think that will condemn her.'

'Oh – what will then?'

'I think it's more likely the fact she was sharing her bed with a servant – in this country that's unforgivable.'

Traherne mused on this for a moment, his expression gradually breaking into a wry smile. 'You could be right,' he said. He then handed Eaves a lunch menu, and turned the talk to other matters – horse racing, summer holidays, a new exhibition of paintings he had just seen. It seemed to Eaves that this man had quite a lot of leisure, and money, to spare. A waiter arrived with their drinks, and Traherne raised his glass in cheery invitation.

'Here's how. Talking of holidays, I gather you're keen on Germany – hiking in the Alps and so on.'

Eaves wondered how he had 'gathered' this. Bowman wouldn't have known, because they had never exchanged so much as a sliver of small talk with one another. And he didn't recall mentioning it at their meeting a few weeks ago. But yes, he admitted, he liked Germany and had made a habit of holidaying there after the war. Traherne knew the country a little himself, having visited Berlin with friends in the late 1920s – the old days of the Weimar.

'We won't see *their* like again,' he added with a half-laugh. 'What do you make of Herr Hitler and his rearmament?'

'Somewhat alarming,' said Eaves. 'If it continues at this rate –' Traherne cocked his head, eagerly expectant. '... I think it will be hard to avoid a war.'

He leaned back in his chair, enjoying the company but not entirely sure as to what he was doing there. He couldn't tell why this well-connected stranger should be interested in his thoughts on Nazi Germany, or on anything else, come to that. Traherne lit a cigarette, shook out the match and observed him through a cloud of smoke.

'How's your German? Did you know the language already?'

'I learned it at school,' said Eaves. 'I'm reasonably fluent ... Mr Traherne, d'you mind my asking – what do you do at the bank?'

He gave a puzzled smile. 'The bank? I don't work at the bank. Roland – that is, Mr Hoyle – well, I'm his godson. He and my father were in the Guards together.'

'So, um, why have you invited me here?'

'Ah. Well. My godfather happened to tip me the wink about a fiendish case of fraud at his bank, and how an employee had taken it upon himself to catch the culprit by an equally fiendish method of his own. I was fascinated – who wouldn't be? – and when Roland was invited by the chairman to meet this amateur detective he suggested I came along. You see, I work in a business that's always looking to recruit such people.'

'You run a detective agency?'

Traherne laughed. 'Not exactly. I work for a government department. A question for you: who do you suppose keeps this nation of ours safe from harm?'

'The police?'

Traherne pulled an ambiguous expression. 'The police are there to contain crime and enforce the law. But they are not equipped to take on the larger enemy – the malign forces who would subvert the body politic and bring the country to its knees. No police force could offer that level of protection. It is a job that demands enormous reserves of patience and watchfulness, because the enemy is often invisible, and his means indecipherable. We fight them, as the poet had it, "as on a darkling plain".'

'The job you're describing,' said Eaves cautiously, 'sounds like, pardon me, a spy.'

'Rather a tainted word, that. It conjures up a glamorous subfusc world – cobbled alleyways, furtive assignments, coded messages. That's not really us.'

'Then what would you call it – the thing you do?'

'Intelligence,' he shrugged. 'Just that. In this country, at present, there is a burgeoning support for Germany – I mean, for the way they run things there. Submission to an absolute leader. Control by a one-party state and the outlawing of opposition. And, of course, a programme of social and racial discrimination. Now, one may argue that such a regime could never win the popular vote here. But five years ago that's what they thought in Germany, too. A nation can lose its head just like an individual.'

A brief silence fell between them, interrupted by the discreet background hum of other conversation. Eaves wasn't sure if he was meant to speak, and as he hesitated Traherne resumed in his assured, even tone.

'The threat comes from a hard core of right-wing fanatics, principally the British Union, though there are others. Our department, known as the Section, aims to neutralise that threat. Not by force – that would be to lend them credibility – but by a process of infiltration. When I heard about your subterfuge at the bank I thought, that might be the chap for us. So we began running some background checks.'

A sudden jolt of excitement – or dread – lurched within Eaves. Was this the way it happened? 'I'm flattered, but what I did wasn't really that amazing. I'm not trying to be modest. Catching out a petty criminal isn't on a par with what I assume would be, well, a full-time job.'

'You *are* being modest. In any case it wasn't just the skill of your imposture that set you apart. It was your discretion. Most people, even if they were clever enough to devise such a trap, wouldn't be able to resist letting others in on their secret. They would need encouragement, or admiration, or perhaps advice. You didn't. You kept mum with colleagues, superiors, and I fancy you didn't confide in friends, either. Am I right?'

'I don't have that many friends.'

Traherne nodded. 'There's a woman, though, isn't there? Jane. Been seeing her for a few years. Surely you mentioned the thing to her?'

'How did you know about Jane?'

'Like I said, we've done our research.'

He gave Traherne a level look. 'If I did have a secret, then the last person in the world I'd confide it to would be someone I held dear.'

'I see. So this woman – you love her?'

'I thought you said you'd done the research.'

Traherne laughed. 'You're a natural.'

He explained what the life would entail. An absolute commitment to long hours of surveillance, and to the monkish regime of sifting information. As well as a steady nerve, an ability to improvise would be invaluable. He would be trained up, of course, schooled in the techniques of counter-espionage – he had already demonstrated a 'theatrical flair' in winning an enemy's confidence. They would even teach him how to use a revolver.

'Think you've got it in you to kill a man?'

Eaves tucked in his chin. 'Who did you have in mind?' he said with a quick laugh. He thought Traherne might meet his facetiousness in the same spirit, but he only stared back at him, expressionless. An answer was required. And at that moment he knew they were serious.

The following Saturday he was back at Haywards Heath station waiting for the London train. Having commuted Monday to Friday he would rather have stayed at home in Wivelsfield. His father needed help repairing some rotten frames in the green-house, and he liked pottering about of a weekend, reading, or doing the crossword with his mother. But Jane, just finished with a job that had lasted weeks and many late nights, had pleaded for him to come up to town. He knew it would be bad form to refuse.

As he stepped onto the platform at Victoria he saw her waiting just beyond the ticket collection. Hard to miss her, actually, for she was wearing one of her brightest outfits, a turquoise summer dress and a silly hat in pillar-box red. Her girlish love of colour had always touched him, the way it expressed something bold yet guileless in her personality. She worked in the copywriting department of an advertising agency, which he supposed was just as well – she couldn't have got away with dressing like that in an ordinary job. They had met nearly three years before. Someone he knew from Cambridge had invited him to a party in Battersea. It was held at a flat, heaving with people when he arrived. He'd been staring out through the French windows at the massed black trees fronting the park when someone who'd been dancing rather close bumped into him and sent his drink flying. 'Gosh, I'm most *awfully* sorry,' she said, and in her fluster introduced herself as Jane Temple. He spent the first few minutes of their conversation feeling beer soak through his sleeve. They had been together ever since.

Jane gave a little jump on catching sight of him, waving as if he'd been gone for years; he acknowledged her with an awkward sort of half-salute.

'It feels such *ages* since I saw you,' she cried gaily, throwing her arms about him. Her friendly, wide-hipped figure pushed against his. 'Have you missed me?'

'No more than I would my ears.' Her momentary confusion as she searched for the compliment in his irony made him laugh. 'Of course I missed you. You're looking nice.' She seemed pleased at that.

They walked out of the station hand in hand, past ranks of growling taxis and shoals of day trippers. The early-June weather had begun rather sullen, but this morning showed promise in the soft air and intermittent spangles of sunlight amid the clouds. They walked through the stuccoed maze of Belgravia and into Hyde Park, the Serpentine glittering in the distance. The grass was springy beneath their feet. Jane was running on with the story of their most recent client, a company that made household cleaning fluids.

'The agency had been sticking with this line "You can be sure with Bagshaw", which I thought sounded *terrible*. Nobody else would say anything, so I gave it a bit of thought and came up with "Bagshaw's is the stuff to give it a buff". And they all loved it – made it the campaign slogan!'

'Bravo,' said Eaves, smiling. 'They should give you a pay rise.'

Jane made a doubtful moue. 'Chance would be a fine thing. But once we knew that Bagshaw's were pleased the staff raised a cheer and sang "For she's a jolly good fellow"! Even Hodge cracked a smile.' Hodge was her boss, and the subject of frequent arias of complaint.

'How long have you been there now?'

'Eight years. And in all that time they've never given me an extra farthing. Same with Doreen. She reckons it's cos we're women and we won't make a fuss.'

'Maybe it's time you did,' he said. 'How is Doreen, by the way?' He knew of her only from Jane's accounts of her forlorn love life.

'Oh. Soldiering on. She said something to me the other day – to get the best out of a love affair one should never ask for more passion than the loved one is capable of giving.' Jane's tone was so thoughtful as she reported this that it caused Eaves to slow, and turn. He found her gaze fixed upon him.

He tilted his head in a ruminative way. 'Interesting. But not as snappy as *the stuff to give it a buff*.'

She laughed, and swung her hand at him playfully. His flippancy had got him out of a corner. But he felt the danger still, hovering like a storm cloud just out of his vision. They walked on through the park, stopping briefly to listen to someone harangue the crowd at Hyde Park Corner about freedom of speech. Among the listeners were a trio of young men, unremarkable but for the black uniform they wore. Eaves looked around to check whether anyone else was giving them the eye. When he mentioned them to Jane a few minutes later she looked at him blankly: Blackshirts? She hadn't even noticed them.

They got a bus along Oxford Street and had lunch at the Lyons on Tottenham Court Road. Jane debated as to whether they should see a film or go to the Emlyn Williams play at the Duchess. The mood between them was fine until talk turned to the visit of the bank's chairman and his friends. What had happened since? Eaves thought for a moment.

'Oh, I was invited by one of them to his club, somewhere in Mayfair. He wanted to chat about ... various things.'

'A club in Mayfair ...' Jane bugged her eyes in a show of curiosity. 'So what were these "various things" you talked about?'

He stirred his tea again, wondering how vague he could keep it. 'Well, he was interested to know how I, erm, brought him down. The fraudster. To be honest, there wasn't a great deal more I could say.'

Across the table, Jane was frowning her puzzlement. 'But he must have asked to meet you for a reason. What does this chap do again?'

'He works in some government department, not sure what.'

'Why won't you –' she began, then dialled her tone down to something less peevish. 'I get the impression – as usual – you're jolly reluctant to tell me things. Why? Do I seem such a gossip to you?' He shook his head, not saying anything; he didn't want to make a wrong move. Eventually, Jane spoke again, in a different voice. 'I always believed that if you loved someone, you had to trust them, too. The one would follow the other. But with you ... I don't know.'

Love. Trust. This was the sort of conversation he dreaded. He wasn't good at it, and in any case regarded it as wrong to burden another person with that much feeling. It was too great a responsibility. But Jane's inquisitive blue gaze did not soften, and he perceived the obligation to answer.

'I'm not sure I agree with that equation.' He reached over the table to take her hand. 'If I don't tell you secrets it's because, by and large, I don't have any. My life's not that interesting! As for the other ... do you honestly feel *un*loved by me?'

He felt the disappointment in Jane's expression. The words he had spoken were hedged about with negatives – to ask a woman if she felt 'unloved' was a poor substitute for the honest declaration of 'I love you'. She perhaps knew him too well to expect effusiveness. He caught her eye, and after a moment she smiled at him. But there was something unconvinced in the smile, and the feeling of a stand-off between them persisted through the afternoon. They went to see a film in Leicester Square just after six, though neither of them was much engaged by it. Such was his distraction he had already forgotten it by the time they were back on the street. They caught a 19 to Battersea and spoke for a while outside her front door. But there was no invitation to stay, and he walked back to Victoria alone.

'Eaves.' He looked up from his desk to find the assistant manager eyeing him coldly. 'Mr Bowman would like to see you. Immediately.'

This time he found the manager alone in his office. Silently he was gestured to take the chair opposite. There followed a meditative pause as Bowman laid his hands on the desk like a pianist stunned into immobility. He was staring at a letter whose contents apparently bemused him.

'I'm rather at a loss, Eaves,' he began. 'May I enquire – have you been unhappy at the bank?'

'Unhappy? No, sir.'

'So there is nothing that might have persuaded you, for example, to apply for another job?'

'No, sir.'

'I ask because I received this morning a letter – from Philip Traherne, who I gather has been in touch with you since our meeting a few weeks ago. A curious letter. It seems he runs a government office concerned with "the defence of the realm". In this capacity he has submitted an urgent request – for your services. Would you kindly explain?'

Eaves made an apologetic frown. 'I'm not sure I can, sir. Mr Traherne invited me to lunch and talked a little about his work. On a later occasion I met some of his colleagues. That's as much as I can tell you.'

'But what does he want you for?'

'I – I don't know. He didn't mention a job when we last spoke.'

Bowman shook his head, querulous now. 'It's most irregular. He asks, or rather he insists, that the bank release you without a period of notice. His "department" wants you to start at the beginning of next week.' He stared hard at Eaves. 'I'm bound to say it's a damned liberty he's taking. What on earth does he imagine *you* know about the defence of the realm?'

Aware that he had nothing to say which might appease his manager, Eaves kept quiet. A few moments later he was out of the door. When he had last met Traherne at his office in St James's he knew that a move was afoot, but he'd had no inkling of its peremptory nature. Traherne had introduced him to his colleagues – Castle, a pouchy-faced, twinkling fellow with a limp, and a woman named Tessa Hammond, whose sharp gaze and brittle manner instantly put him on alert.

'One more thing,' Traherne had said when they were on their way out of the building. 'You'll need a new name. Once you're on the inside, there's a danger that someone might decide to investigate you. We'll kit you out with a new ID, papers and so on. I'm afraid it's RIP Edward Eaves.'

They batted a few ideas back and forth.

'I rather like the name Hoste,' Traherne continued. 'You see, to us it means the person who welcomes a guest – takes them in, as it were. But the ablative case *hoste*, in Latin, means "the enemy". Rather a neat ambiguity, don't you think?'

'Well, as long as it remains ambiguous …'

'Oh, I don't suppose there are many classical scholars in the ranks of the British Fascists. Now, what was your grandfather's first name?'

'John.'

'John Hoste. Hmm. Possibly.'

They were at the door when his new employer squinted at him. 'Jack is better, I think. Friendlier. Jack Hoste.' He offered his hand. 'Welcome to the Section.'

They met in a restaurant on Judd Street, round the corner from the bank. Jane looked tired, he thought, but didn't dare enquire as to why. She wasn't wearing make-up, unusually, which lent her face a scoured, penitential aspect, as though she had just emerged from a religious retreat. Or was perhaps about to enter one. On sitting down her eyes flickered slightly at the bottle of wine: he had ordered it as a precautionary measure.

'Not planning to do much work this afternoon?' she said, accepting the glass he poured for her.

'As a matter of fact I'm not doing *any* work this afternoon. Today's my last day.'

Her hand froze almost as the glass was at her lips. She blinked at him. 'What?'

He quickly explained. The man he had met from the government, Traherne, had arranged it: his employment there was to start immediately. 'It rather took everyone by surprise. I heard that Bowman wrote a stiff letter to them, complaining. Apparently it was "quite beyond him" as to why my services should be required. I must admit, he has a point.'

Jane listened to him in a seeming daze. Eaves had a sense of himself just then as a stranger in her company. His fault, he knew. He had been always too reluctant to confide in her; this new development would not make it any easier.

'So you'll be working for the government?'

'Yes. At an office in St James's.'

'Doing what, exactly?'

He shifted in his seat. 'It's to do with security. I can't really tell you any more than that. They had me sign various confidentiality agreements.'

Jane gave a mirthless laugh. 'I see. That must please you a good deal. You're going to a job that will excuse you from telling me *any*thing.'

He flinched at her sarcasm. 'I hoped you might be proud of me. This job's better than anything the bank might have offered. More money. And I'll be moving to London, too.'

'Have you told your parents?'

'Not yet. I'm not sure they'll understand.'

'I'm not sure I do either,' she said. 'Tell me, once you move to London, how will things change?'

He looked at her, wondering if there was a catch. 'For us, you mean? I don't suppose they'll change at all.'

She nodded, as if his reply had confirmed something. She let her gaze drop, and for a long time she kept perfectly silent and still. 'I had the strangest notion when I heard your voice on the telephone yesterday,' she said in a distant voice. 'At first I imagined you were inviting me to lunch because – ha – you had something to ask me.'

He paused, feeling a panic begin to rise. 'You mean –'

'Yes. I know. Wasn't that silly of me? We might go on for another ten years and the thought still wouldn't occur to you.'

'Jane, you know how terribly fond I am of you –'

'Fond!' she said in a desolate voice. '*Fond* is what you feel about a pet, or a maiden aunt. It's not a word one uses about a – but what's the point in complaining now?'

Her face had been averted as she spoke; abruptly she turned to look at him. Her eyes glistened, but she refused to give way. It pierced him to meet her gaze.

'I should have known, really,' she went on, and took a mouthful of wine as if to help her to the end. 'I remember as a girl staring at myself in the mirror and thinking "No one will ever ask to marry me". And no one has.'

Some minutes later he watched her walk away from the table. At the door of the restaurant she looked back at him, as if there was something she had forgotten to say. But whatever the impulse might have been, she decided against it. Before he could raise his hand in farewell she was through the door, and gone.

March 1944

15

The pub on the corner, where he'd been drinking only the other night, was now a blackened shell. It always struck him how bomb damage was so much more depressing in daylight. At night, with the raids still on, burning buildings had a drama about them. When you got close to the blaze and felt its heat on your skin, there was no denying a certain ghoulish vitality in the spectacle. As an ARP warden he sometimes had to cross fragile ground that might at any moment give way to molten-red vaults below. It reminded him of the trenches during a 'show' – terrifying, with wild periods of exhilaration. Only in the morning, when the rubble was cleared and the fires put out, did the reality of it sink in. Everything looked filthy, and grim, and dead.

After nearly three years of calm, in January the Luftwaffe had come back to London. No one had really believed they were gone for good, even when the skies had cleared. But the longer the planes stayed away the more hopeful became the illusion of safety. For a while these new raids were spasmodic, nothing to compare with the heavy Blitz of 1941. They dwindled, and then in February they began all over again. Bombs rained down from Whitechapel to Whitehall (Number 10 had its windows blown in) and incendiaries came down in ghastly chandeliers of spitting flame. The London Library in St James's Square was hit, and Hoste had gone to help with the clear-up; searching beneath a blanket of ashen debris he found a mausoleum of books lying tattered and coverless. Human casualties were fewer, but the mortuary vans were still busy. He sensed people were less resilient than they had been during the '41 raids. Back then a mood of defiance, of 'London Can Take It', had prevailed. Now they seemed wearier, debilitated by the war and its persistent pilfering of food and clothes and beer. The danger had burrowed down, briefly invisible, but instead of disappearing had renewed itself, and once more the shelters began to fill up.

In the meantime he and his colleagues at the Section had kept close watch over their agents. By 1942 almost all the traffic of German intelligence services was being read: the decrypters at Bletchley had enabled MI5 to identify the enemy and neutralise them. Hoste had heard it confidently said that 'we know more about the Abwehr than the Abwehr probably do'. The corridors were buzzing with talk of the Second Front. An Allied assault on mainland Europe was imminent, but where would it be directed – and when? A network of double agents had been feeding the Nazis false and misleading information for years. Now the deception was to be put to the ultimate test. Germany had to be tricked into believing that an invasion, when it came, would target the Pas de Calais, a smokescreen for the Allies' actual plan of landing on the coast of Normandy. To this end an entire assault plan had to be faked, including dummy landing craft and a blizzard of electric noise to mimic huge armies being prepared where none in fact existed.

The Section had been co-opted into this vast campaign of deceit. The fear was that a rogue freelancer of Nazi sympathies might stumble upon the build-up of troops and somehow channel this intelligence directly back to Germany. Such a leak might hole the entire D-Day operation. Hoste would henceforth report both to Tessa Hammond and a new liaison officer, Richard Lang, who belonged to an outfit called the London Controlling Section. His years in the field would help them identify which German agents should be isolated. Lang, a bristling, athletic character with a pencil moustache, had so far only managed a quick meet-and-greet, such was the pressure they were all under.

Hoste had been too busy to pay him much notice. Aside from his ARP duties he had to keep a lid on the stirrings of dissent within his nest of Nazi cuckoos. Some were demanding active sabotage against the RAF; others were proposing assassination plots and attacks on Parliament. He knew that most of them were cranks. But in this feverish climate of uncertainty loose cannons became dangerous: there was a chance they might hit upon the Allies' plans by fluke and create a panic.

A few nights after the raid Hoste was drinking at a pub just off Hatton Garden with two of his 'regulars', Gleave and Scoult. They were among the more sophisticated of his circle, up from Hastings with news of military preparations on the coast. Scoult, puffing on his briar pipe, had apparently been observing the troops' manoeuvres.

'It's odd, though. From what I can see they're not regular army – they're raw-looking lads without much training.'

Hoste said, 'I suppose they're being kept in reserve. I hear there's a lot of movement along the Kent coast.'

Gleave, looking pastier than usual in the pub light, gave a nod. 'I've been over there a few times. It looks to us like the fleet is going to use Dover as their base. It makes sense – that's the shortest crossing to Calais. Would Berlin be interested in photographs?'

'Of course,' said Hoste. 'Your reconnaissance has been of great value to us. Which reminds me –' He reached into his breast pocket and produced an envelope for each of them. 'For services rendered.'

They murmured their thanks, and Gleave, tapping his envelope on the table, said, 'Looks like it's my shout. Same again, gents?'

Scoult watched him go off to the bar. 'Damned good fellow, that. And loyal as the day is long.'

'I've always thought so,' said Hoste, wondering at his definition of loyalty.

After a pause, Scoult dropped his voice confidentially. 'I shouldn't be saying this, but not *all* of your operatives are so trustworthy.'

'Oh?'

'Our friend Marita has been, um, expressing her concerns. To put it mildly. She complains that you're lacking in ambition.'

Hoste gave a half-smile. 'I've heard that from Marita before. You can't please them all, Mr Scoult.'

'True enough. But it's gone beyond that. The other night I overheard her claiming the organisation has seized up, and that none of the recent intelligence she's given you has had any effect at all.'

'That's a serious claim – and an erroneous one.'

Scoult dipped his head in agreement, and hesitated again. 'Mr Hoste, may I tell you something – in confidence? She reckons that Berlin no longer listens to you. Says you've shot your bolt, and that someone else should step in.'

'I can imagine the "someone" she has in mind ...'

'Correct,' said Scoult, with a worldly-wise lift of his brow. 'I think she'd like nothing better than to take charge – and God knows where that would lead us. The woman sees conspiracy everywhere.'

'What's her latest?'

Scoult puffed out his cheeks. 'Oh, the usual. The Jews are behind everything. Now I'm no friend to them, as you know, but for Marita it's a bloody crusade. To listen to her you'd think every looter and pickpocket in town is a Jew. The Bethnal Green disaster last year? That was their fault, too – "They lost their nerve and caused a stampede," she told me. Madness.'

'Not someone you'd like to make an enemy of.'

'Indeed not. But what I wanted to say was – you can count on us.'

'Glad to hear it,' said Hoste, acknowledging with a glance the return of Gleave with their drinks. 'And thanks for the warning.'

The trees in St James's Park were beginning to show their leaves again. They looked to him less lonely when they gained a bit of green. Once past the sandbags and the road-blocks you could almost forget there was a war on. Hoste came over the bridge and found a bench from where he could watch the ducks on the lake. A cold, troubled sunlight dappled the surface.

Tessa arrived some minutes later. She was wearing a black-and-camel-checked outfit with a chic felt hat he hadn't seen before. She had also become more particular about her make-up. He presumed she had acquired it on the black market, such was its present scarcity. A tiny stone glinted on her finger: her chap, Alan, had recently popped the question.

'You look like a fashion plate,' he observed, looking her up and down. 'Is this what happens to a woman when she gets engaged?'

'That makes me feel I was rather dowdy before,' she replied. She took out her cigarettes and offered him one. 'What are we doing here anyway? You could have just come to the office.'

He pulled a face. 'For one thing I'm not in the mood to deal with the new chap. For another – isn't it nicer to be outside on a morning like this?'

Tessa cast a look of indifference around her, as though a park in spring sunlight had no greater charm than anywhere else. As they smoked, he told her about his meeting with Gleave and Scoult, and the odd feeling he had taken away.

'Why odd?'

189

'I suppose it's because, having been so long in their company, I find myself almost warming to them – Scoult, in particular. He's actually quite a personable fellow.'

She arched her eyebrows. 'Hmm. "Personable" isn't the word I'd use for their sort.'

'I know. All the same … you can't spend that much time with someone and not come to recognise a basic humanity in there. They aren't *evil*, most of them – just deluded.'

'And dangerous. As I don't need to remind you.'

'No, you don't. Which brings me to the matter at hand. It seems there is a mood of mutiny among our operatives – I got this from Scoult – and it stems from Marita Pardoe. She's always thought me too circumspect. Now she's casting doubt on my effectiveness as a spymaster.'

'What's sparked this off?'

He gave a speculative curl to his lip. 'I dare say it has to do with the way the war's going. She's probably realised that Germany can't win – but she's damned if she'll give up without a fight.'

'Marita on the warpath is really the *last* thing we need. Did Scoult know what she's planning?'

'Only this. She has a replacement for me in mind.'

'Herself?' Tessa looked puzzled. 'That would suggest she's found a new outlet for getting intelligence to Berlin. Could she have done?'

He shrugged. 'Unlikely. But I'd never underestimate Marita's capability. If anyone can …'

'What d'you think we should do?'

'Sit tight. In the meantime I need some chickenfeed – some intelligence that she can verify but that won't compromise us.'

'Are you getting worried?' she asked in surprise.

He shook his head. 'Not yet. She knows all the traffic has to go through a Gestapo agent – and I'm still the only one they've got.'

Tessa looked at him. 'The way you said that inclines me to think you almost believe it yourself.'

She was right: he had immersed himself in the part of controller for so long it had become almost a separate identity. When he was in the company of Marita and the rest he found it easy to be convincing, because his imposture had become second nature. His front of self-assurance had never flinched. He had never allowed them to doubt him.

They talked on for a while, until Tessa glanced at her watch and made a movement to leave. He looked at her again, appraisingly. There was some subtle change in her – it wasn't just the clothes or the make-up.

'You look different, I don't know why,' he said, suddenly confused.

She narrowed her eyes, then laughed. 'You think so?' She put her hand on his. 'I was going to wait before I – Alan's decided we should bring the wedding forward.'

'I see. Are you pleased about that?' He was really at a loss to know.

'Very. But there's another reason we're hurrying it along.' She briefly glanced down, to her stomach, then raised her eyes again to his. It took him a moment, but he got there.

'Oh. *Oh* ...' She still had her hand over his. For a few moments he was too surprised to speak. 'Gosh, Tessa – congratulations. When is –'

'We'll marry in June, probably. You know, I really thought I was too old to ...'

'But you've done it! I'll – we'll miss you, of course.'

She laughed again, and rose to her feet. 'I'm not going yet. Not due till September.'

He stood with her, and in a spontaneous rush of feeling he leaned over and planted a dry kiss on her cheek. She beamed at him, murmuring a few words he didn't catch. She pulled her gloves back on, and raised a hand in farewell. He sat down again on the bench and watched as her figure receded into the distance.

He *would* miss her. She had been his case officer for nine years, in which time they had become close. He could not have failed to pick up Tessa's steady yet unexpressed feelings for him. Three years ago her cold-blooded shooting of Billy Adair had been the saving of his life. He had replayed the incident often, recalling the shock of her quick movement – feet planted apart, left hand holding the gun arm steady – and the black smoking hole in Adair's eye. Had the assassin lived to tell Marita of Hoste's true identity it would have been over for him. He could only ever be grateful to Tessa for that. In his heart he felt something more than gratitude, but his recessive character – his neurotic secrecy – prevented him from examining the feeling. Starved of light and hope, it slowly expired within him.

These thoughts preoccupied him on his walk home. His friendship with Tessa would endure. They would always have that secret bond between them. It had roped them together like two climbers on a cliff face. Yet on the surface they treated one another with the same unruffled cool. Only now did he wonder how it might have been if he, not Alan, had popped the question. It made no difference now, but he felt sure that Tessa had wondered about it, too.

16

Amy looked at her watch. The guests would be arriving in about an hour. Outside she could hear the bustle of the hired staff carrying glasses and crates up the stairs. The bureau had last year expanded its premises to the floor above, which would be used this evening for the main bar. She knew she ought to put a spurt on, but the mass of files from '39 and '40 she had been poring over this afternoon still riveted her. All those men and women who had come here seeking marriage partners, first at Bruton Place, then here at Brook Street: it was hard to comprehend the sea of names, faces, that had washed through the door. How many from the thousands could she remember? She and Jo had spent the afternoon trawling through their early triumphs and disasters, misty-eyed with feeling one moment, screeching with laughter the next. The things people had written in the 'Requirements' box would amuse them for hours.

Not a giant, not a dwarf. Not American.

Someone with furniture would be an advantage.

No permed hair. Not too brainy. Of gentlefolk.

No sulkers. Near to Chertsey if possible.

Would prefer a well-off lady. (Jo had written in the margin, *We get a lot of these.*)

Charm, with a sense of the absurd. I emphatically have no money.

No objection to painted fingernails, scent or a dowry.

And yet among the fortune-hunters, the crackpots and the fusspots, there were those driven by an honest yearning for companionship. They didn't want money, or a drudge in the guise of a spouse; they sought only to connect with another human being. Amy took particular trouble over these, and made an effort to match up people she deemed, from their profile, good-hearted. You couldn't be infallible, of course, but generally she had a sound instinct for character, and had scored more successes than failures. Her skill was reflected in the eventual expansion of the marriage bureau; they now employed two junior assistants to help with the volume of mail, and plans were afoot to set up a new branch in Bristol. The war, once feared as the enemy of romantic fancy, seemed to have fired the ardour of the single man and woman.

She was about to close and seal the box-file when her eye fell on a letter whose handwriting seemed to call to her. She unfolded it and read. It was signed by a Miss Gertrude Mayhew, whose face she tried to conjure from the legions who had passed through her office. A vague image of a pale, grey-eyed woman, not unattractive, possibly in her forties – or was she picturing someone else altogether? She checked the details on her application form – worked in an insurance office, lived in Ealing with her mother, had included certain unexceptional details about her life. It was only when Amy read what was written in the 'Requirements' box that she remembered why this one had stuck.

Someone I can fall in love with. I am very lonely.

She examined Gertrude Mayhew's form again. They had arranged a date, there it was, August 1940. There was no follow-up, nothing to indicate what had ensued. There were a few who dropped off the list. Some would meet their assigned match and then disappear – no report tendered of good or ill, just a silence. Others were too embarrassed or dispirited to continue the search, and their details collected dust inside a box-file. Where was Gertrude now? she wondered.

I am very lonely.

Her reverie was broken by Miss Ducker poking her head round the door, checking the blackout precautions: did Miss Strallen want some help? Amy smiled her thanks, and together they unrolled the blankets to hang over the tall sash windows that looked down on Brook Street. Miss Ducker chunnered away excitedly about this evening's occasion, a party to mark the fifth anniversary of the Quartermaine Marriage Bureau. They were expecting around 150 guests – friends, backers, favourite clients and their spouses – so it might be a crush even with the extra floor. Talking of which, she'd better go and check that the junior assistants had blacked out the windows up there; they didn't want the warden coming round.

When she had gone Amy locked her office door and took down the dress, suspended from a hook on its padded hanger. Five years of the bureau. April 1939. The war had been going almost as long. Time was when she would have bought herself a new outfit for a party like this. An impossible luxury today. The dress she was putting on was nice enough, a fitted mulberry-coloured silk thing she had bought at Jaeger, seven or eight years ago. She had had it cleaned for tonight, and the tailor on Avery Row had repaired tears in the seams. Make Do and Mend: a communal piety she cordially detested. Back at her desk she took out a mirror to do her make-up, scrutinising her complexion. No cause for alarm – yet – though the faint circles beneath her eyes betrayed fatigue: the raids had murdered sleep again. She would be thirty-two in October. Thirty-two – and unmarried. When she had last been home even her mother, not generally disposed to prying, had wondered aloud whether Amy mightn't care to keep one of the 'eligible bachelors' at the bureau for herself. How to explain it, the professional matchmaker who had stayed single? Even Johanna, her loyal partner in spinsterhood, had at last broken ranks. She had met a man – a member of the landed gentry, no less – at a house party in Somerset, and married him within a year. Amy was secretly dismayed, but her unworthy hope that Jo's decision was reckless had so far been in vain: they seemed happy together.

There had been affairs, mostly one-sided, all of them ended by her. She disliked herself for this skittishness – she who was so prudent in advising and choosing for others. One of them, an older man, on being given his marching orders had told her that as long as she enshrined 'perfection' as the standard she would always be disappointed. The remark had astonished her, and she later wondered why he had been moved to make it, for she had never suggested to him – or to anyone – that such a state might be attainable. Perfection wasn't even inter-esting; it was the flaws and mistakes that made up a person, the *im*perfection. You couldn't have the pearl without the grit. What she really hankered for wasn't perfection, it was kindness, and wisdom. But experience had shown her that the world was short of kind, wise men.

The party was still in a roar towards midnight. The sounds of a distant raid were ignored; in fact the only panic at Brook Street was the moment someone whispered that the beer was nearly gone. Johanna, who had already moved heaven and earth to round up sufficient booze, went off with a friend to beg for extra supplies from a grand house in Mayfair they knew. Relief arrived twenty minutes later in a taxi carrying half a dozen crates, before most of the party had even heard there was a crisis. Jo's resourcefulness was loudly toasted, and the music started up again.

Amy had been hemmed in by well-wishers near the staircase. She knew only some of them. They wanted to jump on the merry-go-round of congratulations that Jo had set in motion earlier in the evening; her speech had amusingly chronicled the ups and downs of the bureau, sketching an account of their financial scrapes (she praised the forbearance of their 'saintly' bank manager) and the remarkable run of luck that had kept the premises open during the worst of the Blitz. She recalled among certain friends the looks of incomprehension and outright distaste on first presenting the idea of a marriage bureau, and could still remember the tone of voice of 'the prominent cleric' who visited the office one afternoon to remonstrate with her on the subject of public morality. He stayed for tea, and they ended up discussing their shared love of Kipling and thick-cut marmalade.

Jo, saving her most heartfelt words for the close, pondered her good fortune in finding not only a true friend but the very rock on which the bureau was built – 'It could not have enjoyed anything like its present success without the diligence, sympathy, good humour, fine discrimination and unswerving devotion of my partner, Amy Strallen.' A roar went up, and Amy blushed to her roots as the room drowned in applause. She had not had a minute to herself since, and had drunk enough gin to know that she would pay for it tomorrow. It was awful, and marvellous, to hear herself gabble away. And then amid the cavalcade of faces one bobbed into view whose features she was unequivocally pleased to see.

'I spotted you across the room a while ago,' said Georgie Harlow, smiling, 'but I couldn't get near you!'

'Darling,' she cried, hugging her, and grateful for the excuse to wriggle clear of the scrum. They dodged their way to a corner of relative quiet. 'I wasn't sure you'd come.'

This was true. Having moved to a manor house in Sussex Georgie was hardly seen in town any more. Following the

Billy Adair case her confidence had been rocked, and she might have languished indefinitely had it not been for the quiet persistence of her former beau, Christopher – the man whom Amy had originally put her way. Through his kindness he had helped restore her spirits, and when he proposed to her again she accepted him this time without misgiving. Amy was a bridesmaid at the wedding.

'I missed Johanna's speech,' she said, pulling a face. 'Apparently it was all about how wonderful you are.'

Amy laughed, shook her head. 'She overdid it. Probably feeling guilty because I've been running things here while she's away in Bristol.'

'Is it true she's setting up an office there?'

'Yes, which will mean finding someone to replace her. I can't run it on my own. But forget all that. How's the country life?'

'Wonderful, actually. I didn't realise how anxious the job had made me. Chris has been so good about it all.'

'You don't miss London, then?' said Amy, with a nod to the raucous mood around them.

'Occasionally. I still see a few friends from Whitehall, you know ... As a matter of fact, I was up here a few weeks ago and saw that fellow who –' She stopped herself abruptly, and coloured.

Amy stared at her. 'Which fellow?' she asked, and at the same moment she knew exactly who.

'The MI5 man. Hoste. Sorry, I shouldn't have brought it up ...'

Jack Hoste. She hadn't thought of him in a while. Her gaze met Georgie's, and she smiled. 'It's fine – really. Did you talk to him?'

'Very briefly. We only ever met because of what happened. He's one of the top people there, but nobody in our building knows much about him.'

'I imagine that's just how he wants it,' said Amy, and paused. 'There was never anything between us, you know.'

'I know, you said so. I just wondered –' Georgie said, with a gentle, hesitant look that softened Amy's heart. What harm was there in bringing it up now?

'I felt quite bad at the time, after they told me what he was. For a while everything went to pot. I couldn't trust anyone – any man. I felt such a fool to have been taken in. But then I remembered how nice he was, and the bravery he showed when he didn't have to. It's a curious feeling – as if something had happened to me and not to him. I thought I hated him, but I didn't. I couldn't.'

Georgie was still staring at her, the concern vivid in her eyes. She probably wishes she'd never mentioned it, thought Amy, who had never talked about Hoste to anyone in the years since. It didn't matter; she didn't have to feel bad about it any more.

At that moment Johanna came up, somewhat tipsy, accompanied by a friend she wanted to introduce to Amy. His name was Gerard Bellamy, an army officer, tall, dark-haired, velvet-voiced – disconcertingly eligible. Georgie seemed to twig the unspoken contrivance of a match, and tactfully withdrew, mouthing a farewell to her friend. Amy, pasting on a smile, felt frustrated by the interruption, as one does on being woken from a dream that had been promising some revelation. She sensed that Georgie had something else to say about Hoste, and now there would be no telling. The next time she checked her watch it was half past one, by which point even the pretence of sobriety was beyond her. She heard her words come out slurred, and Captain Bellamy was eyeing her with undisguised bemusement. When she decided to call it a night, he insisted upon walking her home: the streets were blacked out, and he was not prepared to let her attempt the journey alone.

On emerging into the night the sudden change of air caused her to stagger. Bellamy, quick on his feet, managed to hold her up.

'Are you all right, Miss Strallen? Should I call a car?'

She shook her head with the vehemence of the dead drunk. She was *damned* if he was going to bundle her into a car. Then might he be allowed at least to take her by the arm? he asked. She submitted to this, and they proceeded at an unsteady bat north up Bond Street. At first she was aware only of his voice at her ear, coaxing, level, unhurried; by degrees she tried to tune in to what he was saying. They appeared to be having a conversation. He wanted to know about her work, it seemed, and she heard herself explain to him the rudiments of matching one person with another. It wasn't a science, this business, it was trial and error, and sometimes they had to rely on intuition. Or whatever. She told him about the 'Requirements' box on the application form, and he laughed when she quoted the silly, self-deluding things that clients chose to write. She liked his laugh, and tried to provoke it again with other stray fragments from the befuddled reaches of her brain.

When he spoke next she was aware that he had adopted a more teasing note: In their place what would *she* write, asked to express her own Requirements? He sounded rather pleased to have turned the question round. But Amy, in her unstable mood, considered the idea with terrible seriousness.

'"Someone I can fall in love with,"' she said, dredging a memory from earlier in the day – possibly from earlier in her life. Before she could stop herself, she added, '"I am very lonely."'

I'm quoting somebody, a client, she meant to say, but she didn't. Something forlorn had hold of her voice. The captain, who seemed to hear it, looked round at her; he was at a loss for an answer. They kept walking, their footsteps on the pavement suddenly louder. He didn't say another word until he wished her goodnight at her door.

17

They sat drinking tea in the Kardomah on Fleet Street, the light dimmed by the cladding of sandbags stacked against its front windows. The traffic of newspapermen through the door was more or less constant; he had never seen the phone booth in the corridor unoccupied.

'I don't know why you like this place so much,' Hoste said, looking around them. 'It's full of hacks earwigging one another's conversation.'

Marita stared across the table at him. 'How typical of you to think like that,' she replied. 'You see a place where strangers may overhear your secrets – whereas I regard it as somewhere to filch *their* secrets for myself.'

'In all the years I've been coming here I don't recall picking up a single bit of gossip of the slightest interest.'

'You have to know what to listen for. People give away things without even realising it.'

'Talking of which, I saw Gleave and Scoult last week – they've observed a build-up of ordnance around the Kent coast. Know anything about it?'

She pulled a sceptical expression. 'All I know is that your scouts are amateurs. If they were to tell me the invasion is being launched from Kent I would assume they had been duped into believing it.'

'Their intelligence has been very persuasive,' he said mildly.

'I would check that personally before you think of filing it to Berlin.' She said this last in an undertone, though their table was set apart from the rest. Secrecy is second nature to her, he thought; she'd sooner kill someone – or kill herself – than get caught. He considered her imperious expression, the dark, illusionless eyes surveying the room, then switching coldly back on him.

'Why are you smiling – what's so funny?' she said sharply.

He couldn't help himself. 'Nothing. Well ... would it be fair to say that, despite all our dealings these last years, you've never much liked me?'

She frowned at the sudden personal tone. 'I've never much liked anyone. As a matter of fact I don't altogether despise you.'

'How flattering. And yet I've been hearing ominous reports that you're disaffected with our arrangement. Apparently you think I'm no longer "up to it".'

'Where did you get this – from that pair of fools?'

'Word goes around. Now what you think of me personally is beside the point: I don't mind being disliked. But when I hear of my professional capability being questioned, then it becomes a different matter. A serious matter.'

A scornful incredulity lit up her eyes. 'What is this?'

'I think we both know what this is. The tide of the war is about to turn. The next months will be the making or the breaking of the Reich. The Abwehr has put its agents on top alert – every scrap of intelligence about the Second Front is vital to them. As their only conduit in London I am charged with keeping Berlin up to date. It is *not* the time to start undermining me or my agents – do you understand?'

'Undermine you – how?'

He narrowed his eyes. 'By putting your own ambition before the job. A job for which you are very well rewarded, incidentally –' She tried to interrupt him, but he spoke over her. 'You're playing a dangerous game, Marita. You have no authority whatsoever to take over this operation. If I get wind of any mutiny I'll know where it's coming from. Your payments will instantly cease, and your position as an agent will be terminated.'

'Well, aren't you the big man?' she sneered. 'We wouldn't need to have this conversation if I could be assured you were doing your job properly. Instead, for three years you've talked and talked and produced *nothing* – not a single initiative – that might help overthrow this government. I'm "well rewarded", as you say, because I've brought you the best and most reliable intelligence of any agent in this country. Yet what use has it been? What good have you done the Reich in all that time?'

'It may surprise you to know that Berlin has always been most grateful. I've given them information they couldn't have come by any other way. It is unfortunate that the results of our work may not be credited for years – may never be. Espionage is a long game. You of all people should know that.'

'Ha. You expect unconditional trust from others, and yet you offer none in return. I would dearly love to know how much of the intelligence we bring you gets to the top. This concentration of ordnance in the south, for instance. How can you be sure they're going to launch from Kent? Wouldn't it be more like MI5 to use that as a decoy and direct the assault elsewhere?'

Hoste waited a beat before answering. She was shrewd, he had to admit; she was always shrewd. 'Or it could be a double bluff. Make a feint to go one way, then just as the enemy become convinced you've got a different plan you switch back to the original. Kent looks the more promising option.'

'Another classic method of the enemy: sow confusion.'

He gave a conceding half-smile. 'I accept that it's all a gamble. But the important question you have to ask yourself is this – in time of need, will I be of more use to Berlin as a rogue agent or as part of a team?' She stared hard at him. This was a moment to test her loyalty: she knew it as well as he did. 'Put it another way. Do you still work for the Fatherland? Because if you do, I want your pledge of support.'

She fell into a sullen silence, pondering. Marita didn't take well to being pushed, but she was pragmatic about the need for alliances. Slowly, with a curl to her lip, she said, 'You have it – for now. Do not make me regret it.'

He betrayed no hint of his relief. The crisis had been averted, and Marita was back on board, for the moment. She was pulling on her gloves, and glanced at him.

'One other thing,' she said, reverting to a more businesslike tone. 'The money. I've been on the same for three years. Would it be beyond our paymasters to give me a raise?'

'I'm sure they can manage something,' said Hoste, realising it was a small price to pay for what he had just got away with. She had risen from the table, and, leaving some coins on the plate, he rose to accompany her.

The cafe was alive with bustle. They were making their way through the tables – she was a few steps in advance – when from nowhere he heard his name being called. Only it wasn't his name any more.

'Eaves!'

He flinched, and there, unimaginably, was Bowman, his old manager at the bank on Euston Road. He looked a little jowlier, his features blurred with age. He had stood up, squinting, his expression clearing to certainty. He had recognised his former employee, though they hadn't set eyes on one another for years. Hoste, momentarily rooted to the spot, caught his breath. His brain was spinning furiously: how to get out of this? There was no possibility of pretending he hadn't heard. If he didn't come up with something fast he was done for. He returned a look of recognition and, as if in a dream, stepped towards Bowman's table, hoping that Marita hadn't noticed.

'I wasn't sure at first if it was you,' said Bowman, offering his hand. 'Must be – what – ten years?'

'Close to,' he said, fixing a grin. Bowman's companions at the table were looking at them both, bemused. Hoste sensed

Marita arrive at his side. 'This is my associate, Miss Berens,' he said, careful to use her public alias. 'I used to be a clerk at Mr Bowman's bank, years ago.'

Marita nodded, politely interested. Bowman's reaction to her dark, striking looks was more pronounced, but he tore his eyes away to ask his old employee a question. 'So what have you been up to since? Or shouldn't I ask?!' He gave a theatrical wink and a laugh that caused Hoste to swallow.

'You really shouldn't ask, Mr Bowman. But I do recall your being a good sport about it at the time.' The two sides of his life were heading for each other, like cars without lights on a blacked-out road. Keep it vague, and *get out of here*. He glanced at his wristwatch, making a face to indicate he was pushed for time.

'I wasn't given much choice,' replied Bowman, with a rueful smirk. 'All very cloak and dagger, as I remember. Never lost an employee to that lot before or since, I might add. Edward Eaves ... Your name was mentioned –'

'I'm so sorry, Mr Bowman, but much as I'd like to reminisce I'm terribly late for an appointment. Would you excuse me?'

Bowman looked nonplussed, but he gathered himself for a valediction. 'Of course. Keep fighting the good fight.'

Hoste turned to Marita, whose gaze was now on fire with curiosity. He made a signal with his eyes that they should exit, and with some reluctance she followed him out of the cafe. They walked along the street for some moments until she angled her head at him.

'You never told me you worked at a bank. And when were you known as "Edward Eaves"?'

'Back in the thirties. The police were on my case, so I had to drop the name and get another. Like you did.'

'He seemed eager to talk. You rather cut him off.'

'Did I?'

She stopped suddenly on the pavement. 'Yes, you did. I've never seen you so twitchy before.'

He shrugged, meeting her gimlet-eyed gaze. 'I don't know what you mean.'

'Don't lie to me. That man back there – he said he'd never lost an employee to "that lot". Who was he talking about?'

'He meant the Midland. The rival bank to his own. They offered me a job behind his back, and he was sore about it.'

'You were a clerk. Why would he get sore about that?'

He clicked his tongue in impatience. 'I've no idea. Perhaps he thought it reflected badly on him. It was a long time ago.'

She fell silent, and they continued along the street. He could almost hear her mind turning over: he wasn't out of the woods yet. He could curse the terrible luck of it, to have run into him in that cafe at that moment, with Marita of all people ... But at least he hadn't specified who "that lot" was.

'Another strange thing for him to say,' she mused.

'What?'

'Your old boss. As we left he said "Keep fighting the good fight". Why would he say that?'

'We're at war, in case you hadn't noticed,' he said in a tone of weary tolerance. 'People say that sort of thing to one another all the time.'

'Nobody's ever said it to me,' she replied shortly. 'He could have just said goodbye – why that?'

Now Hoste came to a halt. 'I don't know why, and I don't care. He's a bank manager. Why don't you ask him if you're so interested?' He looked again at his watch. A bus had just pulled up at a stop, and he saw his moment. 'I'd better get this. Goodbye. I'll let you know about that pay rise.' He felt the abruptness of their parting, but it was imperative to get away. He stood on the passenger platform as the bus moved off. She stared after him, mute, expressionless, before walking on.

He took the stairs to the top deck and found a seat. He felt himself trembling. He scanned the street behind, checking Marita wasn't doubling back to the Kardomah. He had managed not to panic in front of her, that was something. But had he convinced her? He had feigned nonchalance, then impatience, in trying to cover for himself. He had fooled her for this long; maybe his luck would hold, and she'd forget the whole incident. But he knew that wouldn't be Marita's way.

As the bus chugged by Charing Cross Station he quickly descended the stairs and jumped off. He made for a telephone box in the forecourt and rang Tessa's number at work. She picked up on the fourth ring.

'Tessa, listen to me. I'm in trouble.' He described the accidental encounter with Bowman at the cafe.

'Keep calm. You're not burned yet. What exactly does Marita know?'

'My name. The bank. Nothing else for certain. But she's on to me, I can tell. If she manages to track down Bowman the jig is up. She'll get it out of him in no time.'

'I'll get Bowman called in immediately. We can block that. You're sure that she heard your name?'

'Positive. The bloody fool said it twice.'

'That's a pity.' There was a pause before she spoke again. 'We'll just have to come up with something to allay her suspicions. Let's meet tomorrow morning and work it out. In the meantime, try not to panic.'

In distraction he went out on ARP duty, fire-watching, though the raids had thinned out again. He replayed the scene in his head, wondering how he might have been smarter. Should he have ignored Bowman altogether, or pretended not to hear? He had been so taken by surprise there hadn't been time to measure a response. Had his companion been someone other than Marita he would have tried to head them off, said he would catch them up, dealt with Bowman on his own. But Marita was not easily thrown off. In pursuit she was as keen as a terrier after a rat. He returned to the flat in the derelict small hours, still wondering, worrying.

*

The next morning he was drinking tea in Tessa's office at the Section when the new liaison officer breezed in. Richard Lang was tall, sallow-skinned, straight-backed; his tightly clipped moustache seemed to go with his field-phone brusqueness.

'Heard you've run into trouble. Hammond, what's the latest on the bank manager?'

She glanced across at Hoste before answering. 'We've called him in. He'll be apprised of Hoste's situation regarding Marita. If she does track him down to the bank we've put safeguards in place.'

'Good. So that's one danger neutralised.' He looked to Hoste. 'Think we can contain this?'

'If it were anyone else, yes. But Marita's not like anyone else. Once she spots a weakness she'll go for the kill.'

'The female of the species . . .' Lang said, not noticing Tessa's arched brows. 'Well, we must try to stem the wound. If Marita rumbles it as a sham the entire network might fall – Berlin could get wind that we've been running God knows how many agents. Disastrous timing for the invasion.'

'What would you propose?' asked Tessa.

Lang tweaked his moustache thoughtfully. 'There's one way of taking her out of the picture. Arrest her – she's a menace to national security.'

Hoste shook his head. 'Too risky. If she's arrested now she'll know for certain I betrayed her. Then word will get out that Berlin's spymaster in London is a fake, and every home-grown Nazi will vanish into the woodwork.'

'So you're saying it's as dangerous to arrest her as it is to leave her alone?'

'I'm afraid so,' said Tessa. 'We need to keep Hoste in the field, to reassure Marita and the rest that the Gestapo still has a foothold. His integrity remains the key. If one pearl is false, the whole string is false.'

'Can't say I like it,' said Lang. 'With Operation Fortitude we've launched a hugely elaborate deception on the enemy, in advance of the assault. If we can keep their troops and tanks bottled up in the Pas-de-Calais it would give us time to establish a bridgehead in Normandy. One break in the line and the plan could be up in flames. Are you sure you want to let this woman go?'

Tessa didn't flinch. 'Quite certain. I take full responsibility.'

Lang considered this in silence, then said, 'Very well. Keep me informed.'

When he had gone they talked it over again. They called in Castle to see if he could find a solution, but he tended to agree with Lang: wouldn't it be safer to take Marita out of the equation before she could stumble on Fortitude?

'That would be putting our hand in the hornets' nest,' said Tessa. 'What's required is something to expel *any doubts* on Marita's part that Hoste is the Gestapo's man.'

Castle took out his pipe, and lit it. 'What about forging a letter of personal commendation from the Reich Chancellery? You know, "Keep up the good work", or something.'

Hoste laughed miserably. 'She'd see through it in an instant.'

'I gather she accepted her Iron Cross with alacrity.'

'But she's no fool. The timing alone would look too convenient – just at the moment she begins to suspect me a letter of endorsement arrives from Berlin.'

'What about your other agents – Gleave, for instance? Could he not be induced to vouch for you?'

Hoste made a demurring expression. 'She doesn't trust him; she doesn't trust any of them. To her they're all amateurs, or worse.'

A gloomy silence ensued, until Tessa said, almost to herself, 'There must be *some*one she trusts.'

18

Amy stepped off the tram at the Embankment and crossed the road. She had set out early, though she was not the first to arrive. On the bench, calmly facing the river, sat Tessa Hammond. They were meeting here because Amy had refused her invitation to come to the office; she still had unpleasant memories of the last time. The morning was warm, but the sky had a vast leaden lid clapped over it.

'Hullo, Miss Strallen,' said Tessa as Amy approached. 'It's been a while.'

Amy nodded, and sat down without a word. She pulled off her gloves and gazed out at the Thames, a liquid sludge-grey to reflect the sky.

'How's the marriage bureau?' Tessa began. 'You're still there?'

'It's fine. Shall we just get on with this? I know you haven't asked me here to discuss my career.'

Tessa tilted her chin in acquiescence. 'Just to remind you. You're still bound under the Secrets Act – everything said between us is in strictest confidence.' She waited for another indifferent nod from Amy before she continued. 'We're facing a potential security breach which, if we don't act quickly, could be calamitous. It involves Jack Hoste. We think – we have reason to believe – that his cover is about to be blown. By Marita Pardoe.'

'I see.'

'Did Marita tell you what happened?'

'How do you know Marita and I are still –' She stopped herself; of course they knew; it was their job to know. 'No, she didn't tell me. She doesn't talk about her work, and I don't ask.'

Tessa nodded. 'But you're still close, I believe. You see one another for dinner.'

'Every so often. She's been quite busy of late. What do you want from me?'

A pause followed as Tessa took out a packet of Weights and offered one to Amy. They lit up. 'There's an Allied plan afoot. I can't tell you much. At the moment it's so hush-hush there are government ministers who don't yet know. Suffice it to say an invasion is in the offing. Naturally, the exact location of the assault remains a secret, and no – I can't tell you where it is. But I will tell you that German intelligence has been tricked into thinking it knows.'

'How?'

'Because it believes that the British spy network they operate is reliable. It's not. In fact every single agent they run is one of ours. It's the greatest double-cross in the history of espionage. At a domestic level this is what Jack Hoste has been doing. As long as all the intelligence passes through him, we have the fifth column under our control. But a few days ago he was burned – the word we use when a cover's blown. He happened to run into his former boss who knew that he'd been hired by MI5. By sheer bad luck Marita was with him, and though the conversation wasn't conclusive it was enough to make her suspicious. Since then we've heard that she has been in contact with Abwehr agents – mainly in France and Lisbon. It's touch and go whether she's been voicing her concerns to them. But if Hoste *has* been compromised, it could be disastrous – a domino effect across the whole network.'

It was strange to Amy that she'd not thought about Hoste in ages, and now she'd heard his name mentioned twice within a week. 'I'm sorry to hear it. Does this mean that you'll have to arrest Marita?'

Tessa returned a cool, measuring look that unsettled her. 'No. But it's vital we shore up Hoste's credibility. That means convincing Marita that he is absolutely and unequivocally the Gestapo's man. And we've come up with a plan that might enable it.'

Amy took a drag of her cigarette. 'I'm listening.'

'Please understand that it's a temporary measure. Something to buy him time until the invasion plan is under way.' She paused again. 'So, we give Marita a new angle on Hoste. We insert someone into his life, someone who will confirm to her that he really *is* a Nazi spy. It's a ruse, a huge bluff, but if we have the right person it could work.'

Amy began to grasp her part in the deception. 'You think that person is … me?'

'You're the only one we know whom Marita would trust.'

'Even if that's true, why would Hoste take up with me? Think about it. He's supposed to be an enemy agent. What would possibly persuade him to give away his secrets?'

'You fall in love with one other,' said Tessa without flinching.

Amy choked back a laugh once she realised that Tessa wasn't joking. She took a moment to find her voice. 'We fall in love? That's your idea?'

'It's perfectly plausible. You're both single. You've met before. Marita would be the mutual friend who brings you together. Once you "discover" his other life as a Gestapo agent you will confide it to Marita. Her trust in him will be renewed, and our network will be safe again.'

They stared at one another. Amy slowly shook her head. 'It won't work. I couldn't kid Marita I was in love with him. And I'm certain Hoste wouldn't have a clue about pretending to be in love with me.'

'Miss Strallen. You and I both know how to fake things. We put on fronts, we put on masks, all the time. We couldn't get on with our lives if we didn't. Now, you may tell me that you *won't* do this. But don't tell me that you *can't*.'

'Very well. I won't do this. I find the whole idea absurd, and faintly sickening.'

Tessa made a conceding expression, and waited a beat. 'I understand. In that case I must appeal to your nobler instincts. If we do nothing, Hoste is very likely to be compromised. Once Marita knows for certain he's one of ours, the news will crackle across the wires like lightning. Other agents will be suspected. It could seriously set back the war effort.'

'Don't put this on my conscience,' said Amy coldly. 'I've already been through it with your lot. If you need to get one of your agents out of a hole, best of luck. I'm sure you can dream up another subterfuge. But don't ask me to be part of it.'

She picked up the handbag she had placed on the bench and stood. In front of her the Thames flowed unanswerably on. Her eye caught on a little tug ploughing against the grey tide. Tessa had also got to her feet, and said, 'That's a pity – though he did say it was unlikely you'd agree.'

'I'm surprised he dared to ask. Was this his scheme?'

'No. It was mine. As a matter of fact I had quite a job persuading *him* it might work. He saw no way round the central problem.'

'Which is what?'

'Oh, that you detest him.'

Amy bristled at that, and shook her head in irritation. 'He flatters himself. Actually, I haven't given him a moment's thought. But the answer's still no.'

'Very well. I'll tell him. If you change your mind –'

'I won't.'

Tessa shrugged. 'You know where to find me.'

They held one another's gaze before Amy gave another little lift of her chin in token of farewell, and walked away.

She made her way back to Brook Street in a deep trance of preoccupation. Tessa Hammond's level, self-assured voice was still in her ear. She had been prepared for a surprise when the Section had telephoned her, but this had outstripped her wildest imagining. *You fall in love with one another.* That they had the audacity – the *nerve* – even to ask her! She had only to think of the humiliation visited on her three years ago, him putting her under surveillance, insinuating himself into her life, then pulling the rug away to emerge as a spy ... Whenever she thought of it her innards turned cold. What made them think she would consider helping them now?

Hammond, admittedly, had not seemed put out by her brusqueness; she was a professional to the marrow. The casual, matter-of-fact way she had accepted her refusal was nearly as infuriating as the proposition itself – as though she secretly believed a mere civilian wasn't equal to the task. I ought to have given her a piece of my mind, Amy thought, angrily. How dare the woman parachute into my life like this, asking me more or less to *pimp* myself for them? Good God, I ought to have slapped her face!

By the time she was back in the office, with a cup of tea and a cigarette, calm had returned and her heartbeat was steady. A little perspective on the matter had been gained. Maddening and high-handed as the Intelligence services were, she had to accept that they were up against it, obliged to work in trying circumstances. Trying? 'Life or death' would be nearer the mark. With the war entering a critical stage they were presumably going to do everything in their power to confuse the enemy. And if Marita was as dangerous as Hammond said no wonder they were devising such outlandish schemes to neutralise her. It wasn't as though Amy didn't know how to play along. There were times when she had met Marita in company with men whose fly-by-night air invited curiosity. But whenever she pressed her for information Marita would dismiss these passing strangers as inconsequential, or else would say, 'It's probably better that you don't know.' She also allowed Marita to maintain the fiction that the plentiful funds she always seemed to have derived solely from her 'translation work' for a publisher. In fact, Amy had long known where her friend's weekly stipend was coming from.

A light knock sounded, and Johanna poked her head round the door. 'Everything all right, darling?'

Amy smiled back. 'Yes, why?'

'Oh, I heard you stomping up the stairs before and slamming the door. I thought you might be in a foul mood.'

'I'm fine. A minor annoyance that's been cleared up.'

'Righto. Well, when you're ready, let's go through the latest.'

She promised to join her in five minutes. Another phrase of Hammond's had come back to her in the meantime, when she had openly appealed to her 'nobler instincts'. It was just a way of putting pressure on her, of course: lie back and think of England. But hadn't she already done her bit three years ago when she alerted Hoste to Billy Adair's seduction of Georgie? That tip-off had foiled a bomb plot, as it turned out.

There was no use fretting over it, whatever the rights and wrongs. She had said no, and she meant it.

She hadn't set foot in the Ritz for years, and was struck anew by its extravagant spaciousness, its grand cornices and fawn marble, and the velvety crimson carpet she could feel through the soles of her shoes. The management had been determined to keep the war strictly outside its doors, for no spectre of the ration intruded on its table d'hôte or its cocktail list; if you ignored the distant wail of sirens and concentrated on the lounge pianist tinkling through Cole Porter you could imagine yourself back in 1934, or even 1924.

Under the dimmed lights of the bar it took her a split second to recognise Bobby, whose face seemed to be missing some vital element of old. Yet the blue serge of her WAAF uniform and the beaming grin assured her that this was indeed her dear pal, and they hugged one another with fierce tenderness. Of course it was perfectly obvious to her now what was different.

'You're not wearing glasses!'

Bobby fluttered her eyelashes coquettishly. 'Contact lenses, darling. Just had them fitted today at a place on Weymouth Street.'

Amy stared at her, disconcerted by the estranging naked-ness of Bobby's face. Without her spectacles she seemed oddly vulnerable, and younger. Or was it older? She couldn't tell. It would take a little adjustment, and meanwhile Bobby was gaily racing on about her mysterious new 'lenses'. 'I happened to catch my reflection in a shop window and almost shrieked! Honestly, I don't think I'd ever properly *seen* myself before. Who's that creature with the gigantic noggin, I thought, and why is she slouching like that?'

Amy laughed, and blinked. 'They make you look so ... *young*,' she said, grasping the word in the nick of time.

'Do they?' she squealed in delight. 'Well, that's something, because they're *hell* to wear. It feels like I've got two great goldfish bowls clamped over my peepers.'

The Ritz was Bobby's choice, as of course were the reckless martinis which had just arrived. With her first cold sip Amy felt a renewal of confidence and a wild little surge of fondness. Bobby Garnett – no one apart from her mother ever called her Roberta – was in fact her oldest friend; they had been at school in London together, and though their paths had diverged a bond of almost glandular tenacity had held fast. The Garnetts were an aristocratic family – the sort that never had much money – and Bobby grew up with one foot in the world of giggling debs and house parties, the other in a rackety milieu of dismal bedsits and pawned jewellery. Her voice, which Amy loved, was a husky drawl that always sounded on the edge of laughter, as if she had just stepped out of a Coward play. Bobby had some talent for writing and drawing, though she barely made a living from either. Before the war she had dabbled, illustrating for fashion magazines, learning to paint at evening classes, working at Liberty as a buyer in the ladies' department, this last only because it earned her a discount on clothes, which she adored above all things. Even in her WAAF serge she looked chic.

'I bought it at Gieves,' she explained, 'and made a few alterations. I couldn't bear to be dowdy, even in a uniform.'

On joining up Bobby had been posted to the RAF station at Inverness, a place she admitted she had never heard of till that moment.

'How is it there?'

'Well, it's perked up a bit since I last saw you. There are dances again, and with all the ships coming in we can usually depend on company.'

'I seem to recall you were stepping out with someone ...'

'Er ... the Norwegian? That came to nothing. I've been seeing the captain of a Dutch freighter. And last week I met the sweetest young Scots chap, Mungo, who took me out on a shoot. Though of course I was *terrified* by the noise of the guns. You remember as a girl I used to leave tea parties for fear of the crackers? Anyway, next thing he's going to teach me is the Highland fling.'

'Gosh – lowlands *and* highlands. You run quite a broad church,' said Amy, raising an eyebrow.

'Oh yes. All denominations welcome ...' And at that she began a more detailed account of what had been happening romantically, acting out scenes in an expert repertoire of different voices and gestures, then switching back to her own ironic commentary. From another, such monologues might have been insufferable, but Bobby's natural drollery and self-mocking instincts were only endearing. It was the way she played both the stooge and the narrator in the hilarious shambles of her life that captivated Amy. Another round of cocktails came and went before Bobby allowed a hiatus in this part of the evening's entertainment.

'Anyway,' she said, squinting over her glass at Amy, 'you're looking ever so *femme du monde*, I must say. That dress is divine. How's the matrimonial business?'

'Oh, rolling along. Did I tell you we're expanding to the provinces? Jo has just negotiated the lease on a place in Bristol.'

'Good heavens! Who knew there were so many lonely hearts out there? Well, you two did, obviously.'

'We celebrated our fifth anniversary the other week. It's funny, d'you remember that summer when war was coming, we were convinced the numbers would dry up and the bureau would have to close? And then business just took off – tripled, in fact.'

Bobby shook her head wonderingly. 'I suppose there's nothing quite like tying the knot to take one's mind off being bombed into smithereens.'

'I think it made people feel a bit safer. Like a charm against misfortune.'

'Either that or they're terrified of being alone. A friend of mine in the WAAF – Flora – told me about a chap who declared out of the blue he was madly in love and wanted to marry her. She'd only known him a couple of months. Well, she took him back home to dinner, just to test the water. Do you know what he did? Talked to the mother all evening, and more or less ignored Flora until she'd gone to bed! – can you imagine?'

'Don't tell me she married him ...'

Bobby closed her eyes and shuddered. 'Heavens, no. Even Flora's mother – who's rather grand – thought he was a twit. The next day she said, "If that is being in love, the condition has *greatly* altered since I was young."'

A few moments later she glanced at her watch. 'Now, we'd better get cracking.'

'What's the rush?' asked Amy.

'Darling, I've only got a forty-eight, and I intend to squeeze every last drop out of it. I've reserved a table for us at Quo Vadis – so drink up!'

Over dinner Bobby's natural urge to gas relaxed, and by degrees she encouraged Amy to talk more expansively. Amy ate little but drank a great deal, which she felt she'd been doing quite often of late. Wasn't everyone drinking more now? Having performed the comedy of her recent romantic misadventures, Bobby was bright-eyed with curiosity as to what she herself had been 'getting up to'; Amy's shrugging replies couldn't help sounding, in contrast, rather wan. She told her about being introduced at the anniversary party to Captain Bellamy, and his gallantry in walking her home, but she baulked at recalling those forlorn words she had spoken in reply to his humorous sally.

'You mean, you didn't even ask him in for a nightcap?' said Bobby, her face creasing in disappointment.

'I was awfully tight. The poor man almost had to hold me upright.'

'Hmm. I dare say he was hoping to hold a lot more besides. Really, darling, what *are* we going to do with you?'

Amy sighed, and sensed the alcohol loosening her guard. Before she could prevent herself she said, 'You know, Bobs, I sometimes wonder if I'm capable of real love.'

Bobby stopped drinking mid-gulp. 'What on earth d'you mean?'

'I don't know. Oh, I can do all the flirting and chatting and making myself agreeable, that's just instinct. But I hardly ever feel – you know – a real passion. I don't know what it is to be *carried away*.'

'But you've been out with heaps of men. They can't all have been duffers.'

'No, they weren't,' said Amy quietly, 'but that's not the point. Some of them I really liked, and I was sorry when it ended. But when I look back I'm not sure if I can honestly say I was in love. With any of them.'

Bobby retracted her chin sharply. 'That can't be true. What about Mark? And Graham? You were with him for ages –'

'Don't, please, Bobs. Don't go through them all. I couldn't bear it.'

They fell into a silence, lost for the moment in their own thoughts. Amy looked down at her dinner, some sort of fish, almost untouched. She couldn't quite remember ordering it. She signalled to the waiter for another drink. Across the table Bobby was staring at her, perplexed. The turn of the conversation had suddenly knocked the wind from her sails.

The waiter had cleared their table before she spoke again. 'You said "hardly ever" just now.'

'What?'

'You said you'd hardly ever felt passionate. Which suggests that you *have* felt it at some point.'

Amy frowned at the quibble, and seemed to dismiss it. But Bobby's enquiring gaze was like a door held open, waiting for an answer. 'A while ago, I thought – I got to know someone, but no –'

'Who?'

'No one. It was no one. I'd made a mistake, that's all.'

Another round of drinks arrived, which provided Amy with an opportune moment to drop the subject altogether.

Later, a taxi took them from Soho to Queen Anne Street. Bobby was staying the night, and once they entered the front room of Amy's flat she almost hurled herself onto the couch. It was half past midnight, and though both of them were, as Bobby put it, stinko, Amy went off to fetch the gin. A nightcap wouldn't make any difference in their state. When she returned from the kitchen she found Bobby hunched over her kitbag, rummaging for something.

'Here,' she said, drunkenly handing over a brown paper bag. Amy, puzzled, opened it to find two pairs of silk stockings and a bottle of Helena Rubinstein Apple Blossom perfume.

'Oh, Bobs,' she said, tearing open the latter and spritzing her neck with the scent. 'You're such a dear.'

All sorts of contraband came Bobby's way, mainly off the boats; she called them the perks of the port. 'Here's how,' said Amy, handing her a tumbler of gin, and they clinked. The room, lit only by a tiny corner lamp, was steeped in shadow. As Amy fixed the blackout curtains against the window she recalled a song from earlier in the evening, 'Love for Sale', and began singing softly. Bobby joined in.

She went to fetch blankets and a pillow for Bobby, whose voice she could hear running down like a used battery. The overnight train from Inverness and the evening's booze had done for her. Amy made the bed around her friend's slumberous form and tiptoed out.

In her own bedroom she staggered a little as she got undressed. Before she put out the bedside light she remembered the letter she had picked up in the hallway on their return. She got up and retrieved the crumpled thing from her coat pocket. It had been hand-delivered, just her name typewritten on the envelope. She unfolded it and read:

Dear Miss Strallen,
  I know from Tessa Hammond that you rejected the idea put to you some days ago. Would you reconsider

if I explained to you personally why it matters? Please understand that I would not bother you with this were circumstances not of the most urgent sort.

My number is appended below. I do hope to hear from you.

Sincerely,

J.H.

19

Amy closed her front door and turned up the street. The morning had a bright little snap to it. She had seen Bobby off the night before at Euston, having spent the Sunday crushed beneath a colossal hangover. She felt a little fogged even now, and at first didn't notice the shadow drawing alongside her.

'Miss Strallen.'

She nearly jumped. Jack Hoste had abruptly fallen into step with her. He hadn't changed much since they'd last met: the pale, appraising eyes, close-cropped hair, the face, perhaps gaunter, giving nothing away. Still the same watchful saturnine air of a man who haunted places, and people.

'How long have you been waiting there?' she said, feeling no obligation to offer pleasantries, or even a greeting.

'Not long. You read my note?'

'I did, and I'm still pondering it. I didn't expect to have to answer you immediately.'

Hoste nodded. 'I'm sorry, but events have made it impossible to extend you more time. I need a decision from you directly.'

She bristled at his peremptory tone. The arrogance of these people was staggering. 'You said something about urgent circumstances. What's going on?'

'Since Hammond spoke to you there's been a development. Marita has contrived – I don't know how – to bring something new into play. Some*one* new. D'you mind if we stop for a moment?'

They were in Cavendish Square, facing the shattered premises of John Lewis. She glanced at her wristwatch. 'I'm on my way to work.'

'Please,' he said, gesturing to a bench. There was little traffic about. With a reluctant air she sat down. He offered her a cigarette, which was refused.

'I should say straight away that the plan Hammond dreamed up is absurd. You won't persuade me otherwise.'

Hoste inclined his head provisionally. 'I must try nonetheless. Speaking in general terms, you know there's to be an Allied invasion. German intelligence thinks it knows where they are to strike. In fact they have been foxed, the result of a long campaign of deception on the part of our agents. Everything has worked, until now.'

'Marita.'

He nodded. 'She's this close to finding me out. We've had recent intelligence that an Abwehr agent – a real one – may be in London. His name's Heinrich Brunner, one of their top men. We think he's been smuggled in. Marita knew him before the war.'

'If he's the real thing, won't he know that you're not?'

'Not immediately. My story was always that Heydrich recruited me personally. He was assassinated two years ago, so there's no way of proving he didn't. I can keep Brunner at bay if I have to. It's Marita who's the danger. The accident of running into my old bank manager has torn it.'

Up to this point Amy had fixed her gaze straight ahead while they talked, unwilling to distract herself by having to face him. Now she turned her head slightly, sensing the approach of the conversation's crux. It was unavoidable.

'How do you suppose she would be taken in by ... the two of us?'

Hoste, jolted by her sudden directness, considered. 'If we set it up carefully, she would have no reason to suspect. She trusts you – I know, because she's talked to me about you.

As soon as our, um, relationship is established, she'll start to press you for information. And you'll be ready to tell her –'

'– that you're the Gestapo agent you always claimed to be. But where does that get us? Wouldn't Marita expect me to turn you over to the police as a spy?'

He shook his head. 'You're overlooking the vital element. A woman in love wouldn't betray her man.'

'Not even if he were a Nazi?'

'Not even then. Besides, we only have to maintain the pretence until the Allies' assault is under way. If we can keep Marita quiet all's well.'

'Put like that it sounds quite straightforward.' She shifted on the bench and looked out at the square.

'It will be far from straightforward. It might even be dangerous. Believe it or not, that's why I hesitated to ask you.'

'Ah. According to Hammond, you hesitated for a different reason.'

'I have no illusions as to how you regard me. But when I thought it about long enough I became convinced you were right for it.'

'How so?'

'First of all, I knew from the Adair business that you had the nerve. And second –' the ghost of a smile passed over his face – 'who's more qualified for the role than a professional matchmaker?'

She was silent for a long time. There was nothing she liked about this; it seemed to her a desperate and seedy hoax. She quailed at the very idea of trying to fool Marita. And yet the memory of what he had done that night of the Blitz was still alive in her. He had put his body in the way of a blast – had perhaps saved her. He might have used that debt of gratitude as a bargaining chip, yet he had never once mentioned it. She found herself staring absently at the sleeve of his jacket; a button was missing from its hole, and another was hanging by a thread. She thought he probably wouldn't know how to sew.

'How would it work?' she said presently. 'I mean, how would Marita be persuaded that we just … happened to meet?'

He lifted his gaze to the sky to hide the sweet bite of relief. She had thrown him a lifeline. 'Leave that to me.'

'What on earth did you say to her?' asked Tessa. He had called at her office with the news.

'I simply told her the truth. If Marita were to rumble me the whole thrust of Fortitude might be jeopardised.'

'But I told her that, and she still wouldn't budge. You must have some kind of hold on her.'

He shook his head. 'I don't think so. Maybe she felt sorry for me.' Having not seen her in years he was privately taken aback by the feeling she had revived in him. Her features seemed more vivid, her manner more decided, than that of the pale simulacrum he had carried in his head. Her sweetness in repose still affected him painfully.

'And what about – the drinking?' Tessa broke in.

'She looked a bit hung-over. I don't think it's a concern.'

'You should have seen the bar bill she and her friend ran up in that restaurant. I'm pretty sure her hands were trembling when I met her.'

'Look, she couldn't do her job if she was a lush. She likes a drink, and with things the way they are I don't blame her. Anyway, I hardly need remind you this thing was *your* idea.'

'I know. And I hope we don't live to regret it.'

The Luftwaffe raids had died away, and April drifted into May. For those who knew what was coming the atmosphere in London had thickened with omen, yet outwardly all was humdrum. Theatres were quiet, restaurants half empty. The broad, obscuring sprawl of the city felt to Hoste like a warren, a jumble of dilapidated houses and basements – hiding places – from which people stolidly emerged, absorbed the daylight, then disappeared into again. Public shelters at night breathed out a stale, fetid air. He seemed to hear a single question in the chattering of birds, in the rumbling of rails over points: How much longer? How much longer?

He had telephoned Marita to arrange their usual meeting, and suggested the Lyons Corner House at the foot of Tottenham Court Road. It had recently come to her notice that the family who ran Lyons were Jews, and she disliked anything that might help 'swell their coffers'. But to his surprise she made no objection. The Section had not been able to establish whether Heinrich Brunner, an agent based in Lisbon, had made contact with her. In the present uncertainty between them he wasn't sure if raising the matter with Marita might be too risky. Since the incident at the Kardomah, every remark had to be measured with care; he could not afford to make another creak on the floorboard.

The Lyons was nearly full at this hour. Marita was seated, characteristically, with her back to the wall, allowing her an unimpeded view of entrances and exits alike. She greeted him with a sarcastic smirk.

'Why, if it isn't Eaves, the bank clerk,' she said as he pulled up a chair next to her. 'Tell me, do you ever hanker for the old days?'

'Not at all. It was as tedious a job as I ever did.'

'And yet after that you went to work for the Revenue. From one counting house to another.'

Hoste shrugged. 'Steady Eddie.'

They ordered tea from the aproned Nippy and got down to business. From her intelligence – wireless intercepts, spy reports – the Allies were in the final stages of their plan to breach the Atlantic Wall. Preliminary attacks would be launched on the south-west coast of France, near Bordeaux, and another on the coast of Norway. A third would target northern France. This last, Marita said, would be the crux of the entire invasion. But it was still not clear where precisely they intended to land.

'My lot still believe it's Calais,' said Hoste. 'There could be no other reason to amass so many troops in Kent.'

Marita pulled a sceptical expression. 'There *could* be another reason, as I told you. The build-up may be a diversionary tactic. Imagine yourself an Allied leader. Wouldn't you want the German high command to assume your forces would make the shortest crossing? Then surprise them with a different point of attack?'

'Surprise is a useful weapon,' he conceded. 'But like all weapons, it's liable to backfire. A longer crossing involves a larger risk.'

Casually inspecting her nails, Marita said that she had a significant new tip-off, in such a way that prompted Hoste to fish a little.

'More intercepts?'

'I believe this one's straight from British intelligence. There's someone on the inside who's passing information.'

'To Berlin?'

She shook her head. 'To the Russians. By chance an Abwehr agent happened upon it. The Allies have two operations running in parallel. One is the real invasion plan – the other is a fake.'

'Are you sure?'

Marita stared at him. 'Sure? Of course not. One must always remember there are people working night and day out there to mislead and deceive. Doubt isn't just an instinct – it's a talent. If you're not doubting, you're not thinking.'

Hoste held her gaze. 'So which one do *you* think is the fake?'

She looked at him as though his question was as idiotic as the previous one. Their order had arrived. Hoste leaned back in his chair and took out a cigarette. Marita had been surveying the room with indifference when she suddenly jerked to attention. Slowly, with a frown, she raised her hand in greeting: Hoste looked round at the woman approaching their table.

'Someone you know?'

She returned a quick affirmative with her eyes. He watched her as she composed her features in preparation, and detected a flicker of reluctance. The surprise encounter had begun.

'Amy – hullo,' she said.

'Fancy running into you here,' said Amy with an uncertain smile. 'I thought you didn't like these places.'

Marita turned to Hoste. 'This fellow chose it.' There followed a momentary exchange of glances, which obliged Marita to step in. 'I believe you two have met before – Amy Strallen – Jack Hoste.'

They faced one another. From this instant they would be under her scrutiny.

'How d'you do?' said Hoste. 'I once came to your office – perhaps you remember ... ?'

Amy squinted at him. 'Yes. A few years ago. The tax inspector?'

'You have a good memory. Do you still go to the lunchtime concerts at the National?'

'I haven't been in a while. Work and such – you know ...' She looked from him to her, puzzled. 'But how did you two – ?'

'You may also recall putting us in touch over Bernard's tax affairs,' said Marita. 'A confusion about arrears. Well, we met, we became – friendly.' Hoste heard the minute hesitation, and smiled to himself. The word *friendly* had never sounded less sincere. She would rather have swallowed poison than call him a friend.

'Why don't you join us?' said Hoste, pulling out a chair in invitation.

She did so, and for the next half-hour they put on a show of reacquaintance, both working from a long unscripted rehearsal of the day before. Hoste couldn't help being impressed by her. No actress could have done a more natural job of taking her cue (his lighting a cigarette) or of pretending surprise at their meeting. She was not word-perfect – she seemed halting and bemused – and sounded more convincing because of it. He stole an occasional glance at Marita, and felt himself begin to breathe more easily. Beyond her initial reluctance she appeared to have taken the encounter in her stride.

Just as Amy was about to leave them Hoste mentioned, in an offhanded way, that he had a spare for one of Myra Hess's concerts the following week. Perhaps she would care to join him – work permitting? Again, her hesitation, and the demure smile that followed it, was perfectly judged. He told her the date, and the time the concert would start.

'Thank you,' said Amy. 'I shall look forward to it.'

Afterwards, outside the cafe, Marita seemed thoughtful. Cabs and buses rumbled by, and Hoste waited for her to speak.

'She liked you. Did you notice?'

'I liked her,' said Hoste, shrugging. 'Though I'd rather forgotten her. Didn't you once think she was – ?'

'One of us? Briefly. When we were in Germany together, years ago, I thought she might be recruited. But I misjudged her. It turned out she had no interest in politics at all.'

They had begun walking down Charing Cross Road, neither speaking until Hoste turned to her. 'So you didn't mind that I invited her to a concert?'

'Why should I?' she said shortly. 'You're both adults. Amy's been on her own for a long time. She appreciates company.'

Hoste waited a beat. 'Have you heard from Bernard recently?'

'A letter, a few weeks ago. He'll be stuck there until the war ends. Why do you ask?'

'Just what you said, about being on your own. You and he have been separated for years. It must be hard.'

'I can live with it. Others can't.'

He might have known she wouldn't respond to sympathy. He sometimes wondered if there was any softness in her at all.

20

As the Mendelssohn gathered to its conclusion he shot a sideways glance at her. Amy, absorbed in the music, reminded him of a devotional painting in which the sitter might have been transported by the voice of the Divine Himself. The penny programme in her lap had gone unremarked, whereas he had been turning his over distractedly, trying to concentrate. He had suggested that their 'romance', however counterfeit at heart, should bear all the outward appearance of authenticity. So they should behave and talk as though they had just been reintroduced and were eager to create a good impression. 'We have to act as if we're being watched,' he said responsibly, and she nodded her agreement. But it had become apparent from the moment of their staged encounter at the Corner House that he had nothing to teach her. The paradox needled him: she was a natural when it came to faking it.

They came down the steps of the gallery into an afternoon of benign spring gaiety. Trafalgar Square, thronged with promenaders, seemed to have taken a leap back to the pre-war days of uninhibited leisure. Amy threaded her arm through his and briefly pressed herself to his side. He felt somewhat awkward as they walked on.

'What a smashing concert,' she said, with a little laugh. 'Thank you for asking me.'

'A pleasure,' he replied automatically. After a few moments he added, 'I meant to say, that was a very convincing performance of yours at the Corner House. I think Marita bought it completely.'

She waited a moment before answering. 'I hope she did. I've always had the sense she can tell what I'm thinking. How long do you propose I wait before –'

'Telling her about us? It will have to be soon.'

'I'm meant to be seeing her tomorrow night – a party at her house. She'll ask me about you, I know.'

'So you'll be ready, like you were at the Lyons.'

'It might be easier, now we're over the first hurdle.' She offered him an imploring smile.

'Just don't overdo it,' he said, disengaging his arm from hers. Now she looked crestfallen, and he felt annoyed with himself.

'I'll do my best,' she said quietly. 'But bear in mind I haven't had as much practice as you.'

He winced at the implied rebuke – it was deserved. 'I know you'll do your best. We wouldn't have asked you otherwise.'

They said goodbye, and he watched her walk off with a rankling sense of having affronted her.

Marita's flat was situated above a tailor's on Lamb's Conduit Street. She was on good terms with one of the cutters, who would at short notice run up a smart little jacket for her, or a chiffon blouse. How she could afford such things on clothing coupons Amy hardly knew, and didn't like to enquire – she herself was an occasional recipient of some expensive cast-off. The shop mannequin she had commandeered stood at the entrance to her drawing room with the air of an old retainer waiting to usher you inside.

Marita rarely had people round; it had taken over a year before Amy herself was invited. Tonight's gathering turned out to be a special occasion, a party for one of her Czech cousins who had been seconded to the RAF. The crowd was already lively by the time Amy arrived. She looked around for a face she might recognise, and found none. It was very like the hostess to keep her groups of friends in discrete compartments, where she could control them. Finding herself alone and unattended she shyly steered around the edge of the room, stopping to admire Marita's collection of prints and photographs, the latter exquisitely presented in silvery deco frames. She had paused at a picture of a woman frozen in the arc of a dive – nominally in black and white, but really a study in the nuances of dove-grey, charcoal and cream – when she became aware of two men hovering at her shoulder. One was tall, blond-haired, the other swarthier, with an eager, amused gaze. Both wore the dark blue RAF uniform. The blond one gave a little nod at the photograph.

'Beautiful, yes? We have just been admiring it, too.' His voice carried the faint sibilance of a mid-European accent. He introduced himself as Tomas Vachek – Marita's cousin – and his friend as Adam Pavelec. Amy offered them her hand, mesmerised for a moment by Tomas's pale grey eyes and the jolly pink of his complexion. He had the muscular outdoorsy look of someone who climbed mountains and went rowing.

'Marita must hold you in very high regard,' she said. 'She's not in the habit of throwing parties.'

He gave a quick suave tilt of his head both to acknowledge the honour and to suggest it had been worthily bestowed. Adam was the more talkative of the pair, and Amy took to him immediately. She liked his humorous self-confidence. The pair were on leave for two weeks, it transpired, from a bomber crew stationed up in Norfolk. As he talked about his routine Amy felt suddenly conscious of the shameful business following Munich, the way the government had allowed Germany to ride coach and horses through Czechoslovakia. And yet here were two of their countrymen voluntarily fighting on Britain's behalf. Presumably they were taking their leave while they still could.

She said to Adam cautiously, 'I dare say you'll be rather busy in the coming weeks.'

'We've heard rumours, of course. Perhaps you also?' There had come a sly insinuating note into his voice which she took as another of his mischievous darts; but then when he kept silent she realised he was half serious.

'Oh, nothing in particular. The usual whisperings.' They faced one another like card players, none of them willing to show their hand.

As though accepting her reticence Tomas said, 'I have not visited London in some time. The building damage ... it's very shocking. You have lived through all this?'

She nodded. 'We've taken a fearful battering this year. And yet even that wasn't as bad as the first raids, in '41. It's strange what you can get used to.'

She wanted to know about them – she had never met a bomber pilot before, or in fact any other sort – but at that moment Marita interposed herself. She was holding a bottle of white wine, with which she refilled their glasses.

'I'm pleased you've met,' she said. 'Did you know, Tomas, that Amy is one of my dearest friends? We visited Germany together before the war.'

Amy smiled back, quietly surprised. It was unlike Marita to be demonstrative, though it may have been she was putting on a show for her visiting kinsman. When Tomas heard that they'd been to Nuremberg his expression took a quick animated jump, as if he had just returned from there himself. He asked Amy what she'd made of the place.

'It was handsome,' she replied, and looked to Marita for support. 'Like I imagine Rome might have been once. I don't suppose, since the bombing ...'

Tomas gave a slow philosophical shake of his head. 'Not like Rome now. When you see how many tons of explosive are dropped it seems extraordinary that anything is left standing at all.'

Marita cut in. 'Perhaps during your leave Amy might show you both around town – it's not all cinders and dust.'

'We would be honoured,' said Adam, with a little bow, and seemed about to continue when Marita shepherded them onto another loose knot of guests nearby. She drew Amy away on her own, eager to know how far 'things' had progressed with Hoste.

'We heard a violin concerto at the National, then spent the rest of the afternoon drinking. I have the impression that he's ... smitten.'

'And you?' said Marita, her eyes hooded.

'Well, I rather like him. Though I never imagined I'd have that much in common with a tax inspector ...'

There was a pause before she replied. 'Hmm. You'll find Hoste full of surprises.'

'What d'you mean by that?'

'Oh, just that he may seem rather ordinary, perhaps a little dull, on first appearance. But there's more to him than meets the eye.'

'It's strange that you've kept up with him all this time, yet never said. Would you rather we hadn't met like that?'

'Not at all. But a selfish instinct warned me to keep you apart. If things had gone well he might have persuaded you to leave London with him – it could have been the end of our friendship. I wasn't prepared to allow that.'

'So why now?'

Marita returned an ambiguous veiled look. 'Because I know you well enough to trust you. You and Hoste must do what you will, but the bond between us two I regard as secure. Is that presumptuous of me to say so?'

'No. It's not.'

The expression on Marita's face just then flashed on her memory, returning her to a moment she thought she had discarded, or discounted, years ago. They had been in a hotel room together, in Lancashire, Marita sitting on the edge of her bed one night; she had touched her hair, hadn't she, or stroked it? Some confidence had passed between them, some provisional offer made, which was never mentioned again. It had been a mutually agreed irrelevance once Marita had announced she was getting married. Yes, years ago it was; but not forgotten, perhaps, by either of them.

It had gone eight by the time Hoste reached St James's, and the cleaners had set to work on their nightly trawl through the building. Lamps had been turned low, and a mauve light was decanting itself through the windows on the park side. He poked his head round the door, hoping Tessa might have stayed late, but her chair sat empty. There was no one about.

'Looking for someone?'

It took him a moment to recognise Philip Traherne, silhouetted at a corner desk. He took a few steps into the room.

'What are you sitting in the dark for?'

For answer Traherne held up a small flashlight. 'It saved me putting up the blackout. I've been here reading like a schoolboy after lights out.'

Hoste, adjusting his eyes to the gloom, took a seat at the desk opposite. Traherne's flashlight cut a stripe across the room from where he had set it down. He leaned down and pulled out a drawer.

'Since you're here, fancy a drink?' He had pulled out a bottle of Martell and a couple of glasses. He poured a finger of the brandy and handed it across. Hoste felt the weight of the glass in his hand: only Philip could be relied upon to keep crystal tumblers in the office.

'Cheerio,' said Traherne, squinting over the rim of his glass. 'You have the air of a fellow with something on his mind.'

Hoste took a quick swallow and felt the heat of the alcohol bloom in his chest. 'I saw Marita a few days ago and she let slip something that might be –' He stopped himself as his internal security system pulsed out a warning: he was taking a risk even talking about this. Traherne leaned forward expectantly.

'Something …?'

'She knows about Fortitude and Overlord, if not by name.'

'Ah.'

'Apparently an Abwehr agent in Lisbon picked it up. You'll never guess where it came from.'

Traherne shook his head in puzzlement. In reply Hoste made a little circular movement with his finger, indicating their own building. He tried to gauge his companion's expression in the half-light.

After a beat, Traherne said in a hushed voice, 'Impossible.'

'There's more. Marita said this agent came by it from an intercept – to *Russia*.'

A long silence ensued. Traherne was on the verge of speaking, twice, and hesitated. Walls had ears. But the understanding between them was such that Hoste knew they were pondering the same question. By a minute inclination of his brow Traherne asked it.

'Well, my instinct is to start with the one I know least well,' said Hoste.

Traherne spoke in a guarded undertone. 'Lang.'

He nodded. 'Didn't you think it a bit rum, the way he was just parachuted in on us? We've run the Section tight as a drum for years. Not a single breach, in this office at any rate. But – what? – six weeks after he's joined us we've sprung a leak and Marita's got hold of something that might turn the entire war.'

'Could be a coincidence. I'll sound out Hammond and Castle.' He sighed. '*Quis custodiet ipsos custodes?*' He registered Hoste's blank expression. 'Sorry, I forgot you don't have Latin. "Who will guard the guards?"'

He had gone with Traherne to the pub, and after last orders caught a tram back to Charing Cross Road. There hadn't been a raid for over a month, but the habits of the blackout were by now ingrained. On the lightless streets he moved among people reduced to furtive shadows; it was the sound of footsteps that warned you of someone close. The windows of the bookshop below his flat were shuttered tight as any Bond Street jeweller's.

He had just switched off the wireless, yawning, when he heard the dull ring of his doorbell. Moving to the window he pulled back a corner of the blind and looked down. It was so dark in the court he could barely make out a thing; but then a figure took tottering steps backwards and the pale oval of a face – a woman's – swung up. He descended the stairs to open the door, and there, forlorn and bedraggled, stood Amy Strallen. In the shielded beam of his flashlight he saw that her eye make-up was badly smudged and her hair in disarray.

'Miss Strallen? Are you all right?'

'May I come in?' she asked in a small voice.

'Of course,' he said, standing aside in invitation. He noticed her unsteady gait as she passed him into the hallway. Something was wrong, he could see that. As he led her up the stairs he heard her snuffle, like a cat. Was she drunk?

In the living room he turned on a side lamp, sensing that she wouldn't appreciate the full glare of the overhead light. She really did seem in a state; on closer inspection he saw that her stockings were shredded, and blood was trickling down one knee. 'Good God, what happened to you?' 'Oh, I had a bit of an accident,' she replied, and asked him if he might have some iodine and a sticking plaster. He hurried out to the bathroom to fetch his medicine chest, and on bringing it to her he disappeared again into the kitchen. He didn't have any brandy, but there was a bottle of Dewar's, and he took down a glass.

When he got back to the living room the medicine chest lay open but untouched. Amy sat in the armchair, head bowed. At first he thought she had fallen asleep, but then saw the ghost of a tremble in her shoulders. She was crying, silently, or almost silently – a tiny stifled sob, quick as an intake of breath, had just escaped her.

'You poor lady,' he said, which didn't sound right. 'Amy. Here, down the hatch.' He poured out a tot of the Scotch, but she shook her head.

'I can't. I've been drinking all evening. If I have any more I'll be sick.'

Oh dear, he thought. Perhaps Hammond had it right about her being a hopeless drunk. He knelt before her, peering at her skinned knees, and dousing the cotton gauze with iodine he began, gingerly, to dab at the wounds. She submitted with a sharp hiss of discomfort.

He smiled up at her. 'Do you remember doing this for me that night – during the raid?'

'Of course,' she replied, pleased that he should recall it.

His doing so encouraged her to open up. She had been to a party, and had found herself having a long and intense conversation with Marita about him – Hoste – about whether getting together with him could possibly work. At first she wondered if the prospect annoyed her, since her attitude towards Amy had always been rather possessive. But as they talked, the idea of it grew on her. It was the moment Marita warned her that Hoste might not be quite the man he seemed that indicated her belief in the match – she was preparing her for the revelation of his secret life.

'So, you convinced her,' said Hoste, searching her face.

Amy nodded. 'And I felt such a relief that I immediately started tipping it back. Anyway, I thought you'd want to know how it went ...' In her determination to be responsible she hadn't really considered how drunk she was, and that it would make her journey through the blacked-out streets even more perilous than usual. She was crossing Kingsway when a car loomed up out of the night; she hurried to make the kerb but wasn't properly picking her feet up, and stumbled. She went flying and landed in an undignified heap on the pavement, her knees taking the brunt of it but her hands painfully scraping the flags. The car had driven on, unnoticing. She had limped the rest of the way to his flat.

'It was reckless of you to try and dodge through the blackout.' *Especially in your state*, he might have added. 'But I'm very glad you did.'

She smiled at that, and he acknowledged it with a little lift of his chin. Something occurred to him now; he went to the window and, by a minute degree, peeled back the curtain. The court below was a pool of black, but there, in the embrasure of a shop entrance, he thought he detected a movement, some rearrangement in the play of shadows. She could tell from his tensed position that something had caught his eye.

When he closed the narrow slice of curtain and came back to sit down with her he said, 'I think you've been followed.'

'Oh no,' she groaned, 'I didn't –'

'No, it's fine,' he assured her. 'To have put someone on you means she's fallen for it. That's what we wanted.'

He glanced at his watch, and told her that she should stay put for the night.

'You've been shaken up, there's no sense in your going out again.'

'But I have to get up for work tomorrow,' she protested as he began to prepare the divan in the corner of the room.

'I'll make sure you're up bright and early. The bathroom's all yours.'

When she returned, wearing his dressing gown, he had made up her bed and moved the lamp to within her reach. An instinct of modesty made him look away while she settled herself. When he turned round she had pulled the sheet over herself, her hair unloosed and fanned against the pillow. She looked suddenly girlish, and he perched himself at the edge of the bed like a family doctor.

'How do you feel?' he asked her.

'Oh, a bit sore – you know.' Their low voices seemed to intensify the stifled intimacy between them. 'It was odd, just before, when you said – I'd never heard you call me Amy before.'

'You don't mind? It's a fine name. Amy.'

She liked hearing him say it. 'Should I – may I call you Jack?'

He laid his hand, tenderly, on the outline of her shoulder under the sheet. 'I think you should. Isn't that what people in love would do?'

In the half-light he made out the ghost of a smile on her face. They stared at one another for a few moments, conspirators together. He made a movement towards her, and stopped – but she answered it by leaning forward to touch his lips with hers. The contact seemed so tentative it was as though they weren't really kissing at all. Her heart, which had seemed for so long a dim, shrivelled thing, suddenly inflated.

'Amy,' he breathed, before drawing her towards him.

21

Hoste was walking down Victoria Street, a jacket slung over his shoulder. London was drowning in a heatwave. Office workers were out on their lunch hour, strolling in pairs or else loitering outside pubs, wondering if they had time for another half. He had stopped to gaze in a shop window when a voice called out to him and then seemed to fade. He looked around, catching sight of Tessa Hammond on the open platform of a bus that was going the other way. She waved to him, and he waited until she had stepped off and jog-trotted towards him.

'I was just heading to the office,' she said, coming up, beads of perspiration on her brow. 'Where are you off to?'

For answer Hoste held up his tweed jacket, the one Philip Traherne had lent him years ago, and afterwards told him he should keep. It was still the smartest item of clothing he owned – had ever owned. 'I'm taking it to the Hoffman place over there. It needs pressing, and some repair work.'

Tessa had fallen into step with him. 'Any progress with Amy Strallen?' she said with a sidelong look.

He nodded slowly. 'I saw her last night. She's done all we've asked of her. Marita apparently believes we've fallen for one another.'

'Good girl. We need one more push from her and you're home and dry.'

Hoste made a pained expression. 'I wonder if the pressure is too much for her – she was in a terrible state.'

'Oh no. Drunk?'

'She had been drinking,' he said cautiously, 'but only because her nerves were shot. If you knew what Marita was like you'd understand.'

They had reached the cleaner's and stepped inside, setting off the little bell on the door. An acrid whiff of chemicals permeated the air, and from the recesses of the shop came the gigantic hiss of the steam press. By instinct they dropped their conversation while the man behind the counter took the jacket and wrote out a ticket. It would be ready for him tomorrow.

Back on the street Tessa continued to interrogate him. She'd got it from Traherne that he had mentioned a leak – could it be true?

'It could. Marita told me one of their agents in Lisbon had picked it up by accident – and seemed convinced it had come from MI5. Any ideas?'

'Hundreds of people work in that building. It could be anyone.'

'It would have to be someone with clearance at a very high level. They know about Fortitude and Overlord.'

'That doesn't narrow it down either. There must be dozens of people who've been briefed on that.'

'What d'you make of Lang?'

'You mean, as a colleague? Or a suspect?' said Tessa, and allowed a silent beat to pass. 'I don't know. He doesn't seem the type.'

'Is there a *type* who passes secrets to Russia? I would have thought the great trick of the double agent is convincing everyone of his unlikeliness.'

'Or hers,' she said pointedly. 'Did it cross your mind that perhaps –'

'It might be you? I considered it – for about five seconds. No, Lang would be my steer. For one thing, his arrival here coincided with the first serious breach in years.'

'Isn't that a bit too obvious?'

'Perhaps. But sometimes it's the things staring you in the face that are the hardest to see. I've warned Traherne, as I said. And you should keep your eye on him, if you can.'

They had turned off the main thoroughfare and found themselves in a quiet little court. They could hear the life of the city going on around them, but no one else had intruded on the cloistered charm of the enclosure.

'One other thing,' Hoste went on. 'A few weeks ago I heard that Heinrich Brunner was in the offing. Marita had a plan to smuggle him into London. Since then it's gone rather quiet.'

'You don't think he's in London, surely?'

'Probably not. Gestapo agents have a low success rate in escaping detection, as you know. But this one is said to be exceptional.'

Tessa looked consideringly at him. 'I'll put out a warning. We have people in the field who may know something.'

They walked on and out of the court, then stopped again a few hundred paces from the office. Hoste checked the ticket that was still in his hand. He noticed the date the cleaner had written on it. 1/6/44.

'Would you ever,' he murmured. 'It's June tomorrow.'

'Any day now,' said Tessa, shielding her eyes as she looked at the blameless blue sky. 'Let's hope this weather holds for them.'

Tomas, Marita's cousin, had telephoned Amy proposing a day out with himself and Adam. They couldn't do the weekend, so she arranged to take the Thursday afternoon off. There was talk of a visit to Madame Tussaud's, where they agreed to meet at one. At the last minute Adam had to cry off and – another disappointment – they found Tussaud's closed; workmen were still repairing bomb damage inside. It was a sweltering afternoon, so Amy suggested they go for a walk in Regent's Park instead.

'A pity Adam couldn't join us,' she said as they began making their way up the Broad Walk.

'For you, perhaps,' he replied with a sly smile. 'For me – not so much!'

The innocent flirtation of this both amused and slightly unsettled her. It was possible Marita had failed to inform her cousin that Amy was now 'spoken for', and that advances from interested gentlemen, however flattering, were not quite appropriate. She glanced at his face, noticing again the attractively angled cheekbones and the firm mouth. It would be ironic, she thought, to fall for someone just at the very moment she had committed to pretending she was unavailable. Or was she even pretending any longer? The other night would never have happened had she not agreed to the subterfuge. How funny to have shown up at his flat bedraggled like that, and how little she had suspected what might come of it. She hadn't been able to think of anything else since.

They had strolled towards the lake, and settled themselves on a bench. The warmth of the afternoon had slowed the city's tempo. A mother with two children sauntered past, and Amy overheard her scolding the younger one in a heated whisper: 'I told you, you should have gone before we came out.' She smiled, and turned to Tomas to see if he'd heard, too, but he was busy searching for matches and his cigarettes. He offered one to her. The sun, bright all morning, had become quite fierce.

'Flaming June,' she said, squinting into the sky.

Tomas looked at her. 'What is that?'

'Oh, just an expression. "Very hot." It's from a painting, I think, by – someone or other. Bobby would know.'

'Bobby – is your brother?'

She laughed. 'No, Bobby's a woman. Roberta. She knows a lot about painting. She's rather a good artist herself.' He nodded, expelling a lazy plume of smoke, and she added, 'She's in the WAAF now.'

'The WAAF?'

'Women's Auxiliary Air Force,' she replied, and he gasped out a laugh, covering his embarrassment: he hadn't recognised the acronym. She asked him about his life before the war. He had been a student in Prague, and was training to be an architect when the Nazis arrived. He and some friends had managed to get out before the arrests started; he'd gone to Paris, lived there till 1940 and then escaped to England. He had trained as a pilot in Scotland. Amy asked him what it was like to fly missions, but he shook his head.

'Enough. I want to know about you. Marita said you work in a "marriage agency" – is that the name?'

She nodded. 'We take on clients and introduce them to suitable partners. They pay a fee to register, and then pay again if they marry someone we've matched them with.'

'And from this you make a life?'

'A living,' she smilingly corrected him. 'Yes, we do. Fingers crossed. You'd be surprised how many people out there are looking for ... someone.'

'There are many lonely people,' said Tomas, implying that he was not surprised at all.

'That's true,' she replied.

'And you? Marita said you have met a "very nice fellow".'

Her laugh hid a muddle of tenderness and doubt. 'Yes, I suppose he is. His name's Jack. I met him first by chance, years ago. He knows Marita quite well.'

She glanced up at Tomas, who was attending to this with keen curiosity. She wondered if he was the sort who regarded a woman's unavailability as a challenge. The sun's glare was making her woozy; if she wasn't careful it might boil her head, like an egg.

'Shall we find somewhere a little cooler?' she said suddenly.

Tomas suggested they should go for something to drink. Once they reached the shade of the grand plane trees lining the Broad Walk her relief was palpable. The cafe was closed, however, so they walked on. As they emerged from the park and crossed the road, he briefly took her arm – a protective reflex that charmed her. At the top of Mornington Terrace they found a pub still serving the lunchtime crowd. Amy went off to the ladies while Tomas waited at the bar. In the mirror of the tiny WC she checked her face, flushed from the heat; her dress clung damply to her back. She seemed to be undergoing her own personal heatwave. She ran her wrist under the tap and held it against her forehead. That felt better.

On returning to the lounge she saw Tomas talking to a little knot of soldiers at the bar. Spotting her across the room he gave a nod and broke away from them. He set down their drinks on the dimpled brass table – a lime cordial for her, a lager for him. Over his shoulder she noticed one of the soldiers gazing at them, openly, until he caught Amy's eye and turned back to his fellows.

'Been making friends?' said Amy, gesturing with her eyes.

Tomas, in the middle of taking a long gulp, made a wry acknowledgement. 'They are on forty-eight hours' leave. That means – well – something is going to happen, and soon. I asked them where they are stationed, but of course they would not tell me. Careless talk!'

'I'm amazed you dared to ask,' said Amy, accepting a light for her cigarette.

He shrugged, and took a meditative drag on his Player's. 'Even if they had told me it may not signify anything. Perhaps they are part of the decoy operation. You have heard of it?'

She shook her head. It was safer to deny particular knowledge, even though 'everyone' knew an invasion was coming. Months of rumour had prepared the way. She glanced over at Tomas: presumably he and his crew at the RAF base had already been briefed on their own part in the plan; and his admission that he would be back on duty this weekend indicated that the time was nearer than she thought. Maybe nerves had prompted his question. So much hinged on the coming days. What had seemed a distant possibility for so long was about to take real, mortal form. When she had asked Hoste the other night if the Atlantic Wall could be broken he had replied, simply, 'It must be.'

Tomas was encouraging her to have a beer, but she stuck with the cordial: she had been drinking a lot lately, and something warned her she ought to keep a clear head. She watched him at the bar, among the soldiers again. Did she imagine it, or were they somewhat stand-offish with him now? – perhaps they didn't take kindly to his foreign accent, or to his RAF uniform. She experienced a quick dagger-stab of sympathy.

'Everyone's being tight-lipped about it,' she said consolingly, as he set down her drink. He looked at her, not understanding. 'I mean, about Fortitude.'

As soon as the word was out of her mouth she wanted to call it back. What was she thinking, dropping code names into a pub conversation? She looked away, thinking it might not have registered with him. When she lifted her gaze he was staring at her.

'"Fortitude",' he repeated quietly. 'What do you mean by that?'

'I meant about the need for it,' she said, despairing of her bluff. 'Grit. Or "pluck" as we say in English. D'you know that word?'

He shook his head. He seemed distracted, as though something was nagging at him. She couldn't tell what it might be. Presently, Tomas looked at his watch. He rose, explaining that he had promised he would ring Marita at some point in the afternoon – she wanted to know his plans for the evening. He winked at her before he went off in search of the pub's telephone.

When he had gone she allowed herself to breathe again: she had got away with it. But how foolish to have nearly given the game away! *Vigilant at all times* – that was the rule, even among those you could count as friends. Thank God she had only let it slip in front of Tomas. Had it been Marita the mistake might have had consequences ... She had been so preoccupied that she hadn't noticed his return. He was beaming.

'You must drink up,' he cried, quickly downing his beer. 'Marita has organised a trip for us!'

'What? Marita has – ?' She had not prepared for this.

'Yes. I asked her what was happening and she refused to tell me. But she said "Make sure Amy comes with you!"'

Amy looked at her watch. 'I don't know. I have things to do later ...'

But Tomas would not accept excuses. They were going to have a 'jolly time', he said, and Marita had insisted that she join them. He hurried her out of the pub and onto the street, overriding her objections. What on earth had she planned – and why could it not wait? A taxi was approaching, and Tomas let go of her arm to flag it down.

It had come to a halt, its engine throbbing expectantly.

'Tomas, I really haven't the time –'

'Oh, Amy, please,' he said over her protests. 'Marita will be so angry if I don't bring you with me.'

She could almost believe it. He held the car door open in eager invitation, and with a half-sigh she climbed in.

Across town, Hoste was waiting at the counter of the cleaner's in Victoria Street. The man he had dealt with flapped through the shop curtain, bearing his newly pressed jacket. 'Very nice bit of cloth,' he said, stroking a lapel. He indicated where he had made the repairs: the sleeve button wasn't an exact match, but came near enough. 'Looks good as new,' said Hoste, which drew a quick smirk of satisfaction. As he was about to leave the shop the man called him back.

'These are yours,' he said, handing over a couple of items, one of them a box of Swan Vestas. 'We always go through the pockets before we press 'em,' he explained. 'Them matches could start a terrible fire with the cleaning spirit.' The other thing was a folded slip of paper, which he'd found in the ticket pocket. Hoste examined it for a moment; it must have been put there by Traherne, years ago, and forgotten about. Oh yes, they found all sorts in a gentleman's pockets, the cleaner went on. 'I once found a ring in this gown and handed it to my guvnor. Turned out it belonged to the Bishop of Westminster.'

'That was very honest of you,' remarked Hoste.

'Yeah, well,' the man shrugged. 'I got a commendation for it. Though to be honest with yer, I'd rather have 'ad cash.'

Out on the street Hoste unfolded the paper again. It was a laundry list from the St Ermin Hotel, just round the corner from where he stood – a favourite watering hole of the Section, though it hadn't occurred to him that Traherne might also use the place as his laundry. He was about to discard it when he noticed in the margin a faint pencil-written line of numerals and letters. It looked like a cipher. Was that Traherne's handwriting? He wasn't sure.

He put the list back in the ticket pocket, where it had lain hidden, unremarked. It was only when he was back in the office that he took it out for another look. He would drop it by the cryptanalyst department on his way out.

An hour or so later Tessa Hammond stopped by his desk. She had been running checks on the most recent intelligence they had gleaned about Marita. Much of it had come from conversations between Hoste and Amy Strallen, which he would then write up in a report. The last of them dated from the night Amy had attended the party at Marita's flat.

'There's just one query,' said Hammond, riffling through the pages. 'Strallen says she was introduced to Tomas Vachek, a cousin of Marita's attached to the RAF. We checked the base at Norfolk, and they had no record of him. Then we ran it past every other base in the country. Nothing.'

Hoste stared at her. Tomas – she had mentioned his name that night. He picked up the telephone and got through to her office in Brook Street. Miss Strallen wasn't in, said the secretary. He asked to speak to Johanna, who told him that Amy had arranged to take the afternoon off.

'I gather she's meeting her friend's cousin. A chap in the RAF.'

In the cab Tomas at first kept up a stream of talk that seemed as much for his own diversion as for Amy's. He apologised for springing all this on her but Marita's will was not to be defied. 'You know what she's like!'

Amy hadn't heard the address he had given the cabbie but it was clear they were not going in the direction of Marita's flat. They had flashed by St Pancras and King's Cross and were now heading down the City Road towards Old Street. At one moment she glanced at Tomas, quieter now, his expression grimly focused on the gaunt, troubled streets. Shoreditch: unknown territory. Amy wondered now if she had been too compliant with him. She didn't even know this man.

A few minutes later the taxi made a signal and turned right into Curtain Road. It deposited them at the cobbled entrance to a courtyard, inside which an old red-brick paperworks was situated. Tomas paid the driver, then indicated that Amy should follow him. They entered the building, echoing and seemingly derelict, and began to ascend the wide stone staircase. On the second floor they found an office, barely furnished, wooden laths exposed in the wall. Through the far door was a small kitchen and an even smaller bathroom, which showed the rumpled evidence of previous occupants. The desperate shabbiness put her on guard.

'What on earth is this place?' she asked him. 'Who lives here?'

Tomas ignored her, and went around checking the windows. She thought he was going to open them – it was warm in there – but it seemed he wanted them kept closed. At length he said to her, 'Have a seat.'

She looked at him. 'I will once you tell me what we're doing here.'

'All in good time,' he said, and consulted his watch. His manner was no longer one of smiling flirtation; a brusqueness had replaced it. She had an instinct to walk out and leave him to it, but at that moment a slammed door was heard down below, then footsteps hurrying up the stairs. Tomas strode to the door and opened it in time to welcome Marita, whose expression was one Amy hadn't seen on her in a while: her eyes were dark with fury.

She stared hard at Amy before addressing her cousin. 'Why have you brought her here?'

'Because, my dear lady, she *knows*. You will perhaps find this hard to believe, but you have been taken in.'

Then another grim astonishment leapfrogged that one: she and Tomas began talking, angrily, in German. Amy felt a sudden hollowing-out inside her chest. She looked to her friend. 'Marita. What's going on?' Her voice sounded small, and anxious.

Marita shook her head, slowly, sadly. 'Amy ... I cannot believe this. I cannot believe it – you, of all people.'

'Believe what, for heaven's sake?'

Tomas interposed himself. 'That you have been in conspiracy with Hoste – not, as Marita has long supposed, an Abwehr spymaster, but an agent of MI5.' Amused, he turned from her to Marita. 'Look how white she has gone! The game is up, Miss Amy Strallen.'

Amy stared back at him. She briefly recalled his not knowing what the WAAF was, and the hostility of the soldiers in the pub. 'Who are you?'

He returned a pitying look, and glanced over to Marita. 'Who am I? Only now do you think to ask the question! Obersturmführer Heinrich Brunner of the Gestapo. I am here by invitation of Marita, though of course I can hardly introduce myself in polite society.'

At that she looked in appeal to Marita and saw in the bareness of her gaze the knowledge that Amy had played her false. The air between them seemed to bristle with questions – How had it happened? At whose instigation? How long had she been in cahoots? Underneath her fear Amy felt a thin cold trickle of shame, because she knew Marita had trusted her.

Brunner continued. 'I wasn't sure of your involvement until you let slip the code name. The word has been coming up on the wires these last weeks, always the same. Fortitude. *Fortitude*. We want to know what it means.'

There was a pause before Marita said, 'There's no use in asking her. How could she possibly know?'

He frowned at this. 'On the contrary, there is an absolute necessity in asking her. MI5 has been issuing a lot of noise about the invasion. Our intelligence indicates there is a dummy plan – we think it may be known as Operation Fortitude. Hoste knows of it. Therefore *she* knows of it.'

'It doesn't follow –'

Brunner interrupted her in another guttural blast of German, at the end of which Marita sullenly backed away, as if washing her hands of the matter. In the meantime he removed his RAF jacket and with a short gasping laugh threw it on a chair – that he should have fooled so many. He planted himself squarely in front of Amy.

'So. Miss Strallen. You said before that everyone was "tight-lipped" about Fortitude. What is it? Please don't pretend ignorance.'

Amy swallowed. 'I have no idea –'

'There is talk of landings in Bordeaux, in Norway. Then a third attack directed at the north coast of France. The Pas-de-Calais, possibly. Or Normandy. Which?'

'You're not listening to me. I barely know Jack Hoste.'

His expression was sceptical. 'You know him well enough to stay the night in his rooms.' He glanced at his wristwatch. 'There is no more time for bluffing. It would be better for you to speak now –'

'I don't know.'

She seemed to hear the slap before she felt it, his open hand having blindsided her with the speed of a whip. The shock of the blow made her stagger. The room seemed to have tipped sideways.

'I will ask again. Fortitude. What is it?'

She shook her head. 'I can't tell you if I don't know.'

He looked away, disappointed. The second blow sent her sprawling across the floor. The force of it had stunned her, and she whimpered as Marita helped her to her feet. She scolded Brunner, who shook his head as he left the room. From the bathroom came the sound of a tap being run.

In a hushed, urgent voice Marita said, 'Amy, just tell him what he wants. They know already. You're not betraying anyone.'

She looked at her, baffled. 'But I *don't know*, honestly. You think they'd tell me such a thing?'

'It might become very unpleasant for you if you don't,' she said, her face close to Amy's. 'As you can see, Brunner isn't a gentleman when it comes to extracting information'.

Amy's eyes were watering with the pain. Blood was beating in her throat. 'Marita, I'm sorry that I – once I knew about Hoste they didn't give me any choice. I know you hate me for –'

'Shush. I don't hate you. I just want you to tell him – tell us.'

Tell us. And Amy realised: she wants to know as badly as he does. They were working as a pair. This was the technique in action. She tried to think of something she might divulge that would satisfy him – or that would at least make him think twice about forcing it from her. In her mouth she could taste the copper sweetness of blood.

She got to her feet just as Brunner returned, his shirtsleeves rolled to the elbow. He stood in the doorway, hands on hips, his eyebrows raised in enquiry. But Marita shook her head.

'You are merely delaying the inevitable,' he said in a reasoning, almost benign way. 'We will have this information one way or the other.'

He signalled again to Marita with his eyes, then turned away.

'We must get you something to drink,' Marita said, with the half-fearful, half-fascinated air of watching someone on a high ledge, about to jump. Amy allowed herself to be ushered through the door into the kitchen, but had taken only a few steps when she felt from behind his hand locking around her throat, then jouncing her across the room. His grip was intent, and blindingly painful; with his other hand he had crushed her arm up against her back. He was hauling her into the bathroom, its single window clouded and jammed shut. The tub had been filled nearly to the brim.

She heard Marita's intake of breath, and then another shouted exchange. *Was machen Sie?* she cried. Amy twisted about in an effort to free herself, but Brunner kicked out at her ankles and she dropped forward on her knees. She felt something go in her arm. Grasping her head by the hair he plunged her face down into the water. Her panic on swallowing the first cold mouthfuls provoked an animal spasm of resistance, but her rearing up only made him tighten his grip, and she inhaled the drowning flood.

Then he jerked her head back and she was gasping air again, spluttering out the bathwater from her nose and mouth. Her lungs ached with the effort of catching her breath. At her ear came his voice: 'I can stop this right now. Just tell me – what is behind Fortitude? Where will the invasion come?'

Marita's voice rose from somewhere near. 'She *doesn't know*, for God's sake.'

He asked her again, and she shook her head. Before she had time to think she was under once more and staring at the porcelain whiteness below, soundless panicked bubbles escaping her mouth. This time it went on, and she felt her strength start to fade even as she fought against his adamantine hold. Down, down, she seemed to be racing to the bottom of a liquid abyss, beyond help –

When he released her she was almost too exhausted to draw a breath. Slumped against the rim of the bath, she coughed and spat, her lungs clawing raggedly at the air. Brunner, seated on the edge, seemed to be taking a breather of his own. Amy, on her knees, looked round; she saw her through the doorway, her back turned, unable to watch.

'Marita,' she called pleadingly.

Marita moved her head, the merest twitch. But she wouldn't look at her.

'You see, there is no one coming to help you, Amy,' said Brunner, her name sounding a mockery on his lips. He was fixing his sleeve where it had come unrolled. The sporty strength she had admired on first meeting him – when he had been 'Tomas' – now seemed brutish, a means of hurting someone. 'I don't want to continue this. I'm sure that you don't. So kindly tell me what you know, and we can have done with it.'

'He wouldn't tell me,' she half sobbed. 'Hoste. He never would.'

'What? This man you opened your legs for – he tells you nothing?' He was shaking his head, standing up. And without warning he hoisted her upright and thrust her bodily, with a splash, into the bath. The shock of it hadn't time to register before she felt his boot land on her neck, and stay there. Her arms, trapped against the sides, flailed uselessly. Suddenly her head bobbed above the waterline, and she heard Marita beating on his back with her fists. *Let her go*, she screamed. But Brunner pushed her off violently, and Amy saw her land with a thump on the floor.

He was muttering to himself in German as he leaned over. 'Still nothing to say?' he asked. A single word was all she could manage – an agonised whisper. *Please*. She tried to catch her breath, before the next one, but it was too late. He met feeble resistance now as he held her under: she had thrashed her way to exhaustion. The world seemed to be detaching itself from her, it was receding, slipping away, away. To die was not so hard.

A deafening crack tore the air, monstrous in the tiny space. The fugue she had sunk into suddenly dissolved – her mind snapped back into focus. After a split-second delay, like a tree just before it topples, his weight sprawled on top of her. A helpless weight. It wasn't until she felt his stillness that she understood. A hand reached down to pull the plug, and water streaked with blood was emptying, eddying around the hole. Then Marita, the revolver still in her hand, was crooking her arms beneath her, dragging her out of the tub. She had a glimpse of Brunner's lifeless body, slumped face down, a dark crimson perforation just below his right ear.

22

Hoste paid off the cab on Curtain Road and bolted into the cobbled courtyard. Pushing through the door he took the stone steps two a time, his heartbeat plunging and racing ahead of him. This was the safe house where he and Marita had first met, back in '41, the time she had tried to call his bluff with the bogus coppers. He had become used to following hunches, but there was no telling with this one. What if he'd got it wrong, and they had taken Amy somewhere else?

Or if he'd guessed right but was too late?

He burst into the office – and halted. Amy sat huddled on a couch in the makeshift kitchen, a blanket around her shoulders. She looked in a terrible state, bruised around her cheeks and throat, her hair stringy and dishevelled. On the other side of the room Marita leaned against the kitchen counter, smoking. There was something in her expression he couldn't read, something beyond the predatory, ironic watchfulness of old.

He detected the sharp stink of cordite in the air, and stepped towards the poky little bathroom. A man in a blue shirt, head pooled in blood, lay lifeless in the tub. He had been shot at close range – one could tell from the powder residue scorched on his neck. He wouldn't have known a thing about it. Hoste paused for a moment, half mesmerised by the squalid scene. It was how he imagined himself being dispatched one day.

'Brunner?' he said, stepping back into the kitchen.

Marita nodded. 'The Gestapo will want to know how they lost one of their most effective interrogators.'

'I'll take care of it,' he replied, and knelt down before Amy. She appeared to be shivering. She flinched in pain when he touched her arm. 'I'm sorry. I'm so sorry.'

She raised her bloodshot eyes to him. Her voice was gluey. 'I was that close to – if Marita hadn't been there –'

He took her hand in his, and gently raised her to her feet. 'Do you feel strong enough to walk? I'm going to take you to the hospital.' But then he saw that Amy wasn't looking at him; she was looking past his shoulder at Marita. She had the revolver trained on both of them.

'*I'll take care of it*. And how do you propose to do that?'

Hoste met her sarcasm with an unintimidated calm. 'Berlin knows the risks. Your involvement won't come up.'

'Let's drop the pretence, Hoste. It's over. Brunner told me who you are.'

'Brunner. The man whose head you just put a bullet through? I'm sorry, but that doesn't sound like someone you trusted much.'

'He was a good agent – one of the best. He simply confirmed what I'd begun to suspect. No one in Berlin has heard of you.'

'Nor would they have done. That's in the nature of being a covert operative. When he recruited me before the war, Heydrich insisted there should be no record of my service – it would be safer that way. Given that every other agent who tried to infiltrate this country was captured, his precaution was sound.'

'And how convenient for you, now that he's dead. If I had undertaken proper checks I might have exposed your little scheme from the start. And I should have listened to Billy Adair. He always thought you were a fake.'

Hoste felt the walls closing in. But he still knew how to bluff.

'Why would I have been paying you – handsomely, for years – if I were not an agent of the Reich? Why would I have risked my life recruiting people if I were not running a fifth column?'

Marita's lip curled in imperious contempt. 'The risk you took was in making me your dupe. Many have tried to get the better of me and ended up paying for it. Your turn has come round.'

She cocked the revolver. Amy, who had been leaning against Hoste, now took a step in front of him. 'Marita. Please. If you ever had any love for me, please don't harm him.'

Marita's face fell in disbelief. 'What are you saying? I just shot a man dead out of love for you. And I did it even after I knew you'd betrayed me.'

'I never meant to, you know that. But with Hoste – I was in love before I knew it. I had to save him, and the only way to do that was to betray you.'

Marita and Amy stood staring at one another, like actors in a play, neither of them sure of their next line. Hoste was too stunned by Amy's words to know whether they were true or not – he hoped they were. The sands of his life had been slipping through the hourglass, narrowing his time. And just when it seemed too late this woman had declared herself to him. He felt an abrupt and agonising tenderness towards her.

'A touching story. Nevertheless,' said Marita, 'he deserves what's coming. Empty your pockets – slowly.'

He tossed onto the table his wallet, a pen, a packet of cigarettes. His gun, in a shoulder holster, came last.

'I believe it's traditional for the condemned man to have a last cigarette,' he said.

She picked up the packet and tossed it to him. He took one out, and she handed a lighter to Amy. 'Light it for him,' she said.

Amy's hand was trembling as the flame touched the tip. It felt like she had lit a fuse. Hoste gazed at Marita through the smoke. 'One more thing. You told me there was someone at MI5 passing information to the Russians. Did you ever find out who it was?'

She snorted a half-laugh. 'Always working . . . I might as well ask *you* about Operation Fortitude. We have much in common,

Hoste, you and I. Deep cunning, a refusal to trust anything or anyone, a fine talent for deception – and a contempt for humanity.'

He considered this for a moment. 'I would agree with all that, except for the last. Unlike you I don't despise humanity, and I don't hate Jews. That's your disfiguring flaw. It has corrupted your life, and warped your judgement. You were a good agent, but your hatred gives you away like the stink from a wound. I should know – I've watched you at work for three years. Nobody with that much poison in them can survive for long. Not you, and not your friends in Berlin either.'

Amy detected the smallest tremor of feeling steal across Marita's face as she listened. Tears had started down her own. It was an admission, and she knew that with it Hoste had signed his death warrant. He had finished the cigarette, and crushed it under his heel.

Marita said, 'The war is far from over. We shall see who is left standing at the end.' She raised the revolver, drawing a bead on him. 'Amy – step away.'

She shook her head; her eyes were too blurred to focus. 'I can't,' she sobbed. 'Marita, please.'

Her tone in reply was colder than death. 'I'll shoot you as well if I have to.'

Another sob convulsed her, and instead of moving away she tried to put her arms around him; the injured one she couldn't raise. He felt suddenly light-headed in the mystery of her love. How slow he had been to realise it. The time he had wasted . . . His mouth twitched a half-smile at Marita just before he seized Amy in his embrace and turned them bodily about. He began to walk slowly towards the door, his back shielding her. He was ready for the shot when it came, and tried to hold himself steady, until a second shot knocked the breath out of him, and he sank to his knees. But he didn't feel regret. He had been loved. He could hear Amy crying, shrieking out *no no no*, and was glad that she, at least, had breath in her.

They had brought her to St Bart's Hospital. The ambulance men, called to an abandoned paperworks off Curtain Road, had found her lying on the second floor. She had bruises on her face and neck, and a broken arm. The man lying next to her was dead, from bullet wounds in the back. In the bathroom another man, as yet unidentified, had been shot in the head. The anonymous telephone call had come from a woman. The police announced that the killer, whoever he was, was still at large.

Johanna arrived shortly after they had finished putting her arm in plaster. She looked horror-struck on seeing Amy's pale, bruised face. A thug, no doubt some black marketeer, had mugged her on the street. *Well, you know Shoreditch, darling ...* She couldn't be told the real story – MI5, German agents and a home-grown Nazi who was her long-time friend sounded too incredible for words, and there was the Secrets Act binding her to silence in any case. She was touched by Jo's offer to put her up at her place for a few nights, just while she got back on her feet, but she refused; she needed to be on her own.

The following day, Tessa Hammond arranged to call on her at Queen Anne Street. The Section would have to debrief her on the incident. When she saw Amy's arm in a sling she insisted on making the tea. Amy stood gazing out of the kitchen window while the kettle boiled. She sensed from Tessa's brittle mood that she wasn't the only one putting on a brave face.

'He didn't want to involve you,' she said, busying herself with the tea things. 'He hated the idea of putting you in danger.'

'I know.' Amy's voice came out painfully hoarse. 'But I'm glad that I did it.'

She recounted the events as best she could, and managed to keep possession of herself even as she described what

Brunner had done to her. She ought to have known he wasn't RAF – no serviceman would have needed 'WAAF' explained to him.

'We're still not sure how he got into the country. Probably some well-connected Nazi friend of Marita's arranged it,' said Tessa. 'Lucky for us you never knew the detail of Fortitude.'

Amy looked at her. 'I suppose it was. If I had known I would certainly have told him.'

'You can't be certain,' Tessa said with a smile. 'I would have bet on you taking it to the grave.'

But Amy said nothing. They drank their tea, still not quite catching one another's eye. The space between them vibrated thickly with emotion, with the kinship of loss, yet neither woman seemed able to articulate it. Amy got up and drifted back to the window. She found it a comfort to watch the world outside going about its business. Life went on, because it could do nothing else.

'And Marita – anything?' she said presently.

'Vanished, for the moment. She may still be in London, but it's unlikely. She probably had an escape plan worked out. They've set a watch on the ports, and will check private airfields. The security is pretty tight.'

She won't be caught, thought Amy. Even if they got near her, she'd never be taken alive. She pictured Marita now, trying to recall exactly the moment she had pointed the revolver at them. Would she have killed her as well if Hoste hadn't been shielding her?

'It's so hard to judge the person from the face, don't you think?' she said abruptly.

'Sorry?' Tessa looked startled.

'Oh ... It's just that when he first came to the bureau – Hoste – I thought he was rather sweet, but probably ineffectual. You know, hopeless with women. Whereas when I first met Marita she looked so *interesting* and, well, it was like falling under a spell. It was only gradually I came to know how dangerous she was, and by then it was too late.'

'I couldn't speak for her,' said Tessa, 'but you were right about him. He was hopeless with women. It was the work he loved.'

Amy nodded. But in her heart she felt that Tessa, who had known him for years, still hadn't got him quite right. There had been more love in Jack Hoste than she knew. Perhaps more than even he knew. As he lay dying, and she held his hand, he had muttered something in a curious, musing voice: *Exciting times, aren't they?* There was nothing else. Tessa saw her eyes begin to glisten, and gently placed her hand on her shoulder. They stood motionless by the window for some moments.

Later, preparing to leave, Tessa remembered something else. She took from her document case a flimsy slip of paper and laid it on the table in front of Amy. It was a laundry bill from the St Ermin's Hotel, dated from 1940.

'That line of code, in pencil. Would you say that is Hoste's writing?'

Amy scrutinised it. 'I'm not sure. I don't think so.'

'No, I don't either. But I found it on his desk.'

'What does the code mean?'

'Oh. According to our cryptanalyst it's a name and address. Did Hoste ever mention the name Kreshin to you?'

Amy shook her head. Tessa returned the slip to her case, and shrugged. She would let her know about the funeral.

On the day *The Times* reported the first tentative successes of the Allied landings in Normandy, Amy found a short notice in the Deaths column:

EAVES, Edward. 20 January 1899 – 1 June 1944. Beloved only son of the late John Eaves and his wife Marian. Funeral at St Peter and St John the Baptist Church, Wivelsfield, Haywards Heath.

She took out a sheet of writing paper and uncapped her fountain pen.

25 Queen Anne Street, London W.

Dear Mrs Eaves,

I didn't know your son for very long, but in that short time he became a very dear and valued friend. He talked to me about you and your late husband, and I was struck once by a remark of his – that of all the marriages he had known, yours was the happiest.

I can only imagine how terrible must be your grief at his death. So many have been lost in this dreadful war that after a while one feels numb to the fact of their being somebody's brother, or father, or son. I hope in time you will be consoled in the knowledge that Edward conducted his life and work in a way that would have made you proud. It is no exaggeration on my part to say that, had it not been for him, I would not be here, writing these few words to you today.

Please accept my deepest condolences, and God bless you.

Sincerely yours,

Amy Strallen

May 1948

23

Leaning against the parapet she squinted over the terracotta rooftops, trying to trace the route they had walked. Bobby had brought the camera and was taking snaps on the other side, overlooking the Tejo estuary, the purity of its blue almost heartbreaking against the horizon.

They were standing on the terrace of Santa Engracia, with its 360-degree perspective on the city and the river. After stepping off the tram they had made their way up steep, cobbled alleys towards the white marble church. Street life beetled on, the vista patched overhead by drying laundry. In a tiny shop smelling of candlewax and stuffed with devotional knick-knacks Bobby bought a wooden-beaded rosary for her fanatical papist mother – 'To impress her fellow trippers on the way to Walsingham,' she explained. 'Don't they call them "pilgrims"?' asked Amy.

They had set out late from the hotel, where a dusty brindled cat had slunk around their ankles while they ate breakfast. The city traffic honked and fumed under the slab of the noon heat. By the time they spotted the distant dome of Santa Engracia the sun was a savage white glare. A pair of nuns slipped by in silence; otherwise they encountered no one on the winding staircase to the top. They had the entire terrace to themselves. Out on the estuary a little speedboat had carved a white figure of eight on the glistening pane of blue. She felt a drop of sweat trickle down her back.

Behind her a click went off. She turned to find Bobby's face obscured by the camera.

'You had such a soulful pose then,' said Bobby. '*Silent, upon a peak in Darien*. I bet he sailed from here, old stout Cortez.'

'What are you talking about?'

'You must know the poem – Keats? Oh, darling! The conquistador who did for the Aztecs. Of course, when you look at Lisbon on the map it's perched right on the edge, pointed at the New World.'

'It feels rather sad, don't you think?' said Amy, turning back to the view. 'Like a place that's always being left behind. I suppose it's the last of Europe most emigrants ever see.'

''Strue. It's where Ingrid Bergman and what's-his-face are flying to at the end of *Casablanca*, d'you remember, leaving poor old Bogey on the runway?'

Amy smiled. 'Yes, and he put such a brave face on it.'

They made another languid circuit of the terrace; the heat was by now oppressive, and soon they were retreating down the marble stairwell to the ground floor. Their voices echoed beneath the vaulted ceiling. A few other tourists shuffled about the cool, shadowy expanses of the building. Bobby craned her gaze at one or two of the portraits, but Amy could tell from her cursory inspection that she was impatient to be getting on. The real focus of her interest became apparent once they reached the Campo just along from Santa Engracia, where a flea market was under way. It was quite a primitive affair; tented stalls stood about, but most of the wares were laid out on old rugs. Some traders could not run to even this amenity and simply spread their humble bits and pieces on the cobbles. Bobby made a beeline for the more energetic-looking quarter of the market in search of clothes. Her command of Portuguese was unsophisticated, but her expressive use of sighs and her nose for a bargain made her a formidable haggler. She bought two silk headscarves, a floppy straw hat, and a lacquered wooden fan which she immediately put to use.

Amy was amused by Bobby's market savvy, and noticed in one or two of the traders an air of exasperation at her tenacity. 'They expect you to beat them down, it's how the whole business keeps turning.' Amy shook her head, laughing. 'You make it sound like you're doing them a favour.' 'Well, they'd rather have us here than not, darling.' They mooched around for a while longer, and were just about to leave when something caught Amy's eye: it was a citrine ring, square-cut, dressy, not the sort of thing she'd ever imagined wanting. But she did want it, and she knew almost with a certainty as she eased it onto her middle finger that it would fit. Bobby was delighted, and got down to negotiating with the stallholder, a small, shrewd-eyed man whose tanned bald head looked as smooth as teak.

It was soon apparent that he was not going to be knocked down like the others. He kept saying, quietly, *Prata, prata.* Whether it was real silver or not, he didn't seem in a hurry to sell. He listened, with a faint smile, to Bobby's garbled but vehement Portuguese and shook his head. They play-acted a little dispute until she turned to Amy.

'He wants six for it. I'm trying to get him down –'

'Six what?' asked Amy.

'Six thousand. Escudos. It's a lot.' She turned back to the man. '*Nao posso pagar mais do que quatro.*'

The stallholder spread his palms in a pleasant gesture of regret. Amy slid the ring off, and with an answering smile handed it back to him. Bobby had one more appeal in her repertoire. '*Por favor, senhor,*' she said, nodding to Amy, '*significa tanto para o meu amigo.*'

He shrugged. '*E significa seis mil para mim.*'

Bobby's shoulders slumped at last: she had met her match. It was more than either of them could afford. As they walked off Amy called '*Obrigado*' over her shoulder.

Wandering back down to the main drag they found a little cafe where they treated themselves to *bolas de berlim* and tiny cups of coffee as black and bitter as tar. Amy had bought postcards and sat poised with her fountain pen, casting about for something funny to say to her parents. Bobby, meanwhile, a cigarette at the corner of her mouth, examined her little haul from the market, cooing at the softness of the silk scarves and caressing them against her cheek. When she eventually peered across the table at Amy, mid-sentence, something brightened in her eye.

'Are you writing one to his nibs?'

'Dan? Well, I suppose I should ...'

She had already decided to, picturing the look on his face as he recognised her hand on the postcard – in fact, her handwriting had been one of the first things he'd admired about her. She had been seeing Dan – Daniel Collingwood – since last September. They had met earlier that summer when he came as a client to the bureau. He was tallish, early forties, dark hair severely parted on one side and a smile that made his eyes crinkle. He had taught classics at a school in Surrey before the war. After being demobbed he tried to go back to teaching but found he'd lost the heart – or the nerve – for it. Instead, he joined an old friend from university at a literary magazine in Bloomsbury and did some private tuition on the side.

'I must say comprehensively I'm never going to be rich,' he told her, rather seriously, at their first interview. 'Will that count against me?'

Amy tucked in her chin. 'Not with anyone who regards a man as more than a meal ticket. Would you object if I matched you with a woman of ... similar prospects to your own?'

'It would be pretty awful of me if I did!'

His chief requirement was companionship – everything else would follow from that, he believed. Amy read through the short unexceptional list he had made in the Requirements box. She paused only at the last entry.

'"I'd like someone who knows Attic Greek."' She looked across at him. 'Erm, why would that be?'

He wagged his head sideways. 'Well, it's always been a dream of mine to have a girl who might read *The Odyssey* aloud to me. Or *The Iliad*. Just for twenty minutes or so, of an evening.'

Amy stifled a sudden laugh, and blushed. 'I'm so sorry, I don't mean to – I've heard some strange requests in this office, but never that one.'

'Is that unreasonable?' His earnest expression caused her heart to turn over. She felt somewhat ashamed of her mirth.

'No. Not unreasonable. Just a little unlikely.'

He nodded, his brow knitted. 'Yes, I see. Perhaps, then, someone who could recite it in translation?'

Amy eventually set him up with one of their nicest young clients. That didn't spark, so she matched him with an equally nice older one. This proved more satisfactory, but it was plainly not, in the bureau shorthand, an MMIH (match made in heaven). Mr Collingwood – or Daniel, as he now asked her to call him – was game at least, and trusted Amy's judgement: he never refused an introduction she had arranged. They bumped into each other on the street once, and she found herself chatting to him animatedly for ten minutes: the last date she'd sent him on had been a great success, and he was waiting to hear back from her. (She was tempted to ask about the lady's liking for *The Odyssey*, but resisted.) There was nothing from him after that until the end of the summer, when he telephoned her at the office. She was expecting a tale of a triumph, but no, it turned out that the lady he'd been waiting on had 'dropped off the radar'. She had not contacted him after all. Amy was genuinely sorry, and commiserated with him, knowing how disheartened he must feel. Before he rang off he asked her if she would send him a fresh Requirements form; he had decided to rewrite his completely. She promised to put one in the post. A few days later she received a note from him.

273

Dear Miss Strallen,

Would you be good enough to read over the revised Requirements form I have enclosed? I'd be most grateful if you'd let me know your thoughts.

Sincerely yours,

Daniel Collingwood

I am looking for a lady, somewhere in London, who likes to lend a sympathetic ear to the troubles of others. She will be kind, good-humoured, and patient to a fault.

She will be in her mid-thirties, with shoulder-length brown hair, green eyes with amber flecks at the edges; she will always look well dressed.

She will have beautiful handwriting and work in an office, e.g. at a marriage bureau.

She will laugh often, but sometimes will blush if she thinks her amusement has caused pain to her interlocutor.

She will be the sort of person who has no idea of herself as 'a catch' and so spends her life matchmaking others.

She will read Homer aloud to me whenever her time and inclination permit. (This last requirement is optional. The others are not.)

After considering this for some hours, Amy wrote back:

Dear Mr Collingwood,

Thank you for sending the bureau your revised Requirements form. I am happy to report that I have someone here who may suit you. Please call at the office at your earliest convenience.

Sincerely, and always yours,

Amy Strallen

Bobby must have been studying her face, because she now said, 'D'you remember that time, a few years ago – I'm sure we were at Quo Vadis – when you said you weren't capable of "real love"?'

Amy smiled distantly. 'I do. I believed it at the time. Although there was someone –' She broke off, and fell silent.

'Was that him? Jack? I do so wish I'd met him.'

'You might not have been impressed. He wasn't easy to get to know.'

'If *you* liked him, I'd have found a way.' Bobby paused, and Amy sensed what was coming next. 'Did you ever find out how he ...?'

Slowly she shook her head. 'They just said "killed in action". I knew he was brave. He once saved me from flying shrapnel during a raid one night – I must have told you that.'

Bobby nodded, and looked a little nervous. 'Have you told Dan about him?'

'No,' she said. 'But I will. Some day.'

They walked back to the hotel under the white-hot lid of the sky. Up in their room the ceiling fan revolved stoically, whispering into the net curtains. Amy opened the door onto the balcony, but the sultry stillness of the air didn't yield an inch. Even the wallpaper looked parched. Bobby made her laugh when a pigeon suddenly landed right in front of them on the railing of the balcony and she enquired, quick as a flash, 'Any messages?' It was too hot to do anything but lie on their beds.

The turn of the ceiling fan lulled them.

She woke with a start from a dream in which she was trying to leave a party. A few of the guests she knew, but most were strangers; whoever she asked for directions to the exit pointed to this or that door, which led nowhere, and she kept returning to the room to ask someone else. This rigmarole seemed to go on for hours, and left her exhausted. She rose from the bed, her mouth dry and tasting of ashes – that awful coffee.

Bobby slept on her side, unstirring: 'sparko', as she would say. Amy slipped on her sandals, picked up her purse and tiptoed out, having left a note on the bedside table. *Gone for a walk.* Outside, the streets were waking from their siesta. Shopkeepers pulled open their shutters; the cafes were beginning to fill again. The heat remained thick as molasses, stifling. Nobody appeared to pay her any mind, though amid the locals she felt herself to be conspicuously pale. In one of the big squares she wandered for a while; the wrought-iron benches were occupied, mostly by old men with deeply tanned, weathered faces. Pigeons strutted around, chests out, eyes ablaze.

She found a bench of her own in the shade. The funiculars and the wooden trams clanked away in the distance. There was something secretive and antique about the city, its face turned away from the rest of Europe. The war had happened elsewhere. What had they made of it here, aware that the continent was madly tearing itself to pieces? Perhaps they didn't care. It struck her now that Lisbon was the furthest she had ever travelled. She had never been outside of Europe; she had barely been 'abroad' at all. And what did it signify? Who would ever know in time to come that a thirty-six-year-old Englishwoman had sat in this square contemplating her life one May afternoon in 1948? She tried to remember the sad Latin phrase Dan had told her recently, it meant 'under the gaze of eternity'; we live and we die, and the world goes on, not noticing. But to live at all was the privilege.

She remained there a long time, watching the afternoon light turn yolky, until some unfathomable impulse forced her to her feet. She turned in the direction of the hotel, but as the familiar landmarks called her on she decided to walk the long way round. It would enable her to time her return with the cocktail hour. Bobby had been scouring the guidebook for this evening's entertainment. Good old Bobs, still lurching from one love affair to another, unwilling to settle; they would never tame her. And yet she had been a little lost since the war. Many were. She seemed to depend more on Amy, the friend of her youth, and their annual summer holiday had become a kind of ritual that neither dared to break.

She waited at a junction, where the late-afternoon traffic had shoaled and thickened. A tram had halted crosswise right in front of her, its bell clanging. At the windows faces stared, blank as paving stones. For some reason she lifted her eyes to the nearest standing passenger, and her heart took a drastic lurch as the gaze locked on hers. Marita. Amy blinked, thinking to shake the hallucination from her sight. But no: Marita it was, her hair shorter, and a different colour, lighter. Nobody had seen her since that day in June, four years ago. They stared at one another through the glass; it could only have been a matter of seconds (she realised later) and yet the time seemed to swell and slow. Indeed, with the traffic stalled there, Amy felt helpless to resist a natural impulse: haltingly, almost shyly, she raised her hand. Did she expect some acknowledgement in return? She didn't know what to expect, there wasn't time to think about it.

The tram heaved onwards – and just before it did, Marita, who had been holding one of the overhead passenger straps, answered her. She detached her grip, and straightened her arm, hand flat, at an angle of forty-five degrees. It was the gesture of a moment, unremarked by anyone but her.

Amy stood there, immobilised, the boiling traffic filling up the space where the tram had been. When the lights changed again she crossed the road, in a trance. She continued along the pavement, noticing nothing, and no one. It was as though she had been in an accident and was bearing the trauma of it in her bones. The strange mood she had been in this afternoon, the long reverie on that bench in the shade – it was for this,

this, the mood had been preparing her. The wild coincidence of it had thrown her off-centre, like a picture knocked askew. Questions swarmed her benumbed brain. Marita. How long had she lived here? Was this her home now? Or was she in transit? She knew the city was a byword for fugitive war criminals, but she had never thought to see –

And now the expression on Marita's face came back to her. Had there been some rueful tremor on it, some tiny wrinkle of remorse, Amy might have called to her, might have chased that tram down the street to the next stop. But there was not a flicker; only that single movement of her arm. She stopped dead still on the street, absorbing its shock, the implacable cold defiance of it.

When she got back to their hotel room she felt herself shaking, her legs gone to mush. She sat down on the edge of her bed, trying to calm herself. Bobby must have gone out, too, for there on the dresser was a brown paper bag, patched with a translucent stain. After some moments she got up and opened it: her fingers brushed the furry skin of a peach.

She was out on the balcony when Bobby reappeared, swaddled in a huge towel, her face pink and steaming.

'There you are! I've been out myself and had a bath since you've been gone. Where on earth did you get to?'

'Oh, I just wandered around. Lost track of time.'

'I should say so!' said Bobby, towelling her hair and fetching the bag of peaches. 'You must have one of these, they're heavenly.'

So they stood together on the balcony, watching the sun lower over the rooftops, peach juice dripping off their fingers. When Bobby went in to get dressed, Amy was still wondering if she should tell her about the traumatic encounter of the afternoon. But how to begin to explain it? Bobby had not met Marita, and knew little about her even by repute. Marita had never been the sort of friend she would introduce to other people, probably for fear that she would be bored and dismissive, and they would be intimidated. It had sometimes struck her as a mystery that they had been friends in the first place.

She heard Bobby's voice calling her, and went back inside. She had dressed now, and an odd expression was on her face. From behind her back she produced a small black box and handed it to Amy, who returned a puzzled look. She opened the lid. There, nestled on a worn velvet mount, was the citrine she had coveted that morning. It glistened, pale as honey, against the velvet.

She stared at it. 'Oh, Bobs ...'

Well, she had gone back this afternoon. She'd had the most awful feeling it might have been sold, but it hadn't. 'I thought of haggling, only I didn't have the heart to go through all that again, and I'm pretty sure he didn't either. So he polished it up like a tallyman's ink bottle –' Bobby broke off, a sudden dismay clouding her face. Without warning tears had brimmed in Amy's eyes, were rolling down her cheeks; she was helpless to stop them.

'Darling, what's the matter?' said Bobby, but Amy's throat felt too choked to speak. 'It's just a silly old ring. I thought it would make you happy ...'

Amy shook her head: Bobby didn't understand; she could never understand. She saw from Bobby's face that this crying jag must be frightening her. She swallowed hard, tried to gain a semblance of composure. 'I'm crying because –' she had to take another breath – 'because you're such a dear and you always have been and you don't even know it.'

Her eyes were still hot with tears as she fumbled the ring and slid it down her finger. And seeing it there caused her another racking convulsion of sobs. In the end Bobby put her arms around her, and clucked, as if to a child.

'Good Lord,' she murmured eventually. 'I can't imagine the scene if I'd given you something really *valuable*.'

*

They talked on in low voices, Bobby lying across her bed, smoking, while Amy changed into her dress for the evening. The ceiling fan whirred away, a mute eavesdropper. Outside, the night sky had darkened to a granular blue-grey, and lights were winking on across the city. A table for two was awaiting them. They were nearly out of the room when Bobby remembered the bottle of perfume she had bought. She gave them each a long squirt of it. Amy inhaled the scent of violets and orange blossom, sweet as cake. It lingered on them as they walked arm in arm down the wide street.

Acknowledgements

Thanks to Dan Franklin, Rachel Cugnoni, Suzanne Dean, Joe Pickering, Michal Shavit, Victoria Murray-Browne, Richard Cable, Katherine Fry, Anna Webber, Seren Adams. A special tip of the hat to my ace editor, Alex Russell.

The seed of this book was an article by Ben Macintyre of *The Times* (28/2/14) about Jack King and the British Nazi Fifth Column during the war. I am grateful to him for it, and for his book *Double Cross* (2012). *London at War* (1995) by Philip Ziegler, *Wartime Britain 1939–1945* (2004) by Juliet Gardiner, *Marriages Are Made in Bond Street* (2016) by Penrose Halson and *Love is Blue* (1986) by Joan Wyndham were also closely consulted.

I am indebted to Ian Jack, whose knowledge of railway timetables, Clitheroe and British industry in the 1930s was astonishing, even by his standards.

My love and thanks, as ever, to Rachel Cooke, for her encouragement and much else besides.